FLYBOYS

FLYBOYS

Tom Hanley

To order additional copies of this book, contact:
Xlibris Corporation
1-888-7-XLIBRIS
www.Xlibris.com
Orders@Xlibris.com

CONTENTS

TO SHAWN AND LAUREN.

ALSO, TO ALL THE PILOTS AND INSTRUCTORS
I HAVE SHARED THE JOY OF FLIGHT WITH.

CHAPTER 1.

FORBES AIR FORCE BASE

"Die, Yankee dog!"

The hissed threat was evil and insistent, the headphones in his helmet giving the words a startling clarity despite the din of the battle. Immediately, the roar of cannon fire smashed through the warning, hammering Riley's senses with their savage blasts. Each horrific *KOOM-KOOM-KOOM* announced a fresh, deadly piece of lead ripping through the cold sky to kill him. The fiery bullets streaked past his canopy so close that it bathed the dull, green cockpit of the Sabre Jet in a weird, pulsing light. Hell*s bells!* Time to get the heck outta here—time to *fly!*

Lance Riley, Major, United States Air Force, snapped his visor down against the blinding tracers, then slammed the control stick of the fighter hard left while simultaneously kicking the opposite rudder with his heavy boot. Sheesh! thought the Lancester, glancing up at his rear-view mirror—that guy back there matched his wild manuever perfectly! It was Heads Up Time over the Yalu.

"Die? *Moi?*" responded Major Riley to his pursuer, grunting against the savage g-forces. "El doggo Yanqui? No can do, mi amigo." He chuckled, then continued confidently, "Umm, say colonel, where's all your little . . . *helpers?*" There were sixteen of those slimeballs when Riley squared off with them about twenty minutes ago up at 45,000 feet, and this guy was the last one left.

"You schweinhundt pig air-pirate!" fumed the MiG pilot. "You running dog! I know who you are, Rirey, and I have you in my sights—escape is impossible!"

Riley's responsive mount shuddered somewhere from deep within as he rolled the sleek Sabre Jet on its back, furiously yanking the control stick back to his gut, then slammed the throttle into afterburner—Emergency Dive! As he hurtled down through the towering cloud-canyons, the skilled American glanced up to his rear-view mirror and saw the wildly gyrating MiG drop its nose and struggle to maintain position and follow him down. Good. Come *onnnnn* down. Come to poppa, you commie sack of dog poop. Heh heh heh. He could tell from the snazzy, snarly panda emblem on the glistening enemy fuselage that it was Colonel Tomb himself, legendary commander of what *had* been the commies best MiG squadron. The two remaining combatants streaked down through the cold winter sky towards the bleak landscape below. The Sabre rocketed down a dry river bed, its jetwash throwing small rocks into the crowded sky behind it. Riley glanced up to his mirror and saw Colonel Tomb struggling to follow, to dodge the debris and small bushes now in his path. The ticked commie snapped off another burst, but Lance had anticipated it and skidded his aircraft expertly to the left, barely missing a family of water buffalo. He glanced up into his mirror again, and saw Tomb's face centered in the silver frame of the MiG windscreen, screaming expletives at him, raising and shaking his gloved fist.

"You capitarist war-mongering enemy of the masses! You— "

Riley chuckled into his oxygen mask, then shot a quick glance to the snapshot of his woman that he had taped to his instrument panel. The ravishing, dreamy-eyed co-ed looked up longingly at him from the photo, behind her loopy handwriting: 'To My Flyboy, Win The War & Hurry Home! Love, Michelle XXXOOO.' Can-do, good lookin', he vowed to himself. *This one's for you.* In the next instant, it was Speedbrakes OUT and Flaps 20 as Riley slammed the stick up and left, urging his mount to perform a surgical aileron roll, which it did enthusiastically and delivered Lance neatly behind his surprised quarry. Ha! *Gotcha!* thought the skilled and ruggedly handsome American. His eyes were steely—his jaw, lantern. Flaps UP! Speedbrakes IN!

"Perfect bouncing weather, wouldn't you say, Mister Godless-Commie?"

A startled Col. Tomb looked back over his shoulder ... up at the angry snout of the American plane that he had just rocketed helplessly by underneath. Riley's gunsight pipper was now zeroed in right between the eyes of the unbelieving Tomb. Lance thought he noticed the glisten of a tear in the treacherous commie's eye as his finger squeezed firmly on the gun trigger. *Tough ti* . . .

"Breakfast! Time to get up!"

He cracked open one eye, and slowly focused on the doomed MiG as it careened across the sky, the belching smoke like painted cotton, the F-86 Sabre Jet in relentless pursuit. His little brain groggily switched over from full-on aerial battle to real life, reminded him of his up-coming math test (compound fractions), then informed the young warrior that he had to pee. Oh yeah. Shoot! He wasn't Lance Riley, Major, United States Air Force, Hot Rock Stud Pilot. He was just Tommy Riley, Tenderfoot, Boy Scouts of America. A kid. Dangit! And he had almost got that last MiG, too. His maneuvering had really been improving lately—those low-level skids took some hairy cross-controlling, something normally not attempted in an F-86 at 30 feet, but he had them down pat. He'd been practicing for a long time.

He lay there for another moment, hands behind his head now, savoring the slowly disappearing images of the great aerial battle. He had flamed MiGs six and seven with a snap-roll at the top of his outside loop. One burst for both. Beautiful flying. No. Deadly serious flying. He could only imagine how much Michelle would have been impressed by his valor, and how she would thank him: the lingering, delicious kiss ending, then not quite ending, her eyes closed to a dreamy slit, her *mmmmm* of blissful satisfaction, and then, as she raised herself from the bed, her fresh-smelling hair cascading over him, dragging across his tingling skin, tickling his shoulder, his neck, his cheek. She raised herself up slowly, deliberately, a sated cat, and he gazed at her glistening nakedness. Oops. Too far on that one. Confession-list city!

He yawned, kicked off the covers, and had a good, long stretch. It was gonna be a busy day! His feet hit the cold concrete floor, and he stumbled over to switch on his Davy Crockett lamp, put on his waiting clothes, then bolted up the basement stairs. He went to the bathroom, took a leak, washed his hands, then joined his brothers and sisters at the dining room table—where they were already involved in a noisy, routine feeding session. The faint aroma of cigarette smoke and the empty chair at the head of the table meant his dad had already left for work. His mom was wiping some oatmeal off of Markie.

His little sisters spun around to welcome him, and sang out the greeting they had carefully rehearsed the night before, "Good morning, ya' lazy poopy-doo!"

"Girls! Stop that this instant!" A mom-bark.

Tee hee.

Tommy walked nobly past the tee-hee'ers over to the bananas, chose one, then sneered at Diane and Denise, who were still enormously pleased with themselves, giggling between mouthfuls of Cheerios. His mom sang a chirpy 'good morning,' poured a bowl of Wheaties, and positioned it in front of him. He thanked his mom, then sliced the big Chiquita, the pieces raining down in a perfect banana bombing pattern on the hapless flakes. *Sssssbooom! Kaboom!* Bam Bam *Kablooey!* He sprinkled sugar on the ruins, poured the milk, and made a move to dig in.

"Aren't we forgetting something?"

Oh, brother. He bowed his head a little and mumbled the Bless Us O Lord And These Thy Gifts (to his little twerp sisters' delight, of course) then scooped up a spoonful of The Breakfast Of Champions, and his slurping, crunching noises joined the symphony of breakfast sounds rising from the table. When he was finished, there was about half an inch of good, sugary milk left in the bowl, so he raised it up to his lips and prepared to slurp, but then he felt . . . something. Tommy's radar-warning system snapped him 90 degrees to his left, to a cold maternal stare. Dang!

"I've told you umpteen times not to do that, young man. Haven't I?"

"Yes, ma'am," he said sadly, lowering his head, to his sister's continuing glee. Those little scuzmotrons. He got up from his chair and took the bowl back to the kitchen, being careful to accidentally knock Diane's head with his elbow as he walked by.

"Hey you! Mom! He hit me!"

"Oh, I did not. Good grief. Grow up."

"Oh, yeah? Why don't you, huh? He hit me mom, he really did. Ow. I think its bleeding. Do I hafta go to school? I'm dizzy. I can't see too good."

"I can't see too well."

"Yeah. Too well. So do I hafta?"

"Yes, you will go to school. And you, young man . . ." *Heeeere we go,* he thought. "You will apologize to your sister this instant, and there will be no more of that type of behavior at this table."

"Yes, ma'am. I'm sorry."

"Don't apologize to me. To your sister."

Sheesh. No way around it. He was already behind this morning, one to nothing. He sighed deeply, as deeply as he thought he could get away with without getting grounded, anyways. Plus he rolled his eyes up in mock disgust. Perfect. "I'mmm sorrrrrreeeeeeee."

"What was that, young man?"

"I'm SOrry."

"Better. Now rinse out your bowl and brush your teeth, and I don't want to hear one more smart word from you, or I'll report this little episode to your father. Do you want that?"

"No, ma'aaammm."

"Two-nine!" Davey chimed in, not wanting to miss out on this morning's butt-chewing. "Two-nine, two-NINE!" Tommy's little brother was learning to talk, but all that usually came out was "two-nine."

Excited by the morning's events so far, and not wanting to miss out himself, Markie lobbed some oatmeal over at Denise, who shrieked so loud that their mom looked up at the ceiling (or heaven perhaps) and closed her eyes tightly for a few seconds. It was a good hit, the Quaker Oats splayed in a thick, straight line from Denise's elbow all the way up to her neck, a little glob clinging to her hair. It would definitely require a uniform change. As his mom returned to ref this newest battle, Tommy took this opportunity to exit, stage left, to the kitchen. He voted his 'I'm SOrry' to be one point. It was a tie game now, one up.

He finished rinsing off his bowl and spoon, put them on the rack, then did a Frankenstein walk out the kitchen, and down the hall to the bathroom, the huge boots smashing down on the vibrating floor, almost-but-not-quite drowning out the bellowing roar of the peasants back at the table. He walked through the perpetual cloud of diaper pail stink, and started brushing his teeth. He surveyed himself carefully in the mirror, starting at the top. Let's see . . . some hair, brown, used to be a crew cut, but he was letting it grow out a little. He'd probably burr it up good when baseball started this summer. A forehead. A pretty good one, he supposed, with a bunch of freckles on it. Two eyes, bluish grey. A predator's eyes. He scrunched down his eyebrows and snarled. The brows were too light to get scary yet, maybe he could dye them black. Black brows sure worked for his mom! Between the eyes began a nose. It headed south, noselike, where it ended in two nostrils. He flared them, and tried his eyebrows again. Hmmm. He didn't look scary, just agitated or ticked or dizzy or something. A mouth, two lips, with a green toothbrush sticking out between them. A chin. All in all, a good head, he thought. He knew it drove the women wild, or he hoped it would soon, anyway. He finished brushing his teeth, grabbed his books, and raced down the hall for the front door.

Ka*BAM!* The storm door slammed shut and Tommy Riley streaked off the small porch, cleared the hedge in an easy jump, then started picking his way through the muddy spots in the front yard. He heard a bomber starting up, way off in the distance, booming and whistling its shrill whine. He glanced up the street toward the bus stop, and saw three little birds in tight formation zip and wheel up the street, then angle off to the south. Tommy had almost made it to the curb, when out of the clear, blue sky, a voice sang out—in a beautiful church-choir soprano: "Don't slam that *dooooorrr!* How many times do I have to *tellll youuu!*" Cripes! Caught again, thought the young slammer. Two to one. Still, it was gonna be a great day, he could just feel it!

He spun around and saw his mom pretending not to watch him through the open kitchen window. She had recovered from the breakfast wars, and was standing over the sink now, humming away, packing his sister's lunch boxes. Diane had a 'My Friend Flicka,' and Denise had a 'Barbie.' Since Tommy was older now, he only used a paper sack. A lunch box could get a guy beat up nowadays.

"Yeesss maaaam," he answered as sorrowfully as he thought he could get away with, rolling his eyes upward for added effect. He was still trying out some new snotty responses, and was getting pretty good. Tommy was practicing to be a teenager. His mom was practicing to have some around.

"Don't 'yes ma'am' *ME,* young maaaannn," she sang back, never missing a beat.

"Oh, brother," he muttered under his breath. He spun around quickly so she couldn't see his face, then he really scrunched it up good. *"Don't-yes-ma'am-ME-young-man,"* he repeated, his lips, eyes and nose balled up so tight that he could hardly see. It was high and whiney to boot. It was a good one, but he made sure he said it quietly. Almost silently, in fact.

The kitchen operetta continued, "And please wait for your *sisssterrrs!*"

Jeesh, have a cow, why doncha? He just thought that one. He made sure it stayed up in his brain, keeping careful watch that it never even got *near* his mouth. One slip on one of those and he'd be a goner. *"Yeeesss . . . maaaamm,"* he volleyed back. This one was a big, sucky inhale on the 'yes' and a deep whooshy exhale on the 'maam' part. It was borderline, and he shot a quick glance back to the kitchen window to see if it passed. It seemed to, her mom-meter finding the tone and inflection either un-smart-alecky enough, or not worth the fight because of the time. No matter, one point for the home team. It was a tie game now, 2 to 2.

A few seconds later, the storm door banged open again, and his two little sisters bolted out like rodeo animals, squealing and cornering around the hedge, and through the goopy yard. Their big school bookbags, the perfect multi-purpose weapons for little girls, swung straight out, providing gyroscopic help in their maneuvers. The heavy vinyl bags would be used later to claim valuable personal space at the bus stop. His twerp-o-rama sisters liked personal space.

His mom suddenly appeared on the porch, wiping her hands on her apron. She shot him The Look, right at him, no—*through* him! Like a cobra . . . or a nun. He shuddered a little, but there was no time to move, no time to react. Once The Look was delivered, the game went to a new, more dangerous level. Uh-oh, he thought. Did he slip up? What was this? It was definitely an I Heard That or I Saw That Look, but there was no way! Keep cool now. He had pulled off that scrunched face safely, hadn't he? Yeah, *sure* he did, he was positive. He had been facing the durn street when he delivered it, for gosh sakes! His mom was good, but not *that* good. Suddenly, he remembered that he had seen that particular Look before, last Saturday, by the busted Hummel figure. Three sad and silent kids stood there, hovering nervously by the shattered little bits of milkmaid, the no-snitching rule in invisible effect, and The Look was delivered to each kid in turn, until Denise finally broke down and blubbered her guilt. The Look was multi-purpose, so then Tommy knew that the one she just shot over to him was a Look-Bluff, and a good one, too! She would occasionally cast one out there, just to see if a kid would bite and confess to *something*. He had to hand it to the old gal, she was getting pretty good. They were both getting better.

The stalemate ended as he heard his two little brothers back in the house hollering at the top of their lungs, and then a bang and ker-plop that he knew would be Mark's oatmeal bowl. Time-out on the field! His mom rushed back inside (slamming the door a little, he noted). He turned to head up the street for the bus stop, and heard her voice sing out from somewhere back in the house, "Be good and watch your *sisssterrrs.*"

Last chance for a good shot. It was risky, but he felt confident now, on a roll. He yelled, "Okeydokeyyourbuttispokey!" and took off. Ha! She wouldn't be able to unscramble that one in time! He declared himself the winner of today's scrimmage, 3 to 2. A good start for the day. They'd probably have a rematch after school.

Heading up to the bus stop, already way behind his sisters, Tommy's Red-Ball Jets crunched the new gravel that the Air Force recently spread on the streets, which they did every spring. He couldn't figure out why they just didn't pave it, but oh well, what the hell . . . *s bells.* Crunch, crunch. Crunchcrunch*crunch.* Each step sounding about like a platoon on the march. It was a good sound, and great ammo, a gift from the ammo gods, and just in time for summer. It would sting really good up close, even through clothes, and was also great for lobbing those high trajectory scatter-bombs when the enemy was at a distance. Like exactly the distance from the Riley's driveway to that turd-knocker Billy Fitzsimmon's house.

Another use of the versatile little bullets was when the air conditioners came on in the summer, you could scoop up a big handful and drop it straight down through the grill, right onto the big spinning fan, and *BAM!,* it would shoot back up like shrapnel, all over the side of some poor sap's house. The ones who got the most ticked off got the most treatments, naturally. Some of the more excitable ones even came running out in the warm nights with flashlights, yelling and cussing, and sometimes smacking into a trike or a lawnmower. Those were great! (One night last summer, Captain Palmer got tangled up in a clothesline, and sprained his head or something. They had to cool it for awhile after that one.) Lieutenants and captains were the most dangerous, because they could sometimes catch you. Majors or colonels were safer, and usually just hollered out the door, "Hey you kids, knock it off!"

"Knock what off?" answered the high, little voices from the darkness.

"Who's out there!? I see you over there! You . . . you're ah . . . Billy, no Eddie Imean MichaelKontovan*Iknowwhoyouaredammit!*"

I Know Who You Are. Ha! Suuure they did. The housing area would be crawling with kids every evening. With about 20 houses per block, and anywhere from 3 to 7 kids per house, what were the odds? They were great, that's what. It was their turf, they were home free, and they knew it.

All in all, he thought that the base was looking pretty darn good. After the bitter, muddy-snow landscape of a typical Kansas spring, this warm spell meant new life, new hope. Maybe that new bike, what with his birthday coming up. The thin, spring grass was poking up like a green crew cut. The grass-hair was there, a delicate green smudge, but the muddy scalp was still showing through. Still, it was growing, and would be mowable in about a month or so, and at 75c a yard, that meant *moolah!* He continued crunching up the street, and sucked in some good spring smells. There was some bacon in there, and fresh mud, and dog doo, also a little Colgate. That would be him, of course. A whiff of Brylcreem (A Little Dab'll Do Ya.) Also him. Yep, spring was in the air, and after that came summer, which meant school would be O-U-T OUT and that was what every kid at Forbes Air Force Base, Kansas, U S of A was living for.

As he double-timed it up to the bus stop, he looked ahead to the little, chattering crowd. All seemed well so far, no fights yet this morning. As the oldest, he always had to referee their silly little squabbles, and pull them apart if they started pounding each other. They were all obediently waiting, the same bunch of little Catholics, in their same little uniforms, with the same silly arguments, standing at the same corner, waiting for the same bus to take them to the same Saint Luke's Church and School, home of the meanest nuns on planet Earth. He noted gratefully that his little sisters had apparently decided not to bookcase-bludgeon anyone, and were in a one-potato-two-potato circle with Connie and Jenny Griffin.

Soon, the muddy yellow bus crunched around the corner and came to a squealy halt. They all filed in, the doors flopped shut, the kids found the same seats, and boy-howdy-here-we-go-again. They should rename Saint Luke's, Tommy thought sourly, watching the little uniformed prisoners disappear one by one into the bus. How's about Saint Sing Sing? Or Saint Alcatraz?

They were one of the first stops, so the bus took Tommy on a complimentary tour of base housing every morning, before it swung back onto the highway and headed for Topeka. Being an Air Force Base, the houses were all pretty much alike—except for the color. Same house after house after house, all wood siding, a few points added here or there for a trimmed bush, or a birdbath, or bricks lined up in a border, as if to say: This mud over here is the lawn, but this mud over *here* is the garden. So watch your step, bub. Well, at least they were trying. The whole place was only some big wheat fields a few years ago.

The cars were the most interesting and colorful things to check out. General Motors still seemed to have a slim edge over Fords, with station wagons a favorite on both sides. But the new Chryslers were showing up here and there, muscling in on the auto rolls, especially among lieutenant colonels and colonels. Big fins seemed to be losing out, and Tommy would miss them. They made the cars look like *jets!* There were a few exotics: Captain Jenner had a goofy little Renault. Paaaaathetic. The Wallaceses had their la-de-da black Olds convertible, of course, plus a *Porsche,* and their kids suffered for it every single day. There was Lieutenant Campbell's snazzy little MG—it didn't run, though. Well, sometimes, but not often. He'd usually work on it every weekend, and by Sunday afternoon, it was time for a test hop. He could almost always push it back by himself, but if he made it out of base housing, someone would always go look for him before it got dark, and tow him back with a rope. Colonel Komanick's spoiled rotten, juvenile delinquent kid, Chuck, had his candy-apple-red '57 Chevy, with baby moons and dual cherry packs. The gray bondo down at the corners of the door made the thing look even a little more menacing. He smoked already, and peeled out in the commissary parking lot once and got a ticket. Most kids on base agreed that Chucky-Baby'd probably be dead soon. Or at least in the Army.

If you were a lieutenant colonel or above, you got a house with a garage, one-car. Everybody else got half a duplex with a carport. There were a few trees, but they were new and scrawny. Every house had a white plastic plaque, mounted up high by the front door, with black letters. It told you the house number, the guy's last name (they were all guys) his 1st initial, and rank:

12 Dziejowski G Maj

3 Griffin P Capt

6 Berg B Lt Col

11 Ruddy M Lt

Bobby Kontovan thought it should also include the number of eligible girls inside, as if he would know what to do about it.

Finally, the bus hit the stop next to 22 Kontovan F Maj. Bobby and Mike's house, his best friends. The bus stopped, the doors snapped open and Bobby and Mike scrambled on, heading purposefully to the back and their spot. Back seat, right side. They called it, it was theirs. The three boys could see everything, the nosy bus driver couldn't hear or see crap-ola, and plus, they were un-attackable from the rear. In the world of bussed children, they had position.

"Hey, Riley," sneered Michael as he bounced vigorously on the seat. "You better get your dumb book out of our basement. My dad almost found it again last night."

"Yeah, bozo-brain," added Bobby. "I ain't going to Leavenworth for your crazy butt."

The book was the Operations and Flight Manual of the Boeing RB-47, Model H. (Top Secret.) Tommy had kept it hidden at the Konto's since last weekend, when he had spent the night. It was safer there, his room being subject to random searches disguised as dusting. He had found the manual about two years ago, under the basement stairway in one of his dad's flight bags. Tommy didn't really mean to steal it, just to sneak it out to read it, and returned it each time, but eventually it spent more time in his secret hiding places than back in his dad's flight bag. Tommy loved it! It was ten times, a zillion times better than even the National Geographics! Pretty soon, he realized his dad didn't miss it at all—he must have another one somewhere. It wasn't an easy read, but Tommy soaked it up like a sponge. It was fascinating to him, like a treasure map, only better. It listed—by the numbers—everything that needed to be done to make a B-47 come alive and fly (it was a lot!) and Tommy had it completely memorized. All 208 pages.

"Just keep it hid, okay?" sighed Tommy. "I'll get it back as soon as I can."

The bus made the whole loop, then chugged out past the guard shack, and up to the traffic light on the highway. There was the big sign that announced: FORBES AIR FORCE BASE. Under that: STRATEGIC AIR COMMAND. PEACE IS OUR PRO-FESSION. Then a smaller: You Are Entering THE MOST Dangerous Place On Earth, A PUBLIC HIGHWAY. *Fasten YOUR SEAT BELT*. That last one made him edgy. He was a safety conscious Scout, and knew how to drop and roll every time he caught fire, how to lift with his legs and not his back, and how to suck rattlesnake venom out of some poor sap's leg. But the bus, he noted, had no seat belts. Just the big metal frameworks of the seat ahead to stop their little bodies in the event of collision, right about tooth level. He had mentioned this to his parents on numerous occasions, and asked if he had to take the bus to school. Yes, he did. Could he go by bike? Nope. Go-cart? No, he could not. Oh, well . . . some risks you just had to take. They all just hoped that grumpy old Mr. Spence drove better than he looked.

They whined up the highway, and sped past the new Holiday Inn. It had the biggest sign he had ever seen, huge and green, with a swooping yellow arrow with about a thousand yellow lights on it, blinking in rapid-fire sequence. It started at the back of the arrow, and blinkblinkblink in about three seconds, it blinked its way to the point, drawing motorists in. Tommy's eyes tried to keep up, it was mesmerizing. Heck, who wouldn't want to pull in?

Sheesh! It only had everything: ICE-COLD AIR - POOL - RES-
TAURANT - TV - WELCOME FUTURE FARMERS OF BELL
COUNTY - HAPPY ANNIVERSARY ISA + EDWARD. It was
long, low, clean and futuristic. It seemed to have everything, except enough Ls. Still, he bet the Russians didn't have anything
like this!

Four stoplights later, he could see Burnett's Mound, Topeka's
hill. It had a water tank on its side, and was supposed to protect
Topeka's southern flank from tornados. Oh, come *on* now! If he
wrote something like that down on a test, he'd get a D, but if
grown-ups or Indians said so, it was all right. It wasn't fair, of
course. Grown-ups always got away with murder over kids, *just
because.* But Tommy started noticing recently that he got away
with a lot of stuff on the second and third graders, *just because,* so
he sort of knew that kid life was some sort of a training program.

The bus bounced up into the parking lot of Saint Luke's (which
was also the basketball courts) and the kids all spilled out like
chirping chicks. The waiting nuns, herding and clucking and shush-
ing and generally checking them all over, pointed the slippery
load toward the open double-doors, down the hall, then funneled
them into church, littlest kids first.

There was a Mass every morning before school, and frankly,
Tommy was getting a l-i-t-t-l-e tired of it. So was Father Clancy,
he suspected. Father could whip out a fast Mass—the Suscipiats
and Hosannas and Agnus Deis all running together in a blaze of
Latin gibberish. He could mumble out the whole shebang in about
25 minutes, barely taking a breath. His best time this year was
22:28. Those poor little altar boys, with their little white vest-
ments, were stumbling over themselves, trying to keep up. Tommy
had been one, an altar boy, in 3rd and 4th and 5th grade, and had
actually considered it quite an honor, not to mention a huge re-
sponsibility for someone so short. But after a few seasons, it became just another job. Toward the end of his secular career, there
were no scoldings, no performance appraisals, no formal resigna-
tions asked for, only less and less sign-ups for Mass. And then . . .

none. Sister Angelica, who was in charge of the scheduling, knew who was tired, and who the young up-and-comers were. Fine with him, let them have it—he had done his time. Some of the older kids who still liked the game, but just lost a little speed over the years were kept on in coaching or administrative positions, but not Tommy. He opted for full retirement. It was easier now, kneeling at the pew, critiquing the performance of the new kids.

It wasn't like they didn't believe in God and stuff, they did, but the boys just didn't like Mass. At least not this much of it! Counting Sunday, it was six episodes a week. Trying to be still, to be good, trying not to giggle or cut one. Tommy thought about God and stuff a lot around campfires, when all the stories had been told, the marshmallows gone, when the quiet embers glowed their pulsing white. He also thought about Him *real hard* that first time he water-skied up at Lake Shawnee, but not so much in church any more. When you worry so much about proper positioning, about getting all the details just so, you tend to lose sight of the big picture. Come on now! What guys really, really wanted to do was to howl, to beat their chests like it counted, to eat a fire-braised sirloin tip off a stick, and burp, and scratch themselves freely, and if they *did* cut one, to be able to laugh about it. It was just a fart, for God's sake! (Centuries ago, humans had just left the caves and women were getting around to civilizing things with some basic ground rules: no hitting girls, tell the truth, take care of your kids, relieve yourselves *outside* please, and go to church. What women really wanted out of church at first was their smelly, dangerous men trimmed up some and in a clean robe. Obedient and *unarmed* for about an hour a week.)

But girls actually seemed to like Mass, they payed attention. Heck, they *must* have invented it! No man could of thought of a ceremony that long, on a hard bench, wrapped up tight in uncomfortable clothes, showing off big hats and gloves. You want solemn? O.K. Guys could do solemn—*no problemo, Kemosabe.* But choreographed like that? Stand, kneel, stand again, genuflect, stand, kneel, sit down, stand some more, bow over, strike your breast, and then get in a long kneeling line for a wafer? And singing im-possibly high notes all the way through? That was woman-input, sure as shootin'. Anyway, the bishops listened to the girls' ideas, and said they'd think about it. But any man that would aspire to bishophood and dress like *that*, well . . . they were just on the girls' side is all. Mass got womanized.

CHAPTER 2.

SAINT LUKE'S

After Mass, they sang the last song, and filed out, littlest kids first again, then split up and shot down the hallway to their classes. After some shuffling, and book un-loading, and 'I-know-you-are-but-what-am-I's,' all the kids stood by their desks, looked up at the picture of Jesus, put their hands in proper prayer position, and chanted out an 'Our Father' and a 'Hail Mary.' Then they topped it off with a 'Glory Be.' Tommy could do them each in one breath, easy—even the 'Our Father.' Jesus's heart was out there, sort of floating around in front of his chest, a little flame coming off the top of it. He looked down at the whole class, looking sort of sad and disappointed. Plus He had, well, how else to put it, *girl's* hair.

Next, the whole class turned to face the other corner where the flag was, and droned out a Pledge of Allegiance. There were pictures of George and Abe up there, too, bracketing the clock, so Tommy wondered why they didn't throw a prayer or two up at them? They looked as disappointed in the class as Jesus, but with no hearts or organs or anything showing. There were also The Rules Of Whole Numbers over there on the display board (in construction paper) next to the chalkboard. Surely that must have been worth a chant or two. And then, what the heck, they could all turn to the window next, and pray out, way over there, to the swing sets. The Swing Set Psalms! Then, why not pray to the trees, for cryin' out loud, and next, the dumb birds? *Yeah!* Then let's whip back around and pray to the coat rack and the light switch for Pete's sake, and by then it'd be 3:30, and they could just call it a day and get the heck *out* of there! Sister Redempta was watching them all the time, checking for proper enunciation, for slouching, noting who looked a little antsy, or who was smiling a little too much. The ones she would have to keep a special eye on that day. She noticed Tommy Riley was rolling his eyes during prayers.

This year, Tommy was 2nd row, 5th seat. An O.K. seat, not great, but all right. Mike Kontovan was in his row, 2nd from the front. They always kept best friends apart, *just because.* The girl he thought he would marry, when he started liking girls, was one row to his left, two seats up. Michelle Molson. Pretty face, nice brown hair, never threw rocks, and best of all, she was starting to grow, you know . . . Breasts! The first in their class! Big, soft, dazzling. Scrumptious, perhaps. All the girls had little bumps, but these were The Real Thing, buddy boy! They were the topic of consider-able discussion at recess, and had apparently been under the sur-face all the time, like a flower bulb or something. Like lilies in the field, Tommy mused. He'd like to lily *her* field! (Then he stopped himself, and made a quick addition to this week's confession list.) One fine day awhile back, they just sprouted! Both of them! It seemed to have happened during Easter vacation, an appropriate time for new growth, he thought. New life! Tommy wondered what the heck the Molsons had been feeding Michelle this Easter, must have been a magic ham or something. He didn't think choco-late bunny ears could have pulled this off!

From his position, Tommy's eyes could swivel up and over, never moving his head. Sister Redempta would be walking the perimeter, thinking he was reading or writing or generally follow-ing orders, and he could clandestinely zero in on Michelle's excit-ing, new little profiles as they danced and wriggled around under her armpit, trying to keep up as she bent over, scribbling away. She was a furious writer, always took notes, and Tommy appreci-ated it deeply. RIIIINNNNGGGG!

And so began another exciting day of seventh grade. After a spirited religion class (impure thoughts; mortal vs. venial), and English class (participles), and recess (just plain loud), came math.

Mathematics bothered Tommy. He wanted to like it, he really tried, but every year they took the same perfectly good numbers and thought of more and stupider ways to screw them up. Take a 10 for instance—a *great* number. It had built pyramids, had been at Kitty Hawk. You could see a 10, work with a 10. So then they go and divide it by 3. Butcher it! You didn't have a 10 anymore, you had fractions of a ten. Body parts. You knew it made three 3.333s, but why the heck not just start out with a stupid, useless, pathetic little 3.333 in the first place? Why kill a perfectly good 10? What was the point? And this year—the New Math. They finally got the old one so screwed up that they just chunked it, and started all over. And it was even harder! All of a sudden, a 10 didn't even equal 10 anymore at all! Now, $10 = x$! Tommy would like to have met the spas-mo goonball who came up with this nonsense!

Another thing that made Tommy nervous about math, was the serious effect it was having on his future. All their futures. If they wanted to be Air Force pilots, and they all did, they had to get As and Bs in math. In everything! "If you want to be a pilot, young man, you'd better pull that grade up." That admonition was repeated in houses all over base, every report card day, and the admonitioners were serious! Air Force officers liked math, they were *great* with math, it was easy for them. But of course, C students would have never made it to be Air Force officers anyway, never spawned their nervous little charges. Checklists were checked off 'by the numbers.' Planes flew 'by the numbers.' So Tommy tried. If they wanted fractions, he would fraction. If they wanted long division, he would long division 'till the cows came home. He was gonna fly.

After another class or two came lunch. Cuisine de To-Peka. Lunch was eagerly anticipated by all the elite little connoisseurs. The restaurant was okay, with pretty good lighting, but it smelled a little like Pine-Sol. March down to the basement, walk through the door (in line of course) and a nun put a little wax carton of milk in your hand. Then you went to your spot, by your friends. A little minimum security for 25 minutes, time to compare notes on the day so far, to catch up a little. Open up the ol' feedbag—no surprises there! Another Wonder Bread sandwich, which helped Build Strong Bodies Twelve Different Ways, housing some peanut butter and jelly. Grape today. It was wrapped in wax paper as neat as a little present. An apple, two carrot slices, one lonely, lovely Twinkie. Never the pair. Also at their table, Eddie had a drumstick, as usual. He lived on a chicken-and-tomato farm outside Topeka, and couldn't WAIT to trade for a sandwich. Eddie hated chicken.

After a hearty lunch, all the kids got to go outside and choose up for baseball or basketball or something, and generally go nuts and scream as loud as you thought you could get away with. This recess was the Big One, the thirty minute-er, and you could get a good game going. Tommy ran past the slime-ball juvenile delinquents who never played. Today they were huddled around some hapless roly-polys with a little magnifying glass, snickering among themselves, nervously keeping watch. Tommy knew that if God *was* in every living thing, even things with spiracles, those guys were dead meat.

He lined himself up with the other kids by the backstop, and let the captains start choosing. The captains could choose whoever they wanted, but nuns chose the captains, a new one each day, both for the boys and the girls. Tommy and the kids grudgingly admitted it was a good system. He got on a pretty good team, except they had to pick Snotty Scotty Valentine, because the other team had to get William (The Wimp) Hodges. The girls had their own game going on the next diamond, and Tommy noticed that Michelle could still swing away—there was no worrisome interference yet. Good.

The boy's game started, got down to some serious screaming and yelling, and by the bell it was 4 to 3, Riley's team behind, but they had two on base and Billy (Bombshell) Preston was up next. They hurriedly scratched their last positions on a piece of paper. They were going to finish this one tomorrow! Then they all trooped back inside, sweaty and flushed with the afterglow of a good game, comparing scraped elbows, and guzzling water at the hall fountain. A few last shoulders were punched, the last barbs delivered, as the players took some deep breaths and tried to go from recess mode to the unnatural quiet of the waiting classroom.

Tommy squirmed in his seat and listened absent-mindedly to the drone of Sister Redempta discussing sentence structure or some silly nonsense. She wrote on the board (neatly): 'The clouds were like cotton balls, high in the sky.' Oh brother, thought Tommy, rolling his eyes back in his head. The clouds were like *what?*

Suddenly, his alert ears picked up the shrill whistle of jet engines approaching from the distance. The roar became louder, putting a temporary stop to the lesson while the classroom windows trembled insistently. The huge, six-engined bomber passed low over the school toward the runways to the south, it's shadow charging across the playground in a flash. Tommy heard the engines spooling back, and knew that the gloved fist in the cockpit had just selected 45% power and Flaps 25 for the downwind and base approach. Just like the manual. He closed his eyes as his right hand slid silently across the desktop and felt for the Flap lever, moving it back fully to 35 degrees—Tommy now turning for final approach. Keep that nose five degrees below the horizon now . . . steady. His left hand caressed the imaginary wheel, a little to the right, he thought . . . a little more with this wind, maybe . . . showing slightly low according to the VASIs so add some power . . . *powerrr* . . .

"Mr. Riley, were we paying attention?" snapped Sister Redempta.

Tommy looked up and stammered, "Um, uh . . ." as he suddenly landed back in class. Yes. Yes, we *were* paying attention, thought the young pilot. And you would be paying attention, too, if you had 105 tons of jet bomber strapped to your crazy nun butt. He didn't actually say that, though. What he actually said was, "Yes, sister." He saw Michael looking back at him, snickering. Tommy glared at him. *Just you wait, Konto.*

Science class was next, and it was pretty okay most of the time. It was usually stuff like levers and pulleys, and how a light bulb worked, all of which the boys liked. A lot! In fact, last winter, after a few long nights of Dr. Jekyll-like experimentation, Tommy just about had perpetual motion licked again—with some Tinker Toys, his Erector Set, and the spring from the storm door. He was *this close.* He was sure it would work next time, if he would just use model airplane glue, instead of that crummy civilian Elmers. But then his dad told him to put the spring back on the door. He told his dad how close he was, showed him the gizmo, even offered to cut him in on the royalties, but no deal. He had to put it back, just because.

Science this year was mostly "The Wonder Of Life,"and The Wonders Of Life that nuns thought they should know about, were stupid little thoraxes, and pupae, and compound eyes. Like Billy Fitzsimmons. There was a little human anatomy tossed in here and there, but not The Wonder that the boys wanted to learn about. Tommy didn't know much about girls' anatomy yet, but he sure was trying. He could see the bosoms, of course, and was developing a keen eye for those. Girls weren't so mysterious (they were dumb!) but the you-know-what-part between their legs certainly was. Their only guide so far were some ridiculous rumors, and a medical encyclopedia at Bobby and Mike's, with colored overlays showing all the organs and arteries and everything. Veins were blue, arteries were red, muscles kind of a brownish-pink, but everything in that mysterious area on the woman picture seemed connected to bladders or intestines or tubes that loopdelooped at the top. The boys were gonna crack this case eventually, but it was something that did not give up its secrets easily in 1962.

Anyway, this semester was bugs, so they had bug science. Specifically: ant-bug-science. Whoopdedogpoop. They thoraxed and pupaed and aphided and exoskeletoned. Then they colonied and hived and furrowed and burrowed and took a trip down into the mound. They rubbed antennae with the workers and the soldiers and the queen. Said howdy to the marchers and the cutters and the swarmers and the biters. Then Roger piped up without raising his hand, and asked if they had account-ants and consult-ants down there (ha-ha). Oh, *NO!* What was Roger *DO*ing? Twenty-eight children held their breath, mouths tight.

Sister Redempta spun around toward Roger like a gun turret, and didn't even say a word. Her eyes grew wide, quickly zeroing in on the hapless target, then invisible beams of atomic nun-energy rays shot across the classroom sky and smashed right through his eyeballs. The rays ricocheted and blasted around in there, scrambling Roger's petrified brain until his head lowered, turning red. It became deathly quiet, except for sizzling noise of fried brain juice. Minutes passed. Hours. Finally, the ray was shut off, and Sister asked icily: "Are there any other questions about the division of duties in an ant colony?" There were none. She then cleared her throat to signal the end of hostilities, and the tour continued. Roger's head was still down, smoking. Sheesh! They were gonna have to take him home on a stretcher! Holy Moly!

Then Billy turned around to smirk at stupid Roger and started to laugh, but then stopped himself and blew some stuff out his nose. Oh, no! thought Tommy, suppressing a similar event. Things were reaching critical mass. Tommy jammed his arm up in the air and gave the universal 'Gotta Go Now Emergency This Is Serious' hand wriggle. He was looking straight down now, eyes squeezed tight, holding in the volcano. He almost had to pee. Please. Ohplease. *Pleasepleaseplease.*

"Yes, Mr. Riley, you may be excused."

Tommy launched from his desk and out into the cool, silent hall, leaned against the concrete wall, and exhaled tiredly. Man, he was getting too old for this. As he turned to stroll down the hall on that life-saving bathroom pass, Tommy checked things out. The lower classes were just so quiet! Had they ever been timid little sheep like that? The aura of nuns wore off on them a *long* time ago. By about the fourth grade, the boys discovered they were just ordinary human women, only worse. Tragically, as the boys got older and craftier, they were given older and craftier nuns.

If a nun had lots of wrinkles and a little moustache, you weren't gonna get away with jack! This year, Tommy had Sister Redempta, of course, and she had it in for him, no lie! Always making him do it again, till he got it right. Neatly. Please, do not slouch. Read that last sentence again, please, and enunciate. Pay attention. You know, just plain old *mean!* They had heard rumors about this one from the kids who had her last year, and their warnings had proved to be devastatingly accurate.

He returned to class just as the bell rang. He noticed a lot of thin, drawn lips and downcast eyes, as the kids rooted around nervously, waiting for permission to go outside. Sister Redempta was looking out the window, and he could see her jaw muscles twitch as she tried to simmer down. That class had been a rough one for everybody. Man-o-man, they *all* needed a vacation!

After recess, they suffered through a little social studies, then hit geography class and things started really heating up. The last class of the day, finally! Even Pamela and Suzy and all the other smarty-pants were wiggling restlessly. Sister Redempta spent a lot more time ordering the prisoners to sit up straight and pay attention. The natives were restless! Timmy had his hand cupped up to his ear with a far-away look and a weird smile, which meant he had a gnat bouncing and tickling around in there. Lauren was drawing little devil horns on the explorers in her book. Vicki invited Roger to mind his own beeswax (out loud.) Pencils were sharpened a little more aggressively than was warranted, and some erasers bounced their crazy, unpredictable route across the smooth floor. A desk groaned and chattered loudly as it was butt-scooted up an inch, then a book closed a little too firmly. It was the equivalent of out-of-control prisoners smashing and banging their tin cups back and forth across the thick, metal bars, yelling their grievances, demanding to talk to the governor. Maybe not quite so loud, but for polite little Middle American kids, the delicious, rascally intent was the same, so they made do with it. Ha! *Try to stop us, copper!*

Tommy looked out the window as his brain suddenly decided

to go somewhere else for awhile. He saw some little, nervous wrens suddenly spread long, graceful white wings as they circled above a churning boat wake. He squinted up at them in the tropical sun, and heard their boisterous cries— the call of the wild.

"Another sip of beer?" asked Michelle, as her voluptuous body glistened in the hot, tropical sun. She held the cool elixir to his appreciative lips, and Splash Riley took a long pull of the amber liquid, some of it spilling down his straining, muscled chest. Michelle found a towel and dipped it into the ice-filled cooler, soaking it in the freezing, cold, clean water. She pulled it out, shut the lid, and let it drip tantalizingly on the teak deck. Then she walked slowly toward Splash, gyrating in that special manner that she knew drove her man wild, licked her full lips in teasing anticipation, then straddled up to his fighting chair. She slowly wrung the towel out over his tousled hair, the fiery cold liquid cascading down his taut, straining body. "Mmmmmm, still . . . *hot?*" Michelle purred. Then she seductively wiped his head, then his neck, then his chest, lower . . . lower.

"Cool it, babe," Splash grunted. He was enjoying the attention and the soothing, cool water, but the last four hours he had been fighting the world-record marlin, and it was finally beat. He couldn't afford to lose concentration now! He and the huge beast had become as one, connected by a thin, taut, monofilament line, with animal messages of prey and stalker, victor and vanquished, telegraphing themselves continually to each other. Splash knew from these signals when the behemoth would sound, a *split second* before it did so, and released the drag perfectly. He knew when it would jump, a *split second* before it launched its massive self from the ocean, and so had the rod tip up high, the line reeling in just right, the incredible ballet of the two warriors playing out perfectly on the briny stage. The crew, up in the conning tower of the trim vessel, had never seen anything like it.

When the bronzed couple had chartered the boat at daybreak, the crew thought it would be a little trolling, maybe a few martinis, typical requests of the jet-set that these two beautiful people so obviously represented. But when the glistening pair got down to serious business, and gave the captain firm but polite instructions about where to go to find the great fish, everyone was impressed. They even baited their own hooks! Any woman who would dig into a quart of night-crawlers like that was O.K. in their book. And now this! They had never seen a battle so perfectly fought, with no wasted motion, and he with an uncanny sense of timing on the straining reel. The great fish was sounding for the last time, everyone sensed that. The battle was over, the bronzed fisherman had won. They looked down at Splash's straining back as he began the last pulling, raising of the spent beast to the surface. "I'll bring him alongside, then you are to release the hook," Splash announced.

The crew looked at each other in disbelief. "But, this is a record-breaker, sir. Over 2,000 pounds easy! And on 8-lb. test! You'll be famous from Kona to Key West. You—"

"No! We release him," stated the mighty sportsperson. "We'll not tag this great fish, either. That's an order."

"Yes, sir!" answered the crew. Never in their lives had they seen a man so—

"RIIIINNNNGGGG"

The big Simplex clock announced 3:30, their sentence was up! School was O-U-T OUT! Splash and the crew released the fish, then he and Michelle embraced in a last, lingering kiss while the crew looked down, a little embarrassed. Then Tommy got his bookcase, and filed out the hall to the bus.

CHAPTER 3.

RED ALERT

After school, Tommy was still feeling a little tired and salty from the battle, and was still kind of thinking about that last, lingering kiss with Michelle. He thought he just might try a french one next time, whatever that was. He had just heard about them at recess. It might be just the ticket.

He and the Kontos had finished their homework, and were sort of goofing off out in The Field. A clod was tossed. A hit. There was some return fire. Sides were immediately chosen, rules of battle laid out, argued, then agreed upon. There was a 10 second cease-fire declared so the boys could find cover, and man their positions.

How the holy heck had he got into this predicament? Master Sergeant Rock Riley sat hunched with his back up against a large tree, the sound of clods and cannon fire tearing into it and whizzing through the tall jungle grass on either side. He adjusted his small shaving mirror slightly, and saw the reflection of his determined face in it for a second, the two-day growth of beard defining the edge of his the grim, determined jaw. His intelligent eyes narrowed, then he almost laughed as he thought of the crazy, cosmic turn of events that led him into this stinking jungle. Then he caught himself, and went back to work.

In the mirror now, he made out the camouflaged figure of a commie soldier trying to out-flank him, behind and to the right—back by the treeline. He pulled back the bolt on his Springfield, loaded a round, then turned the heavy but trusty rifle around backwards, the barrel resting on his shoulder, pointing behind and around the edge of the tree. He sighted through the mirror again, carefully calculating everything in reverse for windage and elevation. This was a *crazy* way to fight a war! Everything was bass-ackwards! Without waiting for permission from Washington, the grizzled warrior gently pushed the trigger back with his thumb. The heavy rifle cracked, the noise painfully close to his ear. Bullseye! The commie plopped forward, and two compatriots rushed out, each grabbing a twitching leg, and pulled the inert form of their comrade back into the treeline. Riley figured there were about sixty left—he'd have to watch his ammo. He had stumbled onto the enemy camp two days ago, and had been pretty busy ever since. He figured there were about three hundred of them when he first opened up, and they were pretty good! He could tell from the snazzy, snarly bear emblem on their helmets that they were the elite Moscow Marauders, probably the best trained and most well-equipped unit that the commies could field.

He needed to see if their Mauser 880 was still operating. He put his helmet on the end of a stick, poked it out from behind the slowly diminishing tree and Ka*BAM!* He pulled the metal helmet back in, and smiled sardonically. Sheesh! His helmet looked like a smoking colander. The big Mauser was still very much there, he'd say. He'd try to take it out tonight, under the cover of darkness. Rock needed to rest up a little for tonight's busy schedule. The enemy was silent, too—biding its time. Licking its wounds.

He leaned back, relaxed a little, and began philosophizing. He was good at that. He had graduated Magna cum Laud from Harvard, earning his Doctorate in Philosophy. He had enjoyed the East Coast, the tough competition of the Ivy League schools, those vacations at Nantucket, but Rock was always anxious to graduate and get back to the Real Coast, the west one. Just as soon as he did, he opened up a little philosophy shop at Sunset and Vine. There was plenty of parking for the regulars, plus a lot of walk-in traffic, too.

His fiancee, the luscious and vibrant Michelle LaBomba, was a joy to be with, and could turn every head in Tinsel Town. She

stayed busy with her successful art practice, and the Corvette deal-
ership that her proud parents had bought her as a graduation gift.
In La-La Land, she'd earned her Doctorate in Art from UCLA. She
was a pretty danged good artist when she went in, the young phi-
losopher thought, but when she got out of that large, progressive
institution, she insisted on painting the heads on backwards. He
really didn't understand it, but the stuff sold like hotcakes! When
Rock was tired of philosophizing, he'd lock up the shop, then
cruise on down to the Corvette showroom. Mr. LaBomba was urging him to get into management there, even had a luxurious office
set up for him, his name on a brass plaque on the door as a temp-
tation, but Rock would always head for the mechanic's bay. His
heart was in the motors, the pumps, the things that made the
powerful, futuristic 'Vettes often work.

A bullet zinged by his ear, and Sgt. Riley snapped to attention. He carefully put up the mirror, and went back to work. In a
minute, the Marauders were down to fifty-nine, and Rock leaned
back tiredly. His position wasn't good. If the enemy had any sense,
they'd feint left, flank him on his right, launch a scatter-bomb
attack, demand an unconditional, then go home and eat supper. It
was quiet, just too darned *quiet* out there. He cautiously leaned his
head out to see what those sneaky bozos were up to, when more
bullets zinged through the tall grass, and a mortar crunched on
the other side of the tree, spraying him in dirt. Yikes! How the
heck did he ever get into this chicken outfit?

When his draft notice came, he didn't hesitate at all. He knew
he had an obligation to serve, and didn't even mention his Doctorate. The Army noticed how he aced boot camp, and always said
"Yes, SIR" without being told to, so they sent him to Officer's
School. He aced that, too, and attained the rank of colonel in
pretty short order.

There was a new program coming up, and some people at the
top wanted to kick him upstairs to the Pentagon, to head it up. It
was about brush-fire wars, limited engagements, and police actions. There were some civilians pretty high up there who wanted

to use the Army carefully, selectively, to get it out there and win
some hearts and minds. To keep the peace (of all things!) They
asked for Col. Riley's thoughts on the subject. In a nutshell, his
brilliant 287-page report de-bunked the whole philosophy, and
insisted that if *soldiers* were needed to keep the peace, there was
actually a *war* going on, and it was time to choose up sides and get
on with it. But many others (who didn't know a rifle from a
Kelvinator) were excited about the concept. They assured the suits
at the top that Col. Riley's warnings on the subject were old-
fashioned, barbaric, and not in touch with the feelings of the people
who required peace-keeping. It was 'suggested' that Col. Riley
revise his report before the president saw it, but he refused, of
course. The uncompromising, stalwart colonel resigned his com-
mission, busted himself to sergeant, and got back to the guys who
made it happen—the men in the field.

One of the brush-fire police actions was happening right now
in this stinking jungle. Reconnaissance planes had seen what
seemed to be an illegal enemy camp in a "No Enemy Camp Of
More Than 299 Except On Thursdays And Holidays" zone. The
commies denied it, of course, and everybody in Washington heard
what they wanted to hear, and stuck their heads back in the sand.
Riley said the heck with this, and grabbed his Springfield and
some ammo belts. He was gonna go out, alone if he had to, and
find those bastards. Boy, did he ever!

A projectile came flying out from his left, and just missed
him. Oh, no! Those sneaky slimeballs had snuck around! He saw
the next bullet coming right at him, but there was no time to
move. *Whack!* The clod smashed into his chest, exploding into
little dirty chunks.

"You're dead!" yelled Bobby. "Dead as a doornail. Dead as a
dodo! How come you couldn't see us out-flanking ya'? Did ya'
have your dumb ol' spas-mo head in the sand or somethin?!"

They were all arguing loudly about whether Tommy was dead,
or if he was just wounded, when sirens began blaring all across the
base. What the heck!? There weren't any tornado clouds up there,

and it wasn't time for the siren test. The boys stared at each other, wide-eyed. This could only mean one other thing. Something was serious! They ran back to the housing area, where Bobby and Mike split off and Tommy continued on up to his street, huffing his way home. He could smell dinner before he hit the door, and charged in, slamming the door. Oops.

"What's going on?" Tommy heaved, catching his breath. "We heard the sirens, and—"

"Shhhh!" shushed his mom.

His dad signaled for everyone to be quiet. He was on the phone with the squadron commander, and said "Yes, sir" a lot, taking notes. Tommy was still breathing hard, then glanced over and saw Walter Cronkite on the TV. He walked up to the mahogany Motorola, trying to catch his breath. The sound was down low, so he had to listen very carefully. Something big was going on, something about missiles. In Cuba.

That night, and early next morning, bases all across America were on full alert. All the Forbes planes were to scramble, the bombers dispersing out to forward bases in Florida or England or Alaska. All over! The reconnaissance bombers, the secret ones, would go to secret bases. Large transports would follow the bombers with the mechanics and supplies. Whatever was going on wasn't a TDY. TDY meant the dads would be gone awhile, usually months, and they were used to that, but TDYs were usually scheduled in advance, and the families had some time to get ready. Not like this! TDY meant 'Temporary Duty,' which sounded more proper than COTR, or 'Cheese Off The Russians', which was what TDY *really* was. The planes would fly off to who-knew-where, where the main exports were snowballs or camels, and spend the next few months buzzing around the edge of Russia, teasing them, prodding them, rehearsing. Both sides sharpening up their act. Plus, COTR didn't trip off the tongue so well as TDY. In a world of SNAFU, SAC, TAC, NORAD, and MAC, tongue-tripping counted. This here, though, was a full-base scramble, and Tommy had never seen one like it. The whole darn base was packing up. Something big, and a little scary.

The next morning, while his brothers and sisters were still finishing breakfast, Tommy walked quietly into his parent's room. There were lots of clothes and stuff laid out on the bed, his father hovering over the collection, clearing his throat lowly, packing, looking determined. The big, green B-4 bag was opened wide, filling up slowly—by the checklist of course. Socks, blue, A-08s (5 pr.) Underwear, long thermal, grey or green (3.) More items went in, checked off.

"Where ya goin', dad?"

"Can't say, son."

"How long will you be gone?"

"Till I get back. Not long."

"Be careful.".

"I will, sport. Don't worry." He would be gone when they got back from school. Then the final: "You're the man of the house for a little while. Be good and help your mother."

"Yes, sir."

The bus took the same familiar route. The base really *was* scrambling that morning, Red Alert meant *hustle!* The guards at the gate weren't just saluting, they were looking inside cars, checking everybody's faces and IDs, looking for Russians, he guessed. One car even had its trunk open, and APs were poking around in there. But they let the bus go on by, because they knew Russians wouldn't attend parochial school. Everybody was looking really serious, and there was a lot of noise over on the Flight Line.

At school, Tommy just went through the motions. The day dragged when you're wondering what time the atom bombs will start going off. Should he sneak a Twinkie? He might not be there for lunch, y'know. They had a bombing drill—under your desk, cover your face. All the Air Force kids knew it was totally useless, *dumb.* But if it made the civilian kids and nuns feel better . . . He sat there, scrunched down under his desk, knowing that brave men in heavily zippered flight suits, their faces hidden in visored helmets, peering at pulsing green scopes, were *up* there. Men at the brink. There were Russians acting out this same scene on the other side of the line, but not nearly so brave. They were aimed at us under the threat of death, he knew that, with many chained to their seats. Their instruments saying the same things, but in Russian, of course. And not as accurately. Tommy and his friends all made it to 3:30, and managed to survive the bus trip home, too. Things were going a little better than expected.

After school, all their homework was done, so Tommy and Mike and Bobby were just goofing off in The Field, when they saw Mitch and Sam—the Spasmo-Creeps. They were sergeant's kids. Sometimes they would all fight, and sometimes there would be an uneasy truce, it just depended. The boys circled each other cautiously, sniffing a little, like dogs, just to see how it would go today. It seemed to be going okay, but Mitch was sort of dangerous, though. Mitch knew his way around the base. He stole candy bars sometimes, from the Snak Shoppe. One trick he taught Tommy last year, was to wait in the dark, and when an Air Police truck came cruising by, to bolt out behind it, and yell: "Fuzz! Buzz!" then whip back into the dark and lie motionless in the scrawny bushes, hearts pounding, trying to control their gasping breaths, so's they wouldn't give away their position. Trying to disappear in the night, like an Indian.

Tommy didn't much like it. One of these days, they were gonna get *shot!* No *foolin'!* Mitch also taught all the Catholic kids the Johnny Longdong jokes, the whole set. He wasn't the same Mitch today, and the boys didn't fight or anything. Mitch and Sam's dads, both jet mechanics, had also scrambled. Following their awesome responsibilities to wherever the heck they went, wrenches in hand, making sure everything worked just right when it needed to. Mitch was kind of solemn, and there was some simple cussing— venials, mostly. His heart just wasn't in it. There was an eerie silence coming from the Flight Line. Things just weren't normal.

Tommy walked slowly back to his house, kicking some gravel, and could smell supper when he got near the door. Friday was either fish sticks or salmon patties. Tonight it was fish sticks, and Tommy was glad. His mom was a good cook, a *great* cook, but she

had a tendency to dry out the salmon patties a little. A lot, actually. (He would have gobbled 'em up tonight, though. Could be
their last patties.) She tried hard with that ol' salmon, but criminy,
she was a Missouri girl. What the heck did she know about a
salmon? Bluegills, sure, or maybe a bass, but it was apparent that
she didn't have any Indian or Seattle blood in her, which would
have contained the necessary salmon-cooking genes. Still, she was
trying to introduce a little culture, a little *savior-faire* to the dusty
base. Everyone was real polite about it, of course.

"How are the salmon patties?" she would ask hopefully.

"Mmmmm! Good, mom! Great!" They all drank a *lot* of milk
on salmon patty nights. Lots of ketchup helped, too. They blessed,
and started passing the platter of fish sticks around, sort of quiet-
like. Tommy sat at his dad's place. There were some "What did
you learn in school today's?" but they were all unusually quiet,
still a little worried.

His mom was at the head of the table, looking everybody over,
nodding positively, trying to boost morale on the home-front.
Straightening little things on the table. She was real pretty, and
had been elected Homecoming Queen and all that stuff. She had
shiny black hair and perfect teeth. She looked a lot like Elizabeth
Taylor, but unlike Liz, she sang soprano at church, could antique
furniture, mated for life, and was raising five kids. As a part-time
job, her famous coconut cake always got top dollar at Bake Sales.

His little twerp sisters, Diane and Denise, were sitting next to
each other. Sometimes Tommy could tell a few jokes, and get them
both laughing so hard they'd pee in their pants, and then cry. It was
good, clean fun, but he just didn't feel like it tonight, what with
WWIII just around the corner and all. Diane and Denise were in-
separable, and bestest friends when they weren't screaming or scratch-
ing at each other. Their mom had them both in girl-woman training
programs. Last winter was dishes, and the last few weeks was dusting.
Dusting 101. His mom was a *nut* about dusting, but then, she ma-
jored in Home Ec. Every Saturday morning, Tommy would be down
there, cleaning the basement from top to bottom, snickering at his

poor little sister's sentence. The little slave laborers would be upstairs, dusting everything that didn't move. Little girl-women, each with a dustrag and some Lemon Pledge, eyes narrowed, searching for dust . . . to find it, to kill it. They were good! They even got the back of the TV! When the girls were finished with their chores, they could play. They would squeal and run down the hall and back to their room, then set up the doll house. Moving the teensy furniture around, straightening things out. Dusting a little bit.

On the other side of the table were his littler brothers, David and Mark. Davey-o was a pretty good kid, still small, but real strong for his age. Sometimes it took two adults to pry his fingers off something breakable. He usually went for the ukulele, or for Markie. And they never had a cat stick around for long after Dave got really mobile. Dad liked that part! He was really talking now, but had seemed to level off at "two-nine." Give that back! was "two-nine!" Change the channel to Captain Kangaroo and Mr. Green Jeans and Bunny Rabbit, while I drink juice and take a dump in my fresh diapers right here on the floor, was also "two-nine." Where's Kitty-kitty? purred out innocently, "two-niiiine?"

Mark was in his high-chair, up high, royal. He liked it up there! He was going to be handsome and spoiled. Tommy knew about the handsome part, because most babies looked like drooling aliens, but Markie looked good—big, pretty, dark eyes, and wavy black hair. He looked like the Gerber baby, only better. Tommy knew he would be spoiled, too, because between his mom and his two sisters, he couldn't recall Mark's feet ever having hit the floor.

While they were all clearing the table, his mom clicked on the TV. Walter told them that the situation seemed to be worsening. There had been an "incident" in the cold, hostile sky over the Bering Sea near Alaska. Tommy and his mom had both noticed the Underwear, long, thermals (3) being packed that morning. She tensed up a little, but said nothing, so neither did Tommy. They weren't sure where their dad was, but Alaska was a good bet. Walter said that Russia was sending an important message that very night, to Washington, D.C.

Tommy finished helping with the dishes, then went down-stairs to his room in the basement, and lay on his bed, looking up. He and his dad had built his room down there, in the far corner of the basement, and it was pretty neat. He helped his dad measure and cut the 2x4s and put up the walls and hang the door and everything. They even used some New Math on it. It didn't seem so dumb when his dad showed how they could use x to make the shelves come out even. The 2 x 12 studs of the ceiling were covered with maps, the finishing touch that they put up with the staple gun. These were airplane maps, not car ones, with direct yellow routes drawn from city to city, charging across mountain ranges, oceans, and continents. Not wiggly car-map roads—but the straight-line world of flight! The serious red lines meant off limits, or enemy territory. He had the U.S. up there, of course, the Pa-cific, and most of Europe. Alaska and the Kamchatka peninsula were right above his bed—a cold, dangerous place at the top of the world where the two adversaries often met. What had happened up there today? Was his dad okay?

And airplanes, so many model airplanes, hanging from the clear fishing line, Eagle-Claw brand, 8 lb. test. Turning slowly, silently, he knew them all. The silver Americans, the bombers: the huge B-36, the B-47, the B-52, the B-58 Hustler, the not-yet-but-soon futuristic XB-70. That one was all white. The transports: the C-130 (Herky Bird) Hercules, the C-133, the bulbous C-124, the Gooney Bird, and the sleek, new, experimental C-141. And the fighters! He had all the old ones from Korea till now, including all six of the Century Series: the F-100, 101, 102, 104, 105 and 106. There was no F-103, of course—that one turned out to be a real dud. Sometimes those things just happened. The Russians were up there, too, usually in dark green plastic. He didn't know why, but it was a dark, dangerous country. The Russians put up the massive Bison, the Badger, and the new, deadly Tu-95 Bear—they would have to watch out for that one. With a service ceiling of 44,000 feet, and a range of 7,800 miles *with* a 25,000 pound bomb load, it was that psycho Kruschev's Big Stick. Those Tupolev boys were getting pretty good! A little further over, the MiG-15 was belching cotton smoke as it fled silently from the pursuing Sabre Jet. WWII was up there, of course, over by the closet. Just about all the Allied, Japanese and German planes were represented— twirling and chasing—some with black and orange painted cotton trailing from blazing engines, little wood-burner dots marking the paths of the bullets. The T-6 was hanging up-side down, because Tommy knew it was a good little looper. There was a sleek Connie, and a Pan Am 707 over in the civilian corner, sort of staying out of the way. On his desk was a half-finished B-25 laying upside down, balanced on its box. The landing gear was poking up to the ceiling, making it look like a big, dead bug. Rubber bands were wrapped tight around the freshly-glued wing halves, and its freshly painted little crew sat balanced delicately against the cardboard. Boots: flat black; Uniform: olive drab; Mae Wests: yellow; Face: flesh; Helmet and gloves: brown; all waiting to be glued into their Seats: silver.

Airpower (followed immediately by a gutsy ground attack) determined the outcome of wars, of their very lives, he knew that. Airpower was why he was born American, and not some poor Russian slob, or a Frenchman. Airpower was up there tonight, doing something. Determining what his next months and years would be like, and he wished he was up there, helping out. Doing something.

CHAPTER 4.

THE OVAL OFFICE

Sunlight streamed into the tall windows, silhouetting the large, cluttered desk. The famous coconut was at the corner, by the little PT 109 boat model. The Washington monument fairly shone in the distance through the windows in the morning light, but no one was really paying attention to the scenery. Men were shaking hands briskly, rustling about, muttering quietly and choosing chairs. They were all there, all the bigwigs, and this meeting was a Big One. Neatly dressed servants scurried silently, making sure everyone had their coffee or pastries before they got down to business.

The Kennedys were there, of course. The Joint Chiefs of Staff, all four of them, with their adjutants. MacNamara, clutching charts and papers to his chest, his eyes hidden behind thick glasses. Schlesinger was there. Dean. Adlai. Johnson hurried in, trying to tuck in his shirt, wondering what the sam-hill was going on. They all finally settled in, establishing a little pecking order as they claimed the tall leather chairs facing the President's desk.

JFK was reading the brief silently, and when they were finished shuffling about, he looked up. "Well, gentlemen," the President started slowly, in his familiar accent. "They really have us by the, ah, nuts."

From the back of the room came a knowing giggle, quickly suppressed. All eyes shot back to the corner, to the Pink Chair. Damn! He'd forgotten she was still in here! She was really starting to get on his nerves. He said politely, "Ah, Marilyn, could you excuse us please?"

She pouted, and stood up to leave. The entire room craned their eyeballs, appreciating her slow and deliberate retreat. At the door, she turned and breathed out a throaty, "Yes *sir*, Mr. President *sir*," then a wink and a smile, and she spun around and was gone. The loins of the most powerful men in the free world stirred as one, and wanted to follow the figure out the door, and deep, deep into the plush Rotunda, but those loins had a big job ahead of them today, so they all turned back around and got back to work.

"What a ballsy, ah, proposal. Those slimy, brilliant ah, baahstahds." He handed the papers to his little brother. "Please read it for all of us, Bobby."

The young attorney general began: "To the President and Cabinet of the, ah, United States of America: Your unprecedented and completely unnecessary alert status over the Cuban events has heightened the situation to intolerable levels. We now seem to find ourselves at the brink of war. Your Air Forces have gone to full alert, a dangerous and provocative step, and our brave Air Forces have been forced to respond similarly. It seems that one of our aircraft has crossed the Fail Safe line, lured by false imperialist beacons, and is missing and presumed lost. We cannot guarantee that this type of incident won't happen again, with dire consequences."

The President raised his crinkled eyes to Gen. LeMay. "Confirmed," snapped the general, his unlit cigar clenched in his straight teeth, erect with importance. "Got that bastard. A Bison. Off Kiska." His eyes narrowed with warrior intent. *"Never knew what hit him."*

To the left of the general, a large, brooding, balding man slouched in his leather chair. The Vice President hated LeMay, that fancy-shmansy uniform, all that stuff on the visor of his fancy blue hat. Whutinhell was that crap, anyway? From his position, Johnson's eyes could swivel up and over, never moving his head. He squinted to focus in on the silver artwork on the brim of the general's hat. Huh? *What!?* A gol-dang eagle carryin' a gol-dang stick o' lightning!? Now *that* was pretty gol-danged ballsy. How'd ya like to wear something like that to work everyday? Christ Awmighty! All those la-de-da flyboys made him want to puke. The way they all walked so precise, and had their damn precise little haircuts, and pretty little wives, and little silver eagles, and always said *'Yes, SIR!* without being told to. And plus they all seemed to have such pert little, trim little, *perfect* ears. He hated their guts. Johnson swiveled his eyes slowly back to the president's desk. Kennedy had stopped rocking, and was squinting sternly at the vice president. Crap!

"Ahh, Lyndon, this is fairly, ah, important. Were we paying attention?"

"Yessir." *Goddam!*

"Is there, ah, anything you wish to share with us?"

"Um, no sir." *Ya' dang pretty Harvard puke!* He saw LeMay and Adlai grinning silently at each other. *Crap!*

"Good. Continue, Bobby."

The attorney general surveyed the room and went on: "There-fore, in the interest of world peace, and while still maintaining the sovereign right of the Soviet Union and its brave ally, Cuba, to provide whatever weapons it deems necessary for the defense of our people and lands, the Supreme Soviet will nevertheless agree to the, ah, removal of all offensive weapons from Cuban soil." There was an excited buzzing throughout the room. Heck, that was what they wanted, wasn't it? So what's the big problem?

Jack held up his hand for silence. "Continue, Bobby."

He cleared his throat, the famous Kennedy adam's apple mov-ing up and down deliberately. "However, during the time that this removal will be taking place, both the United States Air Force and the Air Forces of the Soviet Union must stand down."

"Outrageous!" LeMay exploded, his voice seething. "This is some kind of trick! Those commie motherf—"

"Easy now, Curtis," warned the President.

'Yeah, easy now Curtis,' mimicked Lyndon under his breath. What the hell kind of name was Curtis anyway? Back in school, he would have beat up somebody named like that. Siddown and shuddup, ya' pretty smartass flyboy, he thought. Boy howdy, just you wait till *I'm* president. *Then* you'll be sorry!

Jack motioned to his brother, "Ah, Bobby, let's hear the rest of it, and then, let's think this, ah, thing through rationally, shall we?"

Bobby's eyes darted around the now-silent room and nervously back to the page, then he continued: "These next days will demand a maximum of calm and trust on both sides, and the constant brinkmanship displayed by SAC and the USAF threatens not only the resolution of this crisis, but could doom our great countries to an unfortunate incident that will not only destroy each other, but could end all civilization in a nuclear armageddon. While our missiles are being removed from Cuba, you will kindly reciprocate and remove your missiles from sites in Turkey. Once these significant events are accomplished, normal but hopefully less aggressive air operations can continue. Signed, N. Khrushchev."

More buzzing.

"Well, we may have to go along with it," announced Kennedy. He stopped rocking and looked around the room. "He's sent copies to all our allies, and they're scared, ah, shitless. They want us to accept. Mac, can we verify this in ah, Cuba, send over some reconnaissance planes or something? Make sure they're not pulling a fast one?"

"Afraid not, Mr. President," McNamara replied. "It would have to be a total stand-down. We have to trust them on this one, sir. Soviet ships left Sevastopol and Leningrad twelve days ago for Cuba to take the missiles back. It's a damn flotilla. They're scheduled to arrive in Havana by Sunday morning to start loading up their missiles. Kruschev and Castro insist not only on absolutely no overflights of Cuba, but an entire stand-down. European and Asian bases, too. If we don't agree to the stand-down, the boats turn around and their missiles stay."

LeMay was looking down, seething.

The President concluded: "Well, the final result, besides a little, ah, black eye for us will be that the missiles leave, ah, Cuba, and we won't have a world war three. So what the heck. I say we do it. We still have our missiles and our subs, and so do they. The airplanes are just the most symbolic."

So that was it, thought LeMay, furiously. We're gonna chicken out.

The next many hours were spent working out the details, and hundreds of highly-skilled executive decisions filled the air. The scenario slowly took shape, and in fact developed into a bit of a photo-op for the administration. By the up-date staff briefing later that night, it was finalized. A Russian contingent was already on its way to the U.S. They would be sent on up to Offutt Air Force Base, headquarters of Strategic Air Command. The Vice President would greet them there. A high-ranking American group was right now winging its way to Monino, the headquarters of the Soviet's Air Force. Stand-down orders for both Air Forces were to be given at the same time, both televised live. A little detente, a little truce. A time out.

The Vice President was scribbling away at his note pad, then reached up and tugged a massive lobe, and realized that this really might work! Why shoot, what if the Reds and us *did* stand down those cocky flyboys? Forever? Think of all that airplane money they could spend in other places—like Texas! It'd be like gosh-danged Christmas! He could give money to unions and even poor people, Lord knew there was enough of them around. He chuckled under his breath. More money was a *good* thing. He wasn't *real* smart, but he knew millions of bucks meant millions of votes. His large brain was a-whirrin' now. He could dribble out little bits of money all over society, and Boom! They would vote for him. Yup. The simplest plans were usually the best, that's what Lady Bird always told him. Imagine . . . the whole high-falutin' country a'lookin up to him, hands out. He'd divvy out that gol-durned Air Corp money like a gol-durn king. It'd be great! It'd be a gol-durned *great* society!

CHAPTER 5.

HANGAR 8

It was a sunny Saturday morning, and the three boys had just finished a game of hot box. It was one of their favorite baseball games, where one kid was on one base, with another kid on the other base, both gloved up and playing defense. Then some poor sap would be in the middle, trying to be a moderate, and feint and charge, and run to the safety of either base, all the while trying not to get tagged out or beaned by a hardball. It had ended when Bobby was in the middle, and a wild throw took out one of the McNally's little ceramic frogs, those silly ones with flowers growing out a hole in their back. Who would buy one of those stupid things anyway?

The boys thought they had done it a favor, putting the pathetic thing out of its misery. They also thought that they had helped to beautify the neighborhood a little, but then Mrs. McNally rushed out and disagreed strongly. *She* said they should buy her another frog, but she could save the pansies. The boys were about to list a dozen reasons why they shouldn't, some of which were that they didn't have any money, plus they had *always* played hot box there, long before she put her stupid frogs in the line of fire when Mrs. Kontovan showed up to talk with Mrs. McNally about it, and said perhaps it was time for the boys to play inside. Now. All right, all right, the boys grumbled, and slunk dejectedly back into the house.

What had actually happened, was the little hot boxers had just got grounded for two hours, but it had happened so fast, they weren't even sure what the heck was going on 'til they were sitting in the cool of the Kontovan's basement. *Sheesh!* Well, if they had to be grounded in any basement, this one was the best. Most basements on base had little couches or end tables, pitiful attempts at decorating a dank, windowless tornado shelter, but the Kontos had none of that nonsense. Their dad had made a long workbench, with good lighting, and with lots of tools and solvents around. Major Kontovan made really great plane models, the *best,* with squadron markings and everything just perfect, and no glue globs either. He also had some radio controlled airplanes laying around, their noses heavy with their big, metal Cox engines. The boys were not allowed to touch those, but did of course.

All the kids that mattered made model airplanes, but what usually happened was you bought the Revell B-29 ($.98, plus tax) and sat down with the best of intentions. All the markings would be absolutely authentic this time, no screw-ups! And then, a bottle of Testor's red paint would just *be* there, and before you knew it, wham! A B-29 with red wingtips, a red rudder, red prop tips maybe. Totally inauthentic, but fun! Kids just couldn't stop it, it was bigger than them—but Major Kontovan could. He was *good!*

Bobby and Mike were reading Boy's Life jokes to each other, lazing on the musty-smelling army cots. Every once in a while, they'd throw one over at Tommy, but he wasn't really paying attention. He was sitting on the big green footlocker, studying his bible again: The Ops Manual of the B-47. How to fly one, step by step. By the numbers. Tommy even made little notes in the margins about procedures he questioned. For instance, he thought that the sequence of on-lining the Station 3 auxiliary pump in case of generator failure, *could* cause problems with the 12th stage compressor bleed air, if that pesky secondary AUX 2 buss switch wasn't isolated first. You know. Little things like that. What the heck were they thinking?

He'd thought of writing to Boeing about it, except they'd probably want to know where he got a classified manual, then there'd be the wiretaps and investigations, and next the black cars screeching up to his house (usually Fords, he didn't know why.) Then the men with sunglasses and walkie-talkies surrounding the perimeter. The neighbors would peer cautiously through their curtains, sadly shaking their heads. "The Riley's boy. Who would have thought it? He seemed like such a nice boy. Who will mow our lawn now?" He'd probably end up in Leavenworth, or at least grounded for a year. Nope, some things were better left alone. It was a monster risk just to have it, but, oh well . . . some risks you just had to take.

He knew every checklist of every crewmember, all flight and ground operations, fuel transfer, engine start, and engine shutdown. He had memorized all standard flight procedures, emergency Bold Face lists, instrument settings, speeds to use for every maneuver at different weights and operating temperatures. He knew that airplane better than Boeing and the Air Force put *together*, and could draw every rivet and panel. He had just never been in one.

"Lunch!" Mrs. Kontovan hollered down the stairway. She left the tray at the top step, careful to let the young men have their basement time. Once she came down the steps too quietly, and suddenly, there she was, in a sensible green dress, holding a load of laundry and standing right smack-dab in the middle of the dirtiest joke they had learned from Boy Scout camp. It was as hard on her as it was on them, except that she didn't get her mouth washed out with soap, of course. Lunch was pretty good today: three bologna and ketchup sandwiches with Velveeta slices, three apples, three big, cold glasses of milk, and six chocolate chip cookies. Fran was a good woman.

After lunch and a game of darts, their sentence was up, and the boys blasted up the stairs, out the back door, and high-tailed it down to the creek. It was actually more like a drainage ditch that skirted the edge of the housing area, took a right, paralleled the gravel road that went down to the baseball diamond, continued down by the joke of a golf course, then turned left and took off straight across The Field.

The Field was still wilderness, the only one they had, and its huge summer sunflowers were redwoods, the creek was their raging river, their ocean. The animals within were savage killers, every rat a panther, every garter snake a python. The boys weren't sure what today's mission was going to be, but once they hit The Field, nature would take its course, so to speak. They were about halfway across it, just past the golf course, when they saw Mitch there, sitting by the creek, half-heartedly lobbing dirt clods at some frogs on the other bank. Some hit the water, some hit the muddy bank. Splish. Plop. Splish. Plop.

"Hey, Mitch."

"Hey," he answered back, but didn't look up.

There wasn't much to say. All the dads were gone, and all the airplanes. It just wasn't normal. They were all thinking about when they'd come back.

It was just too quiet! The far end of The Field, which was really far, and off limits to Tommy and the Kontovans, nestled up to the chain-link and barbed wire fence that was the boundary of the actual base, the Flight Line. They could see the tiny, huge airplane hangars lined up, eight of them, with their backs to The Field. The fronts of the hangars faced the parking ramp—now empty, but normally crowded with hulking aircraft—shimmering in the mirage-waves that radiated up from the acres of hot concrete. Beyond that were the taxiways, and still further out, the runways.

Something that was really missing, though, besides the planes and the men, was the hustle.

Blue or yellow Air Force trucks, with red flashing lights on top, would be zipping around the Flight Line, pulling little yellow carts, which would be unhooked, and then plugged into the belly of a huge, silver bomber. The carts were primed and fiddled with, then started up, idling and vibrating, pumping fluids and explosive stuff into the plane's big, thirsty metal tanks. Green uniformed men, out on the ramp, or up on ladders and scaffolding, would be crawling all over the hulking planes. The jets were lined up 5 deep, 10 or 11 rows of them, with hundreds of miniature men stroking them, and feeding them, and fussing over them like little, green worker ants on big, metal queens. This went on day after day, night after night, seven days a week. No goofing off in SAC, buddy boy! You know, *hustle*.

Something else missing was the noise.

On any normal day, there would be the constant, shrill whistling, booming and roaring of jet engines being started, prodded, tested, winding up and winding down. Then, out at the very end of the runway, connected to the wings of a gleaming B-47, the crack and thunder of six engines together—at FULL BLAST— screaming and blasting, sucking huge amounts of Kansas air through their snouts, each jet delivering it to twelve banks of scythe-like blades, spinning, compressing the air, splashing it with fuel, igniting it, and exploding the whole dangerous mix out the exhaust as sooty, black smoke. The thundering, ear-splitting roar was *LOUD*, even way out in The Field, and would absolutely scramble the eardrums of anybody unfortunate enough to be too close to the thing. You know, *noise*.

Something else missing was the action.

The bomber squatting heavily at the end of the runway, the final check, engines straining on their mounts, vibrating their impatient messages through their metal, up through the wings, down the fuselage, and into the seats and bodies of the sweating crewmembers, who sat there, poised and tense, soaking up the messages, the noises, the dancing instruments, feet standing on the straining brakes, making sure the numbers of a hundred dials said exactly the right thing, feeling the feel and sound of a hundred other motors and valves and switches that made the bomber alive, and then, satisfied, loosed their grip on the massive brakes, and the wheels started their rolling . . . rolling . . . the screaming jets now demanding ever bigger gulps of air, rocketing the silver plane arrow-straight down the runway, faster and faster, until whatever air that it slammed into, and through, and was not consumed by the voracious engines, wrapped itself around the wings, faster and faster and *faster!* until the air became a solid, thick, strong thing, strong enough to bend the metal wings up, pulling the whole thundering, roaring bomber up after them, up, up, up into the brilliant blue sky. You know, *action*.

They missed all that. It was just too darned quiet.

Mitch said there was still one left, besides those wimpy trainers. A *real* B-47. In Hangar 8.

"Liar," said Mike.

Mitch didn't need this shit. "Oh, eat me, Kontovan," he said, still lazily flipping clods at the dumb frogs.

"Eat me?" Mike stared at Tommy. Tommy stared back, then looked at Mitch.

"*Eat* me?" Tommy repeated to Mitch. This was a new one!

"Yeah, turdball. EAT me!"

"So what the heck is *that* supposed to mean?" Tommy demanded cautiously, as Mitch had a pile of good-sized clods right next to him, and closest cover was over ten yards away.

"For your information, ya' frecklefaced turdknocker, what it means is—" Apparently, Mitch had never had to define it before, so he cocked his head a little, and narrowed his eyes, buying a little time, so's he could find the right words.

Well, the heck with this, Tommy thought, time was *up!* He challenged: "So let's hear it ya spasmo —" and was met with a blurring motion that was Mitch's right arm, and a dirt clod coming so fast, all Tommy could do was cringe his eyes and begin to rotate his shoulder up to where his little brain told him impact was going to be. If he had rotated it all the way up to the very top of his right ear, it would have worked.

The clod zinged off the tip of it. "YEOW!" he screamed furiously. It stung like crazy. "Hey *you!*" Tommy yelled. He spun around, found a clod, scooped it up and let Mitch have it.

It was a good hit, smack on his chest, a poof of dust coming off. Mitch jumped up and started to charge him, but then Bobby grabbed Mitch from behind, and pinned both his arms to his sides. There was a little struggle, but Bobby was bigger, so there were some symbolic grunts and shuffles, and then it was over.

Mike was inspecting Tommy's ear —it wasn't bleeding. Mitch was looking down, kicking stuff, muttering, still ticked. Tense seconds went by, slowly, dangerously, and then Mitch piped up: "Just for your information, wise guy, it means stick my . . . um . . . *thing* in your mouth. I think. *So there!*"

Well! This sounded so *unbelievably bizarre* to their little Catholic ears, that they all just froze. Even Mitch seemed stunned as he realized what had come out of his mouth. It got real quiet, and the birds stopped chirping. The bugs stopped bugging. They all just stood there in the sun, eyes wide. There was only the quiet sigh of a dry, Kansas breeze, stirring the tops of the fresh spring weeds. More seconds went by, their little minds still trying to register the . . . the . . . *enormity* of what they had just heard.

Mitch looked down at the dirt, embarrassed now, and continued quietly: "Or maybe it means you put your . . . you know . . . thing . . . in mine. I'm not sure." Mike and Bobby and Tommy were still motionless. Stunned. Absolutely wide-eyed with stunnededness. Who could *imagine* such a thing!? Not them!

Then all of a sudden, Bobby let out a whoop and raised his face to the bright Kansas sky. "Yeeeeeeee haaaaaaaaaaaa!" he yelled. "EAT ME!" Boy, what a cuss word! Wowie-ZOWIE!

Then they all let go, yelling it to the heavens, "EAT ME! EEEEEEEEEEAT MEEEEEEEEEEEEEEEEEEEEE!"

"Hey, look, guys," Mitch pleaded, "I didn't make it up, I just heard it!"

Now Mike and Tommy were really going. Hoo-boy! *EAT ME!* Wow! Where did he ever hear a thing like that? Put my . . . in your . . . ! Ha! So *ridiculous!* Who would *do* that? *Martians?*

They were pounding their fists on the warm dirt now, laughing, tears rolling down their cheeks. Their sides were starting to hurt and they couldn't get up. Whenever they almost got stopped, somebody would let out a horse snort, and they'd start all over again. Man-o-man! That Mitch! *Those sergeant's kids!* Wow! Public school *was* different! After what seemed like forever, the boys finally did get calmed down, and just sat there, heaving in gulps of

air, holding their sides, afraid to look at each other in case they got
going again.

After a little while, Mitch allowed as how an airplane really
was left in Hangar 8, his dad told him so. A B-47. Its transduction
pump was busted and not only that, mister smarty-pants, he knew
how to get into the hangar.

Well, *this* they had to see. And why not? The base was nearly
empty, and this kind of opportunity didn't happen every day!

After a quick vote and a review of likely punishments (prison,
the belt, firing squad, etc.) the four boys were snaking down the
creek bottom, skipping from bank to bank, bounding off rocks
and chunks of concrete to keep themselves out of the shallow, brown
water. Crawdads saw the giants bolt by, their huge, boy shadows
blocking out the sun, automatically making their little crawdad
pinchers raise up in defense, but by then the boys were long gone.
The crawdads stayed on crustacean alert for a few seconds, pinchers up and ready, then the all-clear sounded, and they went back
to crawdadding.

The boys were still bent over so no one could see them, running and bounding down the creek. "Hey Mitch, what *kind* of a
B-47?" gasped Tommy, between breaths.

Mitch's major was tanks, specializing in the Axis powers, 1937-
1945. He had every tank model, even the new Monogram 1/24
scale Tiger. But to him, a B-47 was a B-47. He huffed back, "Shit,
I don't know, Riley, a B-47 is all!"

Well . . . Tommy figured some kids just weren't as smart.
Tommy knew his B-47s, just like he knew his cars. It wasn't just a
Chevy—it was an Impala, or a Bel Air, or a Biscayne. (Major Riley
was a Chevy man—always had been. And, he explained, as soon as
you folded up the matchbook cover about four times and jammed
it between the dash and the windshield to stop that infernal buzzing, you had yourself a darn fine car.) At the bottom, the Biscaynes
had the crummy little hubcaps, and almost no chrome. Next up
was the Bel Air, and the Rileys had a blue one. Lieutenant colonels
or above usually got the top-of-the-line Impala. And it wasn't just

a Ford, either. It was a Galaxie, or a Fairlane, or a crummy little Falcon. Same with the B-47s; there were quite a few to choose from, a bunch! The B-47A models, of course, just to get the bugs out. The B-47B models were the bombers, crew of three, one job only: to bomb stuff. The TB-47s were Trainer Bombers, and a couple of them were left behind over by the tower, out in the open. The B-47E models were mostly bombers (just Bs with bigger engines) but some were customized to do special reconnaissance work, with a bunch of cameras down there in the bomb bay. The Reconnaissance versions were called RB-47Es, of course, and this worked out so good, they made the H model. The RB-47H. Three extra guys were stuffed into the bomb bay to work the radar scopes and stuff. It was a super-secret, reconnaissance-only version, that used a lot of the stuff they learned on the E, but snazzed it up some. For an Air Force kid not to know that . . . *well!* But then, Mitch was a sergeant's kid.

They came to the big pipe that directed the creek under the patrol road. Tommy, Bobby and Mike had never gone farther than that because they weren't allowed to, but Mitch had, and signaled them on. They hesitated, weighed everything in their minds, calculated, gulped, and scurried through the pipe.

The ditch took another right, then got real shallow. They were really scared now, hunkered as far over as they could get and down real low, but guilt was making them Day-Glo orange and ten feet high. All four scurried down the ditch bottom, to where the creek went under the high, chain-link and barbed-wire fence, then dropped to their chests and flattened themselves against the warm, dry bank. They were all breathing hard, saying nothing. This was *great!* Even Mike, who was always the first to chicken out, was grinning between fast, shallow gulps of Saturday air. Saturday air was invigorating! *Dangerous!* Heads swiveled alertly, checking all quadrants. It was All Clear. They were going in!

Where the ditch flowed under the fence, it was about three feet deep in the middle, where the dirty water was, but only about a foot deep on the small, flat bank. Going over was out of the question, so they would have to shimmy under the fence on the bank. It was sharp at the bottom, and ready to snag them with its little, sharp, chain link x'es. Bobby pulled up on the bottom of the chain link, hard as he could, and the other three boys, now in an army and dirt mode, crawled Marine-style through the slot. Once through, they heaved the fence up, and held it for Bobby. His butt got caught on a snag—*yowch!*—but then he un-caught it, and shimmied underneath.

"Dam*nation!* Cool-o-rama," he said.

"Shhhhh!" hissed Mitch. Forget that base was practically deserted, that no one was within a country mile, fear dictated silence. He gave them a hand signal: Come on, it said. But keep it low.

The platoon of boys was hunched over again, really moving. The hangars, which looked so silver and perfect from a couple hundred yards away, started to look big and looming, and a little rusty, like some monstrous metal boxes. They bolted out of the ditch and into some high, dead grass that they wished was higher, dropped to their stomachs, and lay there, panting like dogs. Four nervous little necks bent back, so they could see the teeny side window, right by the back corner, now only about 20 yards away. There were seven other hangars to their left, lined up in front of the ramp toward the control tower, getting small in the distance, but *this* was their target. Hangar 8. The soon to be break-ers and enter-ers couldn't see the hangar front, but the back was solid, and the side was solid, too, except for the tiny window that Mitch said was never locked, and seemed to be the only way in. He'd never gone in himself, he cautioned, but had heard the scuttlebutt.

They jumped up on Mitch's signal, dashed across the last road, then hit the dirt again, breathing hard. In the weeds in front of them, they could make out engine parts, old cans, gaskets, and a bunch of other stuff that had been tossed into the scruffy grass over the years. They waited, breathing deeply, eyes looking to the left, to the right, then carefully behind them. No APs. No nothin'.

A c'mon signal from Mitch. They rushed up just below the

high window, commando-style, and froze, then swiveled around, still low, checking again for danger—*just in case.*

All Clear.

"Mike, you stand watch," hissed Bobby. The other three boys looked around for a box . . . or a . . . *there!* In the grass! They dragged and stacked the wooden pallet up against the hot metal side, and Bobby crawled up it like a ladder to the small window, way over their heads. He slid the window open sideways, peeked in, and announced: "It's a gol-durn bathroom!"

Well, it was a start, anyway. They boosted him up and through the opening. He squeezed, grunted, and disappeared. Then his head popped back out. He reached to grab Tommy's hand, Injungrip style, and hauled him up. Tommy clambered inside, stepping on the tank of the toilet. Bobby then leaned back out, hooked up with Mitch, and pulled him through. Wow! They were *in!* Shhhh! . . . They crept out the stall, past the sink, and over to the bathroom door—still scared—expecting APs to be waiting on the other side, .45s cocked and pointed right between their little trespassing eyes. Bobby turned the handle as sloooowly as he could, then pushed the door open a crack. So far, so good. Then he pushed a little further and . . .

"Hiya!"

"AAAAAHHHHH!" The three boys screamed, bounced around like pinballs against the stalls, sink and wall, fell back on their butts, and grabbed their chests. Mitch cracked his shin, and Bobby skinned his elbow, a good one.

Mike just stood there, looking down at them. They were sprawled on the concrete bathroom floor, eyes wide, panting, staring back up at Mike, who chirped, "Hi, guys!"

"Where the holy heck did *YOU* come from?" Bobby demanded. The bathroom door faced the back of the hangar, and Michael pointed the other way, toward the front. The three boys struggled up, moving cautiously out the door, then turned slowly around and saw all of Kansas through the huge, wide-open, hangar door.

And there it was! The bomber's nose was pointing out eagerly

toward the open door, hulking and huge in the shadows, silhouetted darkly against the bright sky and ramp outside. It was tremendous! Perfect!

They made a few cautious, reverent steps toward the monstrous jet, the boys directly under the tail now. Wide eyes gazed
straight up at the towering tail fins and rudder, which seemed to
go up forever, to touch the ceiling! At the very back tip of the
plane, right straight above their little craned necks, were the two
dull, black cannons, thick as their legs, pointing straight back out
of their swiveling turret. Oh, man! This was soooooo good! The
boys were silent, each lost in their own thoughts, their senses maxed
out, as they slowly inspected the magnificent machine.

Tommy looked down the length of the huge cylindrical fuselage toward the nose, over 100 feet away. The polished metal surface of the bomber reflected the hangar wall, and the floor, and the
lights on the ceiling, like a smooth, curved mirror. Just ahead of
him, all around the bottom of the plane, a few antennas poked
out. Not like car antennas, but like little, swept wings. And scattered around the antennas were streamlined bumps and fairings,
mostly black, one greenish, and some silver, all containing radars
or scanners or something important. Then he knew it was an H
model. *His* model.

He walked forward slowly, to the rear wheel doors. All B-47s
had two main landing gears, with two huge wheels on each, right
on the centerline of the fuselage. The back gear was tucked up,
with only about half of it showing from behind the gear door. The
front gear had a much longer strut, with lights and junk on it,
raising the nose of the jet up higher. It gave the plane a real nice,
sort of *regal* nose-up slant to it as it sat there. Like it was ready to
fly. Ready to get up there!

The B-47s were getting older now, and would be retired in a
few years. Their replacement was the B-52, a bigger, slab-sided,
heavier bomber. Tommy thought they looked like a truck. B-52s
also had a much longer range than the B-47, their fat wings full of
fuel. The wings of the B-47 were thin, like a fighter's, and they

bent down with the weight of the engines as the airplane sat. He could see the wingtip, way over by the hangar wall, only about six or seven feet off the ground. Where the wing connected to the fuselage, near the top, it must have been about fifteen or twenty feet up.

He continued past the rear wheels, and under the high, dark wing. There were two jet engines in a streamlined pod, slung under the wing just in front of him. He stared up at the deep black of their sooty exhaust pipes. From the middle of the pod, right between the engines, a slender silver strut came down with a little wheel on it. These outrigger gears didn't support much weight, he knew, but they kept the bomber from tipping over, so they were pretty important in *that* respect. There was another jet engine out by the tip of the wing, by itself. Three on a side, six total.

As he walked cautiously forward, just to his right, in between the front and rear landing gear wells and on the very bottom of the plane, was a big, long, fiberglass and aluminum hump. In a regular B-47, the bomb bay would be there. In this specialized reconnaissance version, the hump contained a dark, cramped, windowless room, cluttered with secret eavesdropping instruments and radars, with three seats for the electronic warfare officers. They sat in there, strapped in, seats facing backwards. They were called "crows," he didn't know why. Most pilots wouldn't go back there. Some had tried it, he heard, but came back out quickly, and headed straight for the Officer's Club.

Farther up, and out from under the wing now, was the front gear. The two, big tires had deep, straight grooves for tread, and the silver wheel inside was a bright, symmetrical bunch of complex little holes and lines, radiating out from the center hub. Next to the front gear, down low on the fuselage, was the small door panel that opened to plug in the external power.

The fuselage was bright and rounded and looming above him now, the nose up high. There was the entry hatch, the only way inside. The open door angled down toward the ground, and a silver ladder poked out, attached from the inside. Just farther up, painted black at the front, the rest an unpainted, resiny green, was another fiberglass hump (there were a *bunch* of humps on this plane!) It was way above his head now, about six feet long on the bottom of the plane, with another radar in it. That would be the MA-7 bomb/nav radar, of course, from pages 74 through 78 in the manual. And just ahead of *that,* was a smaller, silver square carved into the bottom of the jet, where the ejection seat of the navigator blasted out if they had to bail. There was the little, red, ejection-seat-warning triangle stenciled next to the carving, informing anybody who cared that a big, sharp seat with a rocket strapped to it was nearby, and could explode out at any second. The triangle said something more official than Heads Up, Bozo, but that's what it meant. The three crows all blasted out the bottom, too, back in their fiberglass hump. The RB-47H had a crew of six: four bottom-shooters, and the pilot and co-pilot, up on top.

So, Tommy thought, what if they had to bail out down low? The ejection seats were rocket-powered, the object being to get the heck OUT of there, FAST! If there was time for a vote, all those guys on the bottom would elect the pilot to turn the airplane upside-down, and let *him* rocket down into the dirt. *They'd* go sky-high!

Tommy figured that the pilot could probably turn it upside down for the bottom-shooting guys to blast out, and when they were all gone, whip it back over real quick for him and the co-pilot to eject. But heck, if it was flying that good, why crash it?

The fuselage ended a few feet farther up in a towering, blunt nose, painted black. The other kids were doing their own private, silent inspections. No one talked, they just stood there, looking at the plane, and then at each other, scarcely believing it.

CHAPTER 6.

FLIGHT PLANS

"So. Let's do it," Bobby Kontovan announced bravely.

"Do what?"

"Go inside, what else?"

"Whoah, *wait* a second, buck-o," said Mike. "Wait just a darned minute. Time out. Man, we're already in *so* much trouble for being here," he reported correctly. "When dad finds out, we're gonna get the belt!"

Big Bobby smiled. "Correct-a-mundo on the belt. We're gonna get it, sure as shootin', even if we walk out right now. So we might as well go on *in* the thing, right?"

Tommy stared at him. Man! Those 8th graders could figure stuff that the younger ones couldn't quite grasp yet. They had some logic, boy!

There was some nervous positioning, some shuffling, and Tommy Riley found himself in front. *He* was the one who knew all about the stupid planes. *He* was the one always reading that stupid manual. He had to go first! Dare you!

Cautiously he approached the ladder and looked up into the dark innards of the jet. Man! It was so serious and . . . off limits up there! He swallowed, reached out, put his trembling hands toward the ladder and . . . *touched* it! Nothing. No sirens, no claxons, no APs launching out of the void and down the ladder and onto his face to beat him to a bloody pulp. He stood there, breathing slowly and deeply, gathering strength. Time to go! He raised his leg up high, and climbed to the first rung. (That first step was *up* there, a doozy!)

He was standing on the ladder now, his hands gripped tight on the rail. He looked back at the up-turned, anxious little faces, eyes wide, nodding affirmatively, willing him on up. Go, man, *go!* So he took another step, then another, and another, and another, and his head went up into the dark. He stopped, half in and half out, letting his eyes adjust.

Slowly, the dark, metal tunnel and hatches came into crystal-clear, adrenaline-pumping focus. The inside was painted olive green, exactly like the instructions said to paint them on the models. They got this one *real* authentic. The heady atmosphere smelled like oil or old clothes or rubber or something. A lot of smells all mixed up. He continued on up, cautiously. There was the open bulkhead door to his right, leading to the tunnel—just a crawlway really—back to the three crow's positions. After a few more steps, he emerged through a last pressure hatch that opened in the center of a kind of ledge, right in front of him.

Tommy couldn't believe an airplane that looked so big outside could be so durn crowded inside. Everything was just packed in tight! He grabbed a hand-hold, and swung off the ladder and onto the narrow metal ledge. A catwalk. It sloped down some toward the front and it was scuffed up, the shiny aluminum showing through the olive green paint. It had those black, rough, skid things on it, spaced evenly.

He raised himself up slowly and cautiously, careful not to hit his head or anything on the knobs or switches or boxes which seemed to be attached just about everywhere. The most dangerous one that Tommy almost beaned himself on when he turned around, was a big, sharp-cornered First Aid kit.

Big Konto yelled up, "How is it?"

How is it? *How is it?* It was only super-stupendo perfect, that's how it is! Awesome! The Taj Mahal times ten! Times a zillion! It was the neatest place he had ever been in in his whole life. How is it!? *Mama Mia!* Tommy took a deep breath and calmed down. "Seems safe. Come on up."

He heard some scrambling, and heard the ladder jiggle slightly as the excited boys fought to climb up into the jet. He was facing the pilot's and co-pilot's seats now, inches in front of him, but higher. At the back of the catwalk, by the co-pilot's seat were two more steps that got you up into the rear seat. To get up into the pilot's seat, you put your shoes into some toeholds in the flat, metal wall right in front of you, and grabbed that handhold right up there, and then you just climbed right on up there, like in a treehouse or something. Man, there were about a hundred ways to fall down in this thing! Except that inches away from you, at any position, were scopes and boxes and panels, painted green or black, covered with knobs and switches, and if you tripped, you could either grab onto one to save your life, or be impaled by it, dying, wriggling like a fish—depending on how your day was going.

The pilot's and co-pilot's seats were arranged in tandem, front-to-back, and sat under a long, smooth, bullet shaped canopy. There were only a few skinny metal frames to block their otherwise un-obstructed view, and the view was great! These top guys had it made! The co-pilot could even spin his whole seat around to look straight out the back, which they did to shoot the tail cannons, gun radars and sights and stuff mounted back there. It was so *unfair* to the rest of the crew, down in their little dark compart-ments. They should have spread some of this view around, boy!

Down and to his left, the catwalk continued forward into the dark where he knew it led to the navigator's station, crammed up in the nose, full of scopes and instruments and little tables. He heard some "Wows" and "Gees" and grunts and felt someone push his butt.

"Hey! Quit pushin'!"

"I can't help it, Riley! *He's* pushing *me!*"

"Am not, spas-mo!"

"Are too, creephead!"

"Am not!"

"Are too!"

Tommy needed more room. He was getting pushed. Up. A foot slipped into a foothold, and a small hand reached up for the grab rail. He was dizzy, scared, *excited!* Another foot went in. He couldn't stop it, didn't really try. He went up some more, then some more. Go, man, *go!* And then, suddenly, there he was! *In the pilot's seat!*

He was breathing fast little gulps of air, and his wide eyes scanned the scene. The panels he had memorized all those years were right *there,* every dial, every knob and switch and control, right there! All real and black and silver. He saw some red placards (DANGER) and some yellow ones (CAUTION). The dull, black control column and steering yoke was right in front of him, right there! The only thing out of place was . . . him! This was sacrilegious!

Mitch and Mike started snooping around the hatches and openings down below. Bobby came up the back steps and slid into the co-pilot's seat behind him. Tommy thought this had gone . . . just . . . about . . . far . . . enough! Heroes sat up here, not mortals, and certainly not mortal *kids.* Man, were they in trouble!

Then Tommy noticed a little piece of torn notebook paper, with a little arrow penciled on it. It was taped onto the radio stack, and it pointed to one of about twenty lines radiating out from a selector knob. It wasn't written very neatly, but it said: Preset: SAC link freq.

Now why the heck would somebody write something like that? Then it dawned on him. There were 208 pages of instructions to try to remember about this plane. This was a little, unofficial helper. A crib note. Wow! A *crib note!* In a *bomber!*

Then he saw another piece of paper. Same penciled handwriting, taped to the front instrument panel, right next to the ID-310 Distance Indicator (pages 22,23, and 107; Calibration of.) The note said:

milk
cheese (ched.)
lettuce, tomat.
Schlitz (2)
Wond. bread (2)

fruit (what's on spec.)

5 qts. 30w + filt. for Falcon

Well, hey! *Wow!* These weren't supermen! Regular guys sat up here and did this stuff. And they weren't too bright about car selection, either. Of course! Their dads were regular at home, so why not be regular up in here? Still, he couldn't imagine what a mission with officer dads would be like. He thought it would be so . . . so . . . serious, so official. But they had *crib* notes! Wow! What if they told jokes? Discussed car mileage and junk like that? What if they ate *Snickers* bars up here?!

"So turn something on," Bobby prodded.

Tommy spun around, wide-eyed. That Bobby was a prodder! He was why they were up here in the first place, adding up belt whacks by the second. Still, Tommy knew the checklist, and he thought he might just risk a l-i-t-t-l-e DC partial panel power, as long as he was up here. A click of a switch—*one!*—and energy would surge through select little parts of the bomber. He turned back around, eyeing the panel nervously. Tommy was so *very* careful not to get too carried away with this! That switch was only step numero uno, of exactly 116 more, between the pilot and crew, not including ground link communications or crew peripheral commands, that would get them to Engine Start (pages 88-94).

He engaged the batteries, then found the switch he wanted, swallowed hard, and flicked the toggle up. Click! DC powered needles jumped, and there was a crack and a low hum from the radios.

Tommy couldn't believe what he had just done. His hands were sweaty. When Father Clancy heard this list at confession, he might just come *through* that little window! Too late to think about that! Bobby was right, they were in deep, but hell*'s bells* . . . time to go!

He clicked the black knob over to "SAC link freq." because . . . why not to SAC link freq.? It was good as any other link freq., he supposed.

All the boys were silent now, and Tommy fiddled with the

QL-160 until the bandwidths synchronized *juuuust* right, then he pressed the RECEIVE button and "BLUE DOG 108 DISREGARD RENDEZVOUS VECTORS AND RETURN TO BASE OVER."

The boys *slammed* back, their ears ringing! Tommy's ears cracked with pain, and he hurriedly found the volume control knob and turned it from 10 to 0. Their eyes were spinning, open wide. Mitch and Mike knocked their heads together, and Bobby let out a yelp as he grabbed on to the side of his seat, totally spazzed, trying not to fall down.

Tommy actually looked outside, and tried to see through the hangar wall, over to the tower, sure that they had heard it, too. He was shaking, they *all* were shaking! Holy macaroni! They don't mess around on those bomber speakers, boy! After a few more quivering, wide-eyed, dry-mouthed moments, they calmed down some.

Mitch and Mike stopped crying, but were still rubbing their heads. Bobby was half in and half out of his seat, holding on. Should they get out? Maybe that was some kind of a booming message, like from God or something. Was God in Omaha? Would he be on SAC link freq?

The boys took a quick vote. They would stay, 3 to 1.

"Turn the radio back on, Riley," said Bobby. "Just not so loud."

"No, we better—"

"Come on, Riley, we're already dead meat at home so let's turn it back on. C'mon."

"*Well—*" Tommy gulped nervously as he adjusted the SQUELCH knob. He then delicately adjusted the VOLUME control up to 1, or between 1 and 2. Hidden speakers reverberated their urgent messages throughout the cockpit:

" . . . confirmed Dog Oh Eight, this is SAC command in the clear. All messages now in Code Zulu 2, repeat, Zulu 2 for No Code. Read: break, break—mission cancelled and RTB Minot. Return To Base. All aircraft are to land at forward alert bases at earliest opportunity. This is a command-level stand-down. Over."

"Dog Flight reads and confirms Return To Base order. Formation turning two-two-oh."

"Uh, Ranger Eighteen confirms stand-down order," came a scratchy, far-off call, "But Eighteen has just intercepted tanker track Baker One-Forty at angels twenty-two. Proceed with hook-up?"

"Negative, Ranger Eighteen. Return to base. Kilo Flight, confirm you understand RTB message and are heading back to Carswell, flight level thirty-eight five. Over."

"Ah, that's an affirmative, SAC guard. A command-level stand-down?"

"Affirmative, Kilo. Get 'em back right now. All flights. We just shot down a Bison in Alaska, boys. Things are getting hairy.

"A goddam *Bison . . .?*"

"Uh, SAC Guard, Ranger Eighteen here. Transport flights down, too? And how about reconnaisance?"

"All flights. Repeat, all flights. We understand Russia will pull their nukes from Cuba as soon as we stand down. Big ceremony tomorrow here at Offutt, thirteen hundred hours. With Russian brass."

The speakers emitted a scratchy silence for a few seconds, then: *"Russian?"*

"Commies? replied another aircraft. "In Omaha?"

The boys sucked in a breath. Unbelievably, what they were hearing in the crackling, official-sounding messages back and forth was: If it's up there flying—get it down. If it's down there sitting—keep it down. Some crews questioned it, but only a little. There were some obedient dads up there, buddy boy. Their dad's dad was SAC, and they said "Yes, sir" to their SAC-dad, and did as they were told.

Over the next hour, the story slowly got pieced together, message by message: The United States Air Force was *grounded!* A two week stand-down! Officially: tomorrow. Big ceremony. With *Russian brass,* at *Offutt!* 1 p.m. Unofficially: get 'em down right now, pronto!

The same thing was happening now with the Soviet Air Force. The transmissions went on: Russia was going to remove their missiles from Cuba. Russian ships were on their way right now to take them back, arriving Havana Sunday a.m. It would take two weeks to dismantle and load up the missiles, then everybody could get flight pay again. In the meantime, all air operations were to cease, orders from the President.

They listened for about an hour. No one said much, mostly some "Sssh's," and "Keep it downs," and Bobby was especially quiet. Tommy sat in the pilot's seat, glancing up at Bobby, watching him in the rear-view mirror. He looked like he had his thinking cap on.

"What's up, Bob-o? Looks like you're tryin' to think. Does it hurt?"

"Oh, shut up, Riley!" Bobby snapped. "This ain't right!"

"*What* ain't right?"

"They said a total stand-down. Even recon."

"So?"

"So . . . if they were really pulling those missiles out, they'd *want* reconnaissance photos taken of it, ya' peabrain! They'd want the whole world to see! They'd *insist* on it!"

Bobby didn't trust those Russkies, not one iota. His specialty wasn't planes, it was missiles—he was gonna be an astronaut. As a fledgling astronaut, he knew all about the Russian rocket programs, including the new, deadly SAM missiles that they were producing. He also knew how many mobile, radar-directed SAM sites could be operational in Cuba in two weeks. Lots!

Carefully, Bobby explained all this to the crew. "Doncha *get* it!?"

The boys sat there, stunned. Oh, yeah! Now they got it. That Bobby had some logic. Of course! Those boats were bringing SAM missiles *in,* not taking the other ones *out!* And all those Air Force guys, probably half of them had figured the same thing, but they followed their orders. Probably only the dumb civilians believed it. But if SAC said "stand-down," they knew the dads would stand-down, 100 percent. *Yes, sir!* After two weeks, it'd be a heckuva lot harder to get those missiles out. Those SAMs were good. They'd lose a few dads. But there they all were, standing down, following orders, being good.

"So we better tell somebody about this," suggested Michael.

"Who?" snorted Bobby. "Dad? We don't even know where he is. None of 'em,"

"What about mom?" suggested Mike.

"Oh, give me a break."

"Well, what are we gonna do then, wise-guy?" added Mitch. "Just tell some officer or the mayor? That we snuck in a top-secret airplane and heard this stuff on the SAC channel? Why don't we just ground ourselves for life, and save everybody the trouble?"

"*Ground* ourselves?" mumbled Michael. "Firing squad is more like it."

"You know," said Bobby, after a long, quiet spell, "We're actually . . . civilians."

The boys were silent, stunned. *"What?"*

"Nope, it's true," said Bobby seriously, his head nodding slowly up and down. His eyebrows were furrowed like Perry Mason.

Wow! thought Tommy. It was like finding out you were adopted or something. But Bobby was right! They'd followed orders all their life, dad and mom and nun orders, just because they were supposed to, was all. But what was the point?

Well, the point, Bobby patiently explained, was that the biggest orderer, SAC, *couldn't tell civilians what to do!* They *could* follow SAC's orders, if they *wanted* to, just to be good, but they also *couldn't* follow SAC's orders, if they *didn't* want to. Because legally. They. Weren't. In. SAC.

Sheesh, thought Tommy. How clever! How *sneaky!* If Bobby ever got a C in math and didn't make astronaut, he'd make one heckuva lawyer!

Bobby looked at the instrument panel before him, then down at Michael and Mitch on the catwalk. He then looked back up at Tommy, who was turned in his seat, looking back at Bobby over the confusion of wiring and piping of the pilot's ejection seat. "Plane looks pretty familiar, don't it, Riley?"

"Yeah, so?"

"Isn't this the reconnaissance kind that you've been reading about in that manual all this time? The one with all the cameras and stuff?"

"Yep. RB-47H. Know this puppy through and through," answered Tommy, smugly.

"Could it go to Cuba?"

"With a 4,000 mile range? Easy."

"And back to here? Or to Offutt?"

"From here to Cuba and back? I don't know how far that is. I'd have to check."

"Well, let's check then."

"Why do that? Why would it go to Cuba and back ?"

"Because that's where we'd aim it."

"WHAT!?"

"Because," Bobby repeated, smiling confidently, *"that's where we'd aim it."*

The three younger boys were wide-eyed as it sunk in on them what Bobby was proposing. Impossible! Absolutely impossible! Tommy was shaking his head furiously, and Michael sat slowly down on the catwalk, holding his stomach, making a moaning noise. Mitch and Tommy were both looking at Bobby incredulously.

Tommy stuttered, "Absolutely, positively, *no chance* are we—"

"The Russians are lying," challenged Bobby. "They're bringing in SAMs. And that's exactly the reason they want this standdown. We need photos of those ships in Havana. The President does."

"But—"

"And some dim-bulb just offered to ground the Air Force."

"No, but—"

"And this is the plane to do it."

"Yeah, well, this may be the plane, but how are we—"

"Look, Riley. You've told us a million times how you know all about this plane. In fact, we're all about getting sick of it. Everytime you want to show off, you're spoutin' your mouth off about this system or that system, or this doohickey or that doohickey."

"But—"

"But nothin'. I think you can do this. We *need* to do this. Look, here's the wheel, right?" Bobby grasped the wheel and pulled it back and forth vigorously. It barely moved.

"You're hydraulics aren't on," smirked Tommy, rolling his eyes up. "You're not even *close* to flight control engagement."

"There! See?"

"But I—" Tommy looked up at Bobby, trying to think of something to say, of a way to *stop* this. He knew exactly what to do to start it, sure, and get it going. He knew how to pressurize the systems and operate the ECM gear and camera. But fly it? *"I don't know how to fly this thing!"*

"Well, I'm betting you do, Riley. I'm betting my life on it. Why, the hard part about this thing is probably just starting it up!" Bobby brushed his fingers lightly over the rows of switches to his right, touched the throttle knobs, then put his hand gently back on the control wheel. "Once we've got it goin' and we're on the end of the runway, it's just another airplane. We've seen it a hundred times on TV. Pull back, an' ya go up. Push forward—go down." Then he looked down at Mike and Mitch on the catwalk, and back up to Tommy, grinning hard, squirming in his seat. Bobby wiggled the wheel hard from side to side. He was charged up now! "Left is left. Right is right. We can do this. We *have* to do this. Let's GO!"

Well, after a lifetime of good upbringing, and Catholic school, and Scouts (Cub and Boy) plus those 'Story-Time' segments on Captain Kangaroo, the boys knew that the *right* thing to do was not always the easiest thing, or what everyone else was doing. Moral relativism had already entrenched itself among the beatnik communities of the larger cities, and liberal, elbow-patched professors were making their insidious inroads onto college campuses, but there was none of that nonsense in Kansas—not yet! The boys knew right from wrong.

Bobby explained it all again, and the whole evil, commie plan really began sinking in on the concerned young men. Doncha *get* it? This just wasn't right. This had to be stopped, and pronto.

Then, slowly and carefully, bit by bit, word by word, a plan that seemed so absolutely, completely, stupidly unbelievable was happening! Each objection, each worry, each and every obstacle was met up there in the cockpit, one at a time. Each was discussed, voted on, and either crunched in 8th grade logic, or just went around.

Tommy wondered if this was really happening. Were they actually going to do this? Was this a dream or something? A sudden spitwad from Mitch down on the catwalk said it *wasn't* a dream. They really were in the cockpit of a B-47, there really was a gooey slug of paper sliding slowly down his cheek, and all this *really was happening!*

After about an hour of frantic discussion and arguing (Mike still wanted to chicken out) the boys reached their conclusion. They were sorry that they might have to borrow, no, to *steal* something (like a bomber) but it was a venial, and they would confess it. But this stand-down! To see something this big, this wrong, about to happen, and not try to prevent it . . . well, it could go mortal. Besides, they reasoned, this very plane belonged to a squadron whose job was to find out the truth, to see things as they really are. It was even painted on the side, up over the hatch. *"Videmus Omnia."*

The boys were going to try to stop this stand-down. They just had to. Of course, they'd probably get grounded for life! Oh, well . . . some risks you had to take. A phone call to Omaha wouldn't do it, either. They would have to make a statement! TV was the medium now, this was 1962! No more radio chit-chat, or polite letters back and forth, things were going *visual!*

They decided they would time the mission so they would arrive back at Offutt during the live TV coverage. Right plum smack dab in the middle of it, with the goods. When the bigwigs announced this stand-down at Offutt, the boys would be there to stop it, by gum! They were gonna make a mess of this stand-down nonsense.

There were a million things to do. Tommy was hunched over in the pilot's seat, scribbling furiously on a notepad. Everyone would have to have a checklist, getting everything exactly right, by the numbers.

"B . . . but what about the busted pump?" asked Mitch nervously.

The broken transduction pump was used to pressurize some sensitive equipment down in the crow's bay. It was a no-go item on the checklist, but Tommy was pretty sure he could isolate the thing—they didn't need it to fly. The pump was powered by the Number Two 2,500 volt-amp inverter, one of three, so he thought they could go around it.

Tommy flicked two switches and read a gauge. "The T-pump was slaved to the APA-74 Indicator," he reported to the crew with satisfaction. "I just isolated it, no prob."

Mike and Mitch looked at each other. "Coooooool," they sang in unison.

Tommy smiled. Here they were, in a reconnaissance plane, listening in on the radios, doin' a little recon. This was a sneaky airplane. This baby was just begging to get out there and snoop, to *do* something. This plane was a *go-getter!*

He flicked a few more switches to see how much fuel was in the tanks. Good. They were all nearly full except for the Aft Main, which usually fed #3 and #4 engines. He'd have to show Bobby how to crossfeed some over from Center Main. No problemo. They were goin' to Havana, not Moscow! Then he noticed from the gauges that their considerable eaves-dropping had drained the batteries to below what was needed for internal engine start. Shoot! They would have to use the auxiliary starting cart.

Tommy brought up this newest wrinkle, so the boys discussed it and voted: it would be Mitch's job—sergeant's kids ran the carts.

When he was done, he could get in and help. Mitch said he could do that, the starting part, but his eyes started tearing up. He looked at the other boys, and then looked down as his shoulders shook. "I . . . I can't. I can't fly—" Tearfully he explained that once he'd flown to Wichita to see his grandma, and threw up. He didn't want to go. Sorry.

"That's okay," said Michael gently, patting him on the shoulder. All of a sudden, Michael felt like the brave one. He *wanted* to go! "This is a big airplane, Mitch. There's a lot to do on it. We need a good crew chief."

It was getting close to suppertime, so the mission briefing was voted to continue at the Kontovans. They would all spend the night down in the basement, divvying up the checklists, making the flight plan. Mrs. Kontovan would always let them stay up late on Saturday night, goofing around, and wouldn't come down to bug them. Fran was a good woman. Plus, Saturday night was corn-on-the-cob and hamburgers night—their favorite!

Bobby looked directly at Tommy. "So, Riley, think you can really fly this thing?"

"No sweat, Konto—can do! Piece o' cake."

The boys scrambled out of the jet and the hangar, swiveling low at the front door, just in case, then split down the creek back toward the housing area. They huffed their way along the creek, where Mitch split off at the road and disappeared back up toward the sergeants' side of the housing area to get his stuff.

"Problem, Riley," announced Bobby. "You spent the night with us last weekend. Think we can pull a double?"

"No prob, Konto." Tommy's brain was in high gear. He wasn't about to let some silly 'no back-to-back sleep-over' rule get in the way of this mission. "Listen. It's easy. I'll go home and ask my mom if it's all right if I spend the night again, and say we need to practice some Scout signals or somethin', and say it's all right with your mom. Michael, you come with me for back-up. Bobby, you stay home and make sure you stay on your phone to somebody, *anybody,* so my mom can't call your mom while we're still at my

house to ask if it's okay with your mom, till me and Mike get back
and tell your mom it's alright with *my* mom. Got it?"

"Um . . . yeah! Yeah, I *do* got it, poop-for-brains. That's pretty
smooth. So what are ya' waitin' for? Eggs in your beer? Get goin'!"

A few minutes later, after delivering the request to Mrs. Riley
saying it was all right with their mom if it was all right with her,
Tommy and Mike came blasting back into the Kontovan's kitchen,
and both started jabbering at the same time, out of breath, to
Mrs. Kontovan: "Can we . . . spend night . . . here? Need to . . .
practice . . . Scouts, for the Merit Badge . . . Mitch coming, too . . .
Mrs. Riley . . . already said it was all right with her . . . if it's all
right with you . . . please . . . pretty please . . . we'll be good, can
we? Please? Huh? *Can we?*"

Mrs. Kontovan looked at the flushed, pleading faces, so anxious. So hopeful. Their little chests were heaving as they tried to
collect their breaths, their eyes fixed on hers. Please? Bobby was on
the hall phone, looking back at her (not talking to anyone, she
noticed), but keeping a keen eye on the proceedings in the kitchen.
Hmmm. She knew she would most likely let them, but still had to
do the Parental Pause, keeping the issue in doubt till the last second. *"Wellll—"* she said finally, "if it's all right with Mrs. Riley, I
suppose it's all right with me."

"Yeah! Thanks, mom!" the boys yelled.

Done deal! Bobby slammed down the phone, and the three
boys stomped down the basement stairs to get started.

By suppertime, the four boys were on hour three of the briefing, and Tommy had the crew up to p. 167 (The A-5 Gun-Laying
Radar), skipping a few points here and there, but making them all
pay special attention to their individual duties and the Emergency
Bold-Face lists. Of course, Michael got the heaviest dose (one hour!)
on how to load and operate the K-14 belly camera, and arm and
operate the four downward-firing ejection seats. That took awhile,
but Michael had to have it down *perfect.* Tommy used the Playskool
chalkboard for the abbreviated checklists that each crewmember
would have to copy down. Mitch's attention kept wandering from

his notes toward the radio-controlled airplanes and Tommy and Bobby had to bark occasionally to get his mind back on the class. Those sergeant's kids!

Bobby had the map and compass out—he was the best map-reader in Troop 26. He knew topo maps, mercator projections—he even knew about true north versus magnetic north. They would stay low, *really* low, to keep them under radar, and so they could see the road signs. Then they got out the world atlas, and scribed their route: Forbes to the gulf coast, right about the Texas-Louisiana border looked good. An easy 180 degree route the first leg, just to get started. Then 110 degrees to Havana, get there just before 10 in the morning. Perfect. They figured most Cubans would still be asleep. 1,400 miles, Topeka to Havana. Then straight back to Omaha to the festivities. Bobby calculated the route: speed x time = distance, and was surprised. He figured it again. "If we leave at sun-up, and keep the pedal to the metal, we'll get back by 1p.m. I almost can't believe it! Kansas to Cuba and back by lunch. That's *fast!*"

Every once in a while, Mrs. Kontovan would yoo-hoo down the steps and ask how it was going. "Great, mom! We're really gonna ace that Merit Badge test! Yep, flag signals and um . . . Morse Code. Knots, too! Studyin' hard down here! Thanks! See ya!"

Bobby and Mike also had four younger brothers and sisters, three of them mobile, so a procession of littler Kontovans continuously tried to infiltrate down the basement stairs, but never got past about the third or fourth step before being pummeled by assorted toys and wadded up clothes, then went yelling back up the stairs.

At suppertime, the boys went up to the kitchen to build their hamburgers and butter their corn. Mrs. Kontovan offered to help them carry the trays and milk down the steps, still a little curious, but the boys quickly answered, "No thanks, that's okay. Great supper, mom. Yeah, great supper, Mrs. Kontovan!" Back in the basement, the boys were on the last of their corn when they finished the ENGINE FIRE checklist. Mitch whined and said he wanted to go upstairs to watch Saturday Night At The Movies, but Tommy insisted that they all go over their lists again. The boys grumbled, then they voted and agreed to take a little break and watch the best part of the movie, right toward the end (they had seen it before) where the German tank was closing in on the surviving American platoon, and it drove down into the ditch and then back out to finish them off, and as the roaring Panzer reared up out of the ditch, the brave Americans let loose with their last bazooka round and blasted the tank in its soft underbelly and won the war. It looked easy, but it took guts—with a capital G!

That night, they lay in the dark, scattered among assorted army cots and sleeping bags, alarm clocks (2), clothes and equipment lined up along the basement wall, and let the absolute blackness of the basement encircle them. The more they tried to calm down, the more their little brains spun with the enormity of the task before them. It was so quiet, such a *forced* quiet, that Bobby could hear his mind sending roaring sounds to his ears. Every breath was a noise to him—a waterfall, a rocket launch. He whispered, "Hey, Riley. You scared?"

"Heck no." A pause. "Some—a little maybe."

"Me, too—a little." Bobby cleared his throat quietly. "Think you can do it?"

"We," answered Tommy. "Do I think *we* can do it. If we all do our jobs right and don't screw up we sure as heck can do it. Look. That airplane don't care *who* flys it as long as they follow the checklists. I explained it a hundred times already. Hell's *bells,* Konto—Russians fly, and everybody knows how dumb they are."

"Yeah, you're right I guess," he answered quietly. "Okay. Good night."

"'Night."

"Ooooo! Nighty-night my little spasmo darlings. Do oo need a kissy?"

"Shut up, Michael. Go to sleep!"

"Yeah, shut up over there!"

"Make me, retardo!"

A pair of blue jeans whipped playfully through the dark, except that it had a belt with a slinging buckle on it, and contacted flesh hard enough to warrant a clear mortal response, followed by a tense silence. "Yeesh!" whispered someone.

"Who said *that?!*" All sides prepared immediately for a counterattack, eyes drilling through the dark for enemy movement, tense, measuring. Who's on who's side here? *And where were they?* No one moved. After a little while that nearly overpowering, unstoppable and frighteningly delicious moment for battle was lost. Teeth slowly unclenched, and fists loosened convenient weapons. Silence, only breathing in the dark. And then a fart, a little high one—answered by four giggles. Truce.

After a few more minutes of silence, Michael offered quietly: "Wonder where Billy Duncan is now?"

"Well, he's moved somewhere else, so don't worry about it," snapped his big brother.

"Best shortstop I ever saw," declared Tommy.

"Third base, too," yawned Mitch. "And line-drive hitter. Remember when he ripped one off the pitcher's shoulder and—"

"Well, he ain't *here* no more, so just *forget* about it," countered Bobby, angrily. "Go to sleep!" He really missed Billy. And Theresa, too. And Captain Duncan—all of them.

A few moments of silence followed, then Mike whispered, "Did they ever find out what happened to his dad that night?"

"Dunno," Bobby grunted.

"Or those two other guys?" added Tommy. "I didn't even know 'em yet. Lieutenants, I think."

"Whaddya think happened?" growled Bobby. "They *crashed* is what happened." He remembered the funeral. He tried not to cry, to be brave—they all did. And then, at the end, that guy waiting back by the trees went and played Taps. *Ohchrist,* he thought. He rolled over, smacked his pillow with his fist, and sighed: "They called it pilot error, probably. They always call it pilot error. Makes it easy for 'em." Silence. Clocks ticked pensively as some little lungs did their work in the dark. Shadowy figures rustled to new sleeping positions, then settled in.

"Wonder if they can still see their kids?" came a small voice. "Or us, even. And where they are . . . you know . . . now."

"Ya' mean the heaven and hell part?"

"Yeah, that. And purgatory. Guardian angels, too. All of it."

Mitch piped up: "You guys really believe all that stuff?"

"Prob'ly," Bobby answered quietly. "Who knows? Now go. To. *Sleep.*"

Tommy hadn't prayed a night-time prayer in a long time, but thought—what the heck? He started to dig up something in Latin, but then thought his familiar Now I Lay Me Down To Sleep prayer like he did every night back when he was just a kid. Except this time he said it a little slower, and kind of . . . meant it. It still sounded silly. He remembered a bookmark with a little braided ribbon jobby on it, and a prayer. It showed some guy getting in an F-102 Delta Dagger, and the Blessed Virgin was looking down at him from some clouds. He remembered the picture, but not the words. An Airman's Prayer or something like that. So he silently made up his own Airman's Prayer, and asked that they'd all just, you know, make it. He crossed his hands over his chest, kicked his feet out from under the sheet so's they could breathe, then closed his eyes and got still. *Wonder if they can still see their kids? Or us, even. And where they are . . . you know . . . now?* Go to sleep, he told himself. He didn't see the two shooting stars at that instant, overhead in the night. Then, a few seconds later, another one.

CHAPTER 7.

FIRST SOLO

By 5:00 the next morning, the four excited and scared young cadets quietly extracted themselves from the house, and marched down the creek, following the path they had blazed the day before. Things were A-OK so far, everything by the numbers. They had snuck up the basement stairs and got out of the house okay, with all their stuff, and managed not to wake anybody inside. The McNally's little dog next door yapped at the shadowy group, but Mike offered a hand in front of the nervous little snout. Peppy smelled Mike's hand, checked his I.D., wagged her alert little tail, and waved them on through. The crew had left a note for Mrs. Kontovan: "Sunrise service, Troop 26 only. Forgot to tell you. Home soon." It was unlikely she would buy it, but by the time she woke up and called Mrs. Riley and Scoutmaster Loggins, they'd be long gone. There was enough of a moon still, so they only had to use the flashlights a little bit, and they could walk straight up next to the creek and not down in it. That was a plus.

Tommy pulled up the collar of his Cardinal's baseball jacket in the dark, exciting, chill. He had number 12, Stan Musial's number. Stan the Man. He had dressed specially for the mission, and he wanted to be in uniform for this one. Beneath the baseball jacket was his olive-green Boy Scout shirt, the long sleeve one. No neckerchief, of course. Only those smarty-farty town Scouts ever bothered with that silliness. Not Troop 26! He wore his dress blue jeans and a green army surplus belt, with his favorite Red Ball Jets tennies rounding out his flight uniform. He knew how SAC stressed professionalism, and his clothes made him feel professional. As the Aircraft Commander for this mission, Tommy was going to do this thing right. Mike was also in his Scout uniform, but Bobby opted for his favorite red shirt—showing off as usual. Mitch wore sergeant's kids clothes.

They got under the fence okay, didn't even get wet, and began the final sprint to the hangar. At the front opening, they peeked cautiously in, checking to be sure it was still deserted. All clear! They were actually gonna *do* this! The mission was not meant to hurt anyone, but to show the strength and resolve of young Americans in a way that would make the world pay attention. It would be similar to the Indian practice of "counting coup," sneaking up on another person, but instead of bashing their heads in they would just tag them, or steal a little something, or perhaps leave something—just to show them they'd been had. *Gotcha!*

The huge plane was waiting for them, hulking and silent in the cavernous hangar. The lights were left on all the time, and after the dark hike they felt really exposed, naked in the harsh light. If someone came by, they were dead meat, that was just all there was to it. No time to worry about that now.

They plopped their stuff down, and took out their checklists. Time to go! The boys had a lot of work to do, and it all started right *now!* They gathered in a circle and did a time hack, little Christmas Timexes clicking together at 5:22:00. Numero uno on the list had all four tug and scoot the APU (auxiliary power unit) around to the side of the plane and plug it in. They used a 4x4 as a lever to get it moving. Then, Mike and Mitch went scurrying back down to the creek with some of the empty buckets that were stacked up by the back hangar wall.

Tommy and Bobby began their pre-flight inspection of the outside of the jet, following the manual. By the numbers. Then they marched up the ladder, and began waking the sleek, sleeping bomber up, step by step. After about an hour, the horizon was turning purpley-red, silhouetting some low buildings and poles off to the east. Tommy slipped out of his seat, and clambered down the ladder and out the hatch. The bomber was humming with life now, hydraulic fluids pulsing through pumps and hoses, relay switches directing current to hundreds of motors and dials. They were on step 112, almost to engine start, and took their break, according to the plan.

The boys all gathered under the high, dark wing and made progress reports. Mitch was ready with the starter unit, and had all the 'Remove Before Flight' ribbons stowed. He and Mike had the K-14 loaded with film, spare cartridges in their feed belts. Mike had strapped the leaky bombs to the downward-firing ejection seats, with Mitch's help, but needed about five or ten more minutes to finish securing them in position. Tommy and Bobby had the transduction pump by-passed, and all the other systems were up and going, and had been checked off according to the list. They were actually eight minutes ahead of schedule. Some coffee would have been nice, they thought, if they drank coffee. The perpetrators moseyed around a little, stretching and yawning, giving the plane a last once-over.

There was other neat stuff in the hangar. Along the wall was a yellow towing tractor, with oversize tires. It had a long, yellow and black striped pipe hooked to it, that would attach to the front gear of the planes and pull them around. Pulled up next to the plane, of course, near the hatch, was the big, yellow APU. It was idling slowly, directing current through the bomber to get the show rolling. It had a muffler poking out on top, and its thick, black cables were plugged into the plane through the little access panel door by the front gear well. At the very back of the hangar up against the wall was a big, yellow stairway on wheels which could reach the tops of the planes. There were also engine stands back there, along with some test equipment, and some scaffolding.

Near the back corner, by the little bathroom, were some grey lockers with helmets and flight suits hanging inside, and heavy black boots—for the guys who test-flew them after they got them fixed, they guessed. Mike was checking those out, doing a little window shopping. He pulled out a helmet, gave it a once-over, and plopped it on his head. He looked a little top heavy, but the little-boy face disappeared in the shadows. He had been a very short trespasser. Suddenly, he was a very short *airman.*

Bobby yelled over at him, "Hey, ya' look like a spasmo spaceman! Like a stupid Roger Ram-Jet retardo! Take it off, ya' peabrain!"

Mike stood there, his face dark in the shadow of the heavy white helmet. He seemed to swell up his chest a little, trying to get a little bigger, to keep the helmet from squashing him any shorter. He put his hands on his hips, then he bared back his teeth like a little boy-hyena. His teeth were bright up in there, about all they could see of his face. Mike liked that helmet! It *did* something to him, made him feel brave, made him feel like . . . a tenth grader! He looked straight back at his brother, still smiling. Everyone stopped what they were doing, looking at Mike. They were a little uneasy. After all, his brother had just told him to take it off. His *older* brother. There was a long silence, then Mike hissed, slowly and deliberately: "Eat me!"

The boys were stunned! Wowie-zowie! Mike said that?! Yep, he sure did! No kidding, no lie! They heard right! Hmmm, those helmets must do something for a guy—Tommy and Bobby started thinking maybe they should be wearing helmets, too. Yep, *definitely!*

They each grabbed one from a locker, then Tommy called for a huddle, and made a quick addendum to his crew's checklists, showing the eager young cadets how to activate and use the oxygen and intercom features of the heavy, white bone domes. (Pages 3-5, and 108).

Tommy, Bobby and Mike, fully-helmeted now, scrambled up the ladder and back into the bowels of the hulking jet to their positions. Time for the final checks, time to *go!* The airplanes were normally towed out of the hangar before starting the engines, but the big yellow machine sat unused in the shadows. Tommy could see it down there from his cockpit seat, parked up against the hangar wall. It would have been nice to be able to use, but it had clutches and stuff. They could have probably handled an automatic, but not one with clutches. Plus, none of them really knew how to drive yet, soooo . . .

Time for engine start! Bobby was reading out the fuel pressures, when Tommy's little brain suddenly went to AUX DUMP OVERLOAD. It snapped. He froze, total freeze-o-rama.

"Hey, up there! Yoo hoo! Knock, knock," Bobby sang out.

"Unnhhh—" Tommy couldn't answer. The checklist fell to the floor, his hand paralyzed. His throat was dry, his mind suddenly blank. Nothing in there—nada. Zilch. He was starting to feel dizzy.

Bobby stared up at the back of the motionless helmet, five feet ahead of him. Criminy! What now? "Whatsamatter, Riley? Turning *pansy?*"

That did it. Tommy yanked the helmet off his head, pinioned it on the steering yoke, grabbed the instrument panel with his right hand and swung *fast!* straight out of his seat and then bam! straight down onto the scuffed catwalk. He skipped the treehouse steps part completely. He shot an angry glance back up at Bobby, opened his mouth, and then remembered that if you're not going to say something nice, don't say anything at all, so he bent over, face out, and clomped down the ladder toward the open hatch. He almost jumped straight down through the opening, but at the last second his hands reached back and found the railing of the boarding ladder, and he stopped himself. He stood swaying over the opening, feeling dizzy, and looked down the eight feet to the hangar floor. He had to get out! To do something! He loosened his grip and clambered down the last steps, jumped down off the bottom rung to the hangar floor, and raced past Mitch and the power cart, straight back to the bathroom.

Tommy's guts were going round and round, and he was thinking very seriously about throwing up. It seemed like an appropriate thing to do, but a throw-up had its own rules, its own checklists, and Tommy hadn't checked them all off yet. Still, his stomach *hurt!* He leaned against the wall, hands on his gut, eyes shut tight. Man-o-man! What the holy heck were they *doing!?* He had never been so nervous, not even when he was lead altar boy at

Christmas Midnight Mass, and that durned incense wouldn't light!
Ooooh, man! He hurt! But . . . wait. Wait a minute.

Let's try *this,* thought Tommy's brain, going down the sick
tummy checklist. He walked in the bathroom door, opened the
stall door, rushed in, and spun around. He pulled down his pants,
hovered, and a had a quick b.m. There! Much better! He'd forgot
to have one this morning in all the rush and excitement, and it was
amazing how it helped. He gave himself a quick wipe, hopped up,
and fastened his pants. He hummed a little "and away go troubles,
down the drain," then stopped himself. He immediately felt a
little guilty about thinking that as he turned and looked down,
inspecting it like he usually did.

It was a good one, a one-piecer, and real aerodynamic—blunt
up front, with a nice trailing edge. It had been a part of Tommy for
the last 24 hours, and they had gone through a bunch, those two.
They'd broken bread together (broke a little corn too, he noticed),
inspected a bomber, learned a lot about time-management techniques and delegation, and made some checklists. But now it was
time to part company. Tommy was going on to Cuba while his
little friend would stay back here in Topeka, and spend the day
swimming. A day at the lake with his little brown buddies.

Tommy saw the light start to come in the little entry window
above the toilet. It *would* be a nice day at the lake, actually. He
stayed a sec to watch the flush, going round and round . . . mesmerizing . . . drawing him in. But it didn't, of course. Then he
spun around and went over to the sink and drank straight from
the faucet, four good, long, slurps, water trickling down his cheek
and drip-dripping from the bottom of his chin. He stood up and
deliberately brushed the wet away with the back of his hand. Aaaah!
If his mom knew he did that in a public rest room, there'd be heck
to pay, but he did it anyway. He straightened up, took a deep
breath, walked to the door, and leaned tiredly against the door
frame. He felt a little better now, but was still kind of queasy. This
just wasn't *safe.*

Bobby came out the hatch and down the ladder, a last little squeak echoing distantly as his sneakers hit the hanger floor. He had his head lowered, and he just stood there for a sec. The motor of the auxiliary starter continued its muffled putt-putt-putt, with Mitch standing obediently beside it, wondering what the heck was going on. Bobby knew he shouldn't have said that, the pansy part. He looked over at Tommy, leaning there, way over by the bathroom door, and knew that there was no other seventh grader he would rather fly a jet bomber to Cuba with, but of course he couldn't say that, being a guy and all. He knew he should be kinder, and set a good example—because he was older. All those things.

But Bobby was edgy, and not just because of the mission. He was majorly worried about school next year. He'd get Sister Alice Ann (a toughie) plus he had his first pimple last week. He hid it with a band-aid, and told his mom it was a cut. He also wasn't so sure about heaven and hell and purgatory and all that anymore, either. Eternal fire for one "god damn?" Even if a hammer smashed your thumb (God's will, right?) the word coming out, just like blood? Then a meteorite smites the bejesus out of you a few seconds later, before you can get to confession? What if you were building a convent? For free? One good, caring lifetime cancelled out by one cuss word? He bet Joseph even cussed sometimes. *All* carpenters cussed, all that he had heard anyway. And then to burn for eternity? It just seemed a little extreme, is all. A hundred things went through his mind, but they would just have to wait. They had a job to do, and Tommy needed help. Maybe he'd apologize, he'd have to see how it went.

He walked slowly out from under the high wing of the bomber, on over toward the bathroom, trying to look nonchalant. His red Ban-Lon shirt and Levi jeans contrasted civilianly with the white, heavy helmet on his head. The thick green visor was in the up position, and his oxygen mask dangled by his neck and shoulder. He put both hands on his hips and sort of looked up, at nothing really, then down at his feet. He drew a few little invisible lines on the concrete with the tip of his tennis shoes, and let out a small "Whooosh".

Tommy watched all this, and knew why he was coming over, and really appreciated it, but still felt like he might throw up.

Bobby decided to start with a little small talk. "So how about those Jayhawkers?"

Tommy sighed deeply, looking down. "Yeah, yeah. Lookin' pretty good this year, I suppose."

"Good, heck. They're a cinch to take State. They'll go Regional for sure." Bobby paused, waiting for a response, got none, so continued. "So how's your mom and dad?"

"Fine."

"School work going okay?"

"Pretty good, I guess. Having a little trouble with fractions," Tommy mumbled.

"Who isn't?"

"Yeah, who isn't?" There was some pained silence. "So enough already!" Tommy cried out, "I don't think I can do this! I can't, *I can't!* Look at that thing! It's so big! I don't know how to fly it and neither do you! What if we crash? Huh? What *if?* This isn't *safe!*"

Bobby stood still, silhouetted in the early morning light. He was the oldest, he had to set an example, to do something. Mitch was looking silently on, standing by the power cart. They could hear Mike scraping and banging around inside, going over his checklists, the bomber sounding like a big, metal drum. Bobby took a deep breath and knew what he had to do. He was gonna have to use the big one—the ol' chicken approach.

"Isn't safe? Isn't *safe?!*" he admonished Tommy. "Look, bozo-brain. If ya' can't start it we're *safe,* right? And if you can't get it out of the hangar, we're *safe,* right? Plus if you can't steer it, we shoot across the ramp into the mud and ain't goin' nowhere. *Safe,* right? But if you *do* get it to the end of the runway, and you *do* manage to take the thing off, *then* you can start worrying. But's that's why we're here, Riley! To fly it! To do a job! That's our mission, remember?! This is about guts, Tommy Riley, not about being safe! I always thought you had guts. Remember when you ate that crawdad? Raw? Feet and eyeballs and everything? Now that took guts! Show some guts now, why doncha! Either ya got guts or ya *don't!*" Then Bobby let him have it, right between the eyes: "Don't. Be. A. *CHICKEN!*" That word echoed once off the hangar wall, accusingly. Bobby then looked to the floor, and added quietly: "Plus, I'm sorry I called you a . . . you know . . . pansy."

Tommy tried to measure a little . . . hmmm. Pansy. Versus chicken. Nope. "Chicken" was way, way worse! The ultimate, basic, put-down, centuries old, never improved upon. David stood in front of Goliath, looking up, squinting, going over his options one last time. This Goliath guy was *big!* Dave wanted to turn tail, to run! Then, from the back of the crowd . . . "Cluck, cluck, BWOCK! *Chicken!*" That was all it took! History was made. That word chicken was a powerhouse!

Tommy smiled slowly, the fever broken. Bobby was right, some risks you just had to take! He slapped his pal on the shoulder, and they spun around and headed back to the ladder and destiny. They had a mission to do. No chickens here! What about the crews who knew they wouldn't come back? The ones who flew off to Ploesti, to Berlin, to Tokyo. Did they chicken out? No way! They had Guts! With a capital G! Let's GO!

They ran back to the nose of the waiting jet and up the ladder, Bobby first, Tommy following. Tommy gave Mitch a thumbs up, and then quick, up into the jet, pulling the ladder up and securing the hatch behind him. He climbed up the ladder to the cockpit through the last pressure hatch, then scrambled up into his seat onto the two telephone books, and pulled the heavy helmet over his head. Tommy then reached back over his shoulder for the maze of belts and pulled them down over his chest, connecting their heavy stainless-steel buckles with the straps from the lower seat, pulled up through his crotch. He shifted, letting the heavy green webbing work its way into the most comfortable positions on his now smoothly-functioning body. He brought the oxygen mask across his small, determined face, and snapped it to the other side of the helmet. He then found the end of his rubber oxygen hose, inserted it, and twisted it a quarter turn clockwise into the oxygen regulator panel to his left. Oxygen valves to ON, and cool, fresh air surged down his confident young throat. Also at the end of the oxygen hose was the plug for the radio and intercom, which clicked easily into its slot. From now on, they would all talk through the intercom, their voices crisp and professional through the built-in speakers in their helmets.

Tommy crackled, "Do you read me, Bobby?"

"Rojahhhhhhhh," Bobby answered coolly. He had always wanted to say that.

"Do you read me, Mike?"

"You *betcha,* Tommy Riley!" Mike was excited! His first transmission! Mike's intercom would be on and off throughout the mission as he moved to the various positions needed to get everything ready—but for take-off, they wanted the little fella strapped in back there. Michael was Head Crow and Chief Bombardier for this mission.

Tommy's black high-top tennies were now firmly positioned onto the blocks that Mitch had cut from 4x4s, and strapped to the plane's rudder pedals. The young pilot shifted and wriggled, took a deep breath, sucked in some good bomber smells, and looked out to the orange Kansas sky. This was it—Engine Start!

"Okay back there," he radioed to Bobby. "Set and confirm starter-generators to START position on engines one through six. Just like we practiced, daddy-o."

Bobby swallowed slowly, his throat dry, as he put his checklist down on his lap. Time to do it! He held his breath as he clicked a switch-guard down, aimed a trembling finger and hit the switch, watching the #1 voltmeter jump to life in the heavy silence. He did it! Man! And nothin' blew up or *nothin'!* He let out a whoosh as he did the next five: click-click-click-click-CLICK! The six spring-loaded switches were now toggled down, their green paint chipped from years of use. "One through six set to START," said Bobby excitedly.

"O.K. boys, hold on to your helmets, *heeeeere we goooo!*" Going by the book, Tommy engaged engine #4 first. With the press of the well-worn turbine accelerator boost-switch, the rpms were now coming up, a far-off dynamo hum. Bobby confirmed 18 volts at 5 per cent rpms, so at 10 per cent, Tommy quickly slipped the #4 throttle forward to FLIGHT IDLE. Two sets of wide eyes watched intently as the rpms continued to clock upwards, listening to the whine increase, louder, faster, *louder!* and at 26% Riley hit the #4 igniter, and BoomwhoooooooshKa*BAM!* and it was going, *just like that!*

All pressures right where they should be, the exhaust temp in the green. Tommy's hands were a flurry of activity over the switches and throttles as the other engines followed in their correct order, and soon all six were going good! The shrill whistle was *loud* to the crew, even through the thick plexiglas canopy and the heavy helmets. Mitch was holding his ears down there, off to the left—it looked like they hurt. Tommy gave him the "cut" signal, drawing his hand across his throat. Mitch acknowledged the signal, then disappeared from sight, so Tommy knew he would be under the bomber, unhooking the power cables, closing the access door, pulling the wheel chocks, and then racing to his position by the hangar door to help guide the plane out the hangar and out onto the ramp.

In a minute Mitch re-appeared, looking up at the cockpit. He gave Tommy the "okay" signal that the APU was disconnected and his other pre-taxi duties were finished.

"Set starter-generators to GENERATOR," commanded Tommy. "Confirm 40 per cent IDLE and exhaust temps okay."

Bobby toggled the six switches up to their generator position. "Engines one through six set to GENERATOR," he confirmed. "All set to 40 per cent IDLE, exhaust temps green, and fuel pressure's steady at 290. Crossfeeds on." He added, "This is so cool, Riley! Just like you said! Follow that durn checklist!"

While Tommy and Bobby watched, Mitch ran over to the hangar door, and carefully peeked around the corner, hands still over his ears. He then spun back around, looking up at the cockpit, eyes and mouth open wide, sure by now that the whole *world* knew what was going on. He was jumping up and down—totally freaked—spinning around, looking back to the tower, pointing quickly at something behind the roaring jet, then putting his hands back over his ears again. More jumps, more signaling. He was nervous as all get-out! Dirt and dust swirled around outside the canopy.

"Looks like our crew chief is spazzing out," radioed Tommy. "Major wiggleworm city down there."

"Reading you five-by-five on the spazzing wiggleworm," came Bobby's crisp reply. He just loved to hear his voice over the intercom. It sounded so, so . . . serious, maybe. Confident. Studly, perhaps. He couldn't *wait* for the opportunity to say "Wilco," or even "Five churnin' and one burnin'." Except, of course, for that last one he'd have to wait for an engine to catch fire first. Who knew? Maybe he'd get lucky.

But what Mitch could see, and the bomber crew couldn't, was the dozens of 4 x 8 foot corrugated panels that made up the back wall of the hangar were shuddering, and bulging, and rattling like they were coming apart at the seams—which was exactly what they *were* doing. Tommy and Bobby finished the Before Taxi checklist, gave Mitch a sharp salute, and released the brakes.

Tommy opened up the throttles a little more to get the big jet going, and finished the job of blowing out the back wall of Hangar 8. Huge sections of metal wall were banging, tearing off, and hurtling away backwards, spinning crazily in the blast and smoke, skipping through the flattened weeds and grass, and then the back wall of the hangar was just gone! Nothing was left but the grey iron framework, with a bent, yellow ladder twisted up against it, shuddering in the hurricane current of blasting jet exhaust.

Bobby saw Mitch's excited gesturing, cranked his head around, and saw the back of the hangar had flat-out disappeared! Jeepers creepers! He could see the baseball diamond and base housing and *everything*, way over there. What a mess! Pieces of metal and busted light fixtures and engine mounts, and what looked to be pieces of a toilet and a sink and some lockers were scattered all over tarnation. Aye-carumba! So *that's* why they started these big ol' noisy mothers outside.

CHAPTER 8.

FUZZ

Airman Second Class James (Jimbo) Santini was a New Yorker in Kansas, and he didn't like it, not one bit. He had joined the APs because he wanted to be an Air POLICEman, to POLICE stuff, to get in some good butt-kicking, a little action, and he wasn't getting any. Everyone was so damned polite around here. Yes sir'ing and Yes ma'm'ing each other, even when they didn't have to, and no one ever pushed or cut in line. When he pulled people over for little things, they always had up-to-date licenses and registrations, and co-operated fully. Nobody ever tried to run, or pull a gun on him. Most wouldn't even argue!

He hated it, he was losing his big-city edge. Even the blasted teenagers and kids around here, what a joke. On weekend nights, Jimbo would cruise base housing, looking for a little action, somebody to beat up. Nothing. Zip. Sometimes little kids would bolt out of the dark as he drove by, and yell "Fuzz! Buzz!" or "Try to catch us, cherry top!" or something else disgustingly, parochially Kansan, and then charge back into the darkness, giggling at their larceny. He wouldn't even slow down. New York kids would eat these punks for lunch, make pets of 'em, make 'em do tricks—just before they killed them.

And now . . . booorrrinnnng! The base was about empty. There were a couple of gutless B-47 trainer bombers parked in front of the tower, with their wide, bright, orange training bands painted on the fuselage and wings saying: "Excuse me, pardon me, pardon please, coming through! I'm just learning, thank you!" Even the freaking bombers around here were polite. There were also two old transports down there on the ramp, one with an engine off, and a tiny little silver T-33, way over by Hangar 7, looking like a toy. But all the other planes, and all the men had shot off to who-knew-where the other day to kick some Russian butt. *He* wanted to kick some butt, any butt. Plus now, all the dang butt-kickers were gosh-dang *grounded,* so he was up in the control tower, at some ridiculous hour in the morning, when most New Yorkers would just be heading home, for chrissakes. He was shooting the bull with Smitty, a dickweed from Baltimore, but at least he was from somewhere.

Santini was sipping his coffee (four sugars) and making small talk when he heard a far-off explosion, then a muted roar. Huh? He scanned the sky, then the runway. Nothing. The roar was increasing—a train? He looked back around to the tracks by the warehouses. Nothing there. He then spun back around to the ramp. No movement down there by the trainer bombers, and the noise was still growing. The thick glass in front of him shuddered slightly. What the . . .?

Suddenly, something caught his eye—off in the distance, over by the hangars. *Holy shit and shine-ola!* He spat his coffee out in a brown, messy cloud onto the huge window. "It's a freaking TOR-NADO!" he screamed. Smitty spun around from his radio, his eyes growing wide. Sure enough, a tornado was demolishing the hangars! Funny though, he couldn't see a tornado. And this early in the morning? It wasn't even cloudy, but—

Santini grabbed a pair of binoculars and aimed it out at the storm. Sure enough, a tornado was chewing up the last hangar! Huge metal chunks and debris were flying through the air, somersaulting through the dust and weeds. "Holy Moly—LOOK! There goes a toilet!" he yelled, watching the white receptacle bounce and twirl, disintegrating into a shower of tiny white fragments. Wow. Now *this* was something a New Yorker could appreciate! An entire Air Force base was being demolished, and he had free parking, and a perfect view of it. Hot damn! This kind of luck didn't happen every day!

Santini looked around for a chair and grabbed the box of donuts over by the radarscope. Quick, don't wanna miss any of this! *Soooooo* good. There! He settled down, put his feet up, and got ready for the show. Santini was smiling now, chuckling lowly, his chair tilted back, binoculars raised to his appreciative eyes, a little powdered sugar on his lips. This was gonna be great! A little of the ol' *ellll-destructoooo*, when suddenly, he noticed the black nose of a . . . a . . . bomber! slowly emerging, glistening, like in slow motion from the shadows of the disintegrating hangar, and out into the weak dawn light. What the hell!? He thought all the bombers were gone! What the hell was going on around here? The jet continued moving slowly out, showing more and more of its sleek profile to his unbelieving eyes. He made out the pilot and co-pilot, helmets swiveling, making sure the wingtips cleared the hangar door, and a . . . a . . . kid! A damned *kid!* Jumping up and down by the disintegrating hangar, holding his ears!

Smitty was on the radio now, trying to call the plane, clicking switches and turning dials, looking for the right frequency. "This ain't right, Jimbo!" he stammered. "There's something fishy about this here. They just can't *do* that, they need clearances, flight plans! And they usually don't take off during tornadoes, either. There's rules against that, I think! This ain't good!"

Wrong! thought the San-Man. This wasn't good. This was *great!* And that warn't no freaking tornado, either! His highly-trained police brain was gathering input and visual clues, deducing stuff, little brain cells sparking and synapsing to AP attention. He started a slow smile, his New York body tensed for a fight. Finally! There was some *major* perpetrating going on down there! Jimbo smacked a tight fist into his palm. He had a lot to do. He was gonna pull a bomber over, and kick some butt! He turned and blasted down the seven flights of stairs, three steps at a time, and out the door to his waiting AP truck.

The B-47 pulled out of the disintegrating hangar and hung a

hard right, away from the tower. It steered easily with the rudder pedals, and all the controls handled just like the manual said. Tommy headed it out toward the end of the empty ramp, where he'd then take a left onto the taxi-way that led over to the end of the runway. He squirmed in his seat, trying to calm down. All those years of reading the manual were paying off. Wow! His first solo. He liked it up here, he could see forever! He had never been this high before—he felt like he was flying!

Bobby twisted around, and looked back toward Mitch and what was left of Hangar 8 to wave 'bye. Then he saw the flashing red light. "Uh-oh," he radioed to Tommy. "We've got company behind us. Check six, amigo."

Tommy glanced up into the rear-view mirror, looking straight behind them, and sure enough! "A cherry-top," he yelled. "Hell's bells! An AP! He's got his lights on! He wants us to pull over," Tommy jabbered excitedly.

"Of course he does," sighed Bobby. "He's an adult, and this looks like fun. He'll try to stop it, he has to, but he can't, so just keep on driving."

"Why can't he stop us?" Tommy asked, still worried.

Bobby sighed again. Kids! "Because we're bigger than him, ya' moron. Plus he can't reach the door—it's over his head."

"Oh, yeah!" Tommy smiled, and kept on driving, watching the little red light on the little blue truck swerving around back there. Looking ticked.

The San-man was ticked! Royally ticked. He had his lights and siren on, and what with the blast from the jet engines added to that, it was loud back here! Plus that damned plane was buffeting his truck, and his eyes were watering from the hot, blasting exhaust. The windows were up in the morning chill but his truck was a freaking Dodge—it leaked like a sieve! Plus the jet didn't seem like it was going to pull over.

He thought about shooting it with his pistol, but Jimbo was staring down the barrels of some pretty bodacious cannons. He guesstimated that they were four or five feet long, and seemed zeroed in on his rattling dashboard, so he thought the better of it. He was ticked, not stupid! The bomber led him down the ramp, turned left onto the taxi-way, drove a little bit further out to the end of the runway, turned left again to line itself up on the centerline of the runway, and then it stopped! It *stopped!* He did it! He pulled over a freaking bomber! Wait'll the gang at the Chat 'n Chew back in Brooklyn hear about this one! He was gonna add resisting arrest to the other charges. He was gonna get out and kick some bomber butt.

Tommy stopped the airplane, and he and Bobby started going down the Before Take-off checklist, but they were hurrying now, skipping a few, nervously watching the authorities right behind them. The blue truck was shaking and bouncing in the jet wash, and it looked like the AP was pushing up against the door now, trying to get out. Well, the heck with *this,* thought Tommy. Time to GO!

The San-man was really ticked now, you'd better believe it! The noise and smoke and smell of kerosene was making his head hurt, plus he couldn't get the ding-dang, god-danged *door* open. Every time he got it open a little, the jet wash would slam it back shut. He'd call for a freaking back-up, if there *was* a freaking back-up. Enough of this! He pulled out his gun, a big, no-bullshit .45. He was gonna shoot that freaking bomber right through the freaking windshield of this freaking piece-of-shit Dodge truck! He was gonna shoot some butt! Nobody messed with the San-Man!

The runway loomed straight out in front of Tommy, disappearing to a point on the horizon. He had tried to calculate take-off speeds last night, at their weight and estimated temperature and density, but it had a lot of fractions. He'd even tried some new math on it, but by then they were all getting pretty tired. He knew they didn't have to worry about calculating rotation speeds because of the pre-set AOA (Angle Of Attack) of the wings (p. 33) so he figured he'd just drive as fast as he could, right down the middle of the runway, and when he got to the other end, he'd just V^1 and V^2 and everything, and haul it the heck on up there! Sky

King did it every day: roar down the runway, pull back on the wheel, and Penny got smaller, waving, looking up at her flyboy. Now *she* had some nice titties!

Tommy put his right hand·on the throttles, said a quick "Glory Be," and shoved them forward, out of idle, to the stops.

Back in the shuddering, rattling Dodge, the noise of the jet went from a thundering roar, to an unbelievable, piercing, hellish, howling scream and Santini was right in the middle of it! What's happening?! This can't be happening!

The huge plane started rolling away, and the noise became downright painful! The last thing Jimbo remembered (before he woke up in the base hospital three days later) was the front of his truck lifting slowly up, and James Santini was staring, unbelieving, his gun pointed straight up to the Kansas sky. He yelled at the top of his lungs, but his screams were swept away in the hellish cyclone that encircled him. His truck pointed straight up, teetered, then flew—dreamlike—straight on over backwards! Santini watched incredulously, still screaming, as the concrete rushed up to meet him, then closed his eyes as the glass exploded.

Up in the tower, Smitty was watching all this through the binoculars. "Yikes," he gasped. A gol-durned truck loop! Shit, man, those Big Apple boys *loved* a scrap. He watched, fascinated, as the leaky blue Dodge began a crazy, unreal, smashing and rolling, over and over, off the end of the runway and into the scrubby weeds, toward the eastern boundary of the Flight Line. Toward New York.

Heading swiftly in the other direction, Tommy saw the end of the runway coming up fast, so he pulled back on the wheel, and the boys went up into the air, *just like that!* Gear UP! Wowee-*zowee!* This was certainly different! He was looking DOWN at the TOPS of the trees. And by the time he blinked at this new vision, they were someplace else. Things were just happening so . . . fast! His movement through the sky was sort of . . . *slippery.*

He could turn the wheel to the left and few seconds later, the big jet slewed in that general direction. He could pull back on the wheel and a few seconds later, the boys would be a couple of hundred ding-danged feet up . . . like magic! It was a weird feeling, like a go-cart ride and a trampoline mixed together. Lots of weight as the jet was climbing, then no weight at all as he aimed back down toward the fields, his checklist momentarily floating off his lap. Cool! Leaning left, then leaning right. Up and down and left and right was a constant, changing *liquid* sort of movement. Whenever he looked straight down over the side, he tended to drift and got all wiggly. But when he focused far ahead, things smoothed out a little.

The plane felt a little sluggish, though. He didn't know what it should feel like, but he sensed something wasn't right. B-47s weren't known as wallowers, and this one was definitely wallowing. Think. *Think!* Oh NO! Now he remembered! He'd forgotten to set Take-Off Flaps, step 18 on the list. That darned AP had distracted him a little—a lot, actually!

By this time the jet had accelerated through 200 knots, and the need for flaps was decreasing every second. Tommy should have know that, of course. It was mentioned twice, once on page 14 and also on the chart on page 107. However, considering he had only about 10 seconds of actual flight time, he was a little nervous, and reached for the flap lever anyway. It wouldn't budge. He shoved down harder, trying to steer the plane with his other hand, and the lever started moving—there—but at the bottom of the arc, his hand slipped off the flap knob, smashing against the console. Yowch! He checked his finger. Awshoot! He got a *cut!*

The flaps came down, the plane ballooned up dangerously, and the stall warning alarm sounded. Tommy knew that you do *not* want to stall a bomber this close to the ground, that's how people got hurt! He shoved the nose down for some more speed. "Hey!" radioed Mike angrily, "Knock it off! You're doin' that on purpose, so cut it out! I'm tryin' to work down here!"

Sheesh, Tommy thought, have a cow, why doncha! They were all a little nervous and testy, he reckoned. They had never stolen a B-47 before. Still, he had rarely heard young Michael so mad! He hoped it wouldn't affect the mission. If there was a mission. He knew that they were dangerously close to crashing, and was trying to think of a way to mention it to the crew without sounding, you know . . . negative . . . but he couldn't, so he just went and yelled: *"Whoooahh Nelly!"*

Tommy wrestled hard with the control column as the plane continued to gyrate, nose up, then down, wings all over the place, barely missing the small trees and fence posts. Dang! If he crashed it, the darn report would probably say Pilot Error. It always said Pilot Error.

Bobby screamed into the mike, "What'd you just *do* up there?"

"The flaps!" Tommy shot back angrily.

"Then *un*-do 'em, Bozo!"

Oh! Well, for pete's sake, thought Tommy. Of course! A good co-pilot could see the big picture. That was the co-pilot's job, to sit back there and give the pilot advice and suggestions, reminding him of correct procedures, and admonishing him for any sloppy techniques. Pilots appreciated that, and knew that a good co-pilot was worth his weight in gold. Tommy undid the flaps, his hand still smarting, and the jet smoothed out. Whew! That was a close one.

Tommy still felt nervous, and the instruments were all over the place. He was trying to make sense of all the numbers, and still miss the trees. He was flying, all right, he knew he *could,* but every time he looked down to one of the spinning dials, he'd start to steer toward the ground.

Bobby radioed up to him, "Try not looking at your instruments so much! Just look out, keep the horizon level on the nose, and calm down, for cryin' out loud! Either ya' got it or ya' don't. And try a little smoother turns, too, why doncha. I almost fell out of my chair back here!"

He was right, of course. What an excellent co-pilot! Okay, Tommy thought. Calm down. Look out. Fly the plane. *Don't let the plane fly you.*

Mike piped up again from down below, "Hey, Riley, your

turns are maj-o-rama stink-o's!"

Tommy had just about had it up to here with that young
man. "Michael Kontovan!" he transmitted angrily, "do you wanna
drive?"

Silence crackled from below.

"O.K. then, let's keep it down back there. I don't want to have
to pull this thing over!" Hell's *bells!* This crew needed a little discipline.

Tommy floored it. They had a mission to do, they were gonna
make some noise! They'd decided it would be mostly symbolic
noise, starting with the TV coverage at Offutt. But a B-47 at tree-
level made more than just cliche noise. It also made some *real*
noise. Kind of like Krakatoa, East of Java, or maybe the explosion
of a small planet. Only much, much louder.

They flew over the edge of town, the nose of the jet swerving,
hunting, sniffing for the correct route. There was the Holiday Inn,
its teensy green and yellow sign flashing at them. Wow, this was
neat! thought the young pilot. There was the Katz, and the Van de
Kamp's grocery, its little blue Dutch windmill turning slowly on
its sign. Most of the cars were swerving around or pulled over, and
the few people he could focus on were either lying down, or running around like loose chickens. Off to his left, he could see the
Capitol building and the big grain silos, even with him, or maybe
a little higher, receding in the distance.

Maureen had always been an early riser. She would go out into the
still morning air, thank the Lord for this new day, say good morning to her husband, Lawrence, and his parents, and watch the sun
come up. She dearly loved Lawrence, just as she loved mornings.
He was lying over there, next to the zinnias, facing California.
Lawrence's father and mother had meant to get to California, as
had Lawrence. But the Lord, in his infinite wisdom, decided they
would all stay in Kansas, and farm this beautiful land, and raise
fine families. So there they all lay, over there by the flower garden.
There was a place saved up for Maureen, too, right next to them,

but she wasn't ready yet. The warm coffee cup was comforting her hands in the cool morning air, and the smell of the brew was heavenly. Her eyes reveled in the purpley-orange of daybreak, and she thanked the kind Lord for the ability to see, to smell the sweet air, to even feel the warm smoothness of the cup. After 74 productive years, Maureen had few regrets. Her children and grand-children and great-grand-children were a pleasure, and her life had been good, but quiet.

She glanced to the northwest, and saw the hawk hurtling low across the barley field. Strange, she thought. She had never seen one thermal this early, and it had bumps on its wings and smoke behind it and *wait*. This was no bird. Too fast! *Oh my!*

Maureen turned to run toward the house and looked back up at the huge thing, and then it was ON her, and blocked out the sky–Ka*BAM!*

She suddenly found herself sitting quite firmly in the yard, her spilled coffee warming her legs through her bathrobe. Something was different, she felt, *wrong*. The crackling roar of the low, smoking jet chased its speeding silhouette off to the orange horizon. Excited birds chirped their alarm, and their melodious alerts stunned and dazzled Maureen. The family of squirrels that she had silently fed through their generations scolded and fought, and relayed their skittery messages up and down what was left of the old walnut tree. Back at the house, a few surviving panes of glass held on as long as they could, then let go, tinkling themselves to pieces on their windowsills.

Looking back to the sky, she heard the roar of the jet become a low rumble, then a whisper, and then it was gone. A worried bug flew past her face, the delicious *bzzzzzzz* tracing its flight swoopily out toward the barn. The birds kept discussing the event, the squirrels quarreled, and Maureen just sat there, collecting her thoughts. All her life, she had always had that one silly hope, that one "if I had just one wish" dream. She thought that if it ever did come true, it would have been through prayer, or a miracle, or an as-yet-undiscovered medical treatment. Not an *airplane!* But the Lord worked in mysterious ways! Boy, did she! But Maureen would take it.

She sat there, her eyes wide, her ears savoring the early morning sounds, the melodious masterpieces, sweet beyond belief. That jet was her miracle. 'Ka*BAM*' was the first sound she had ever heard in her life. She sat there, stunned and thoughtful, and began composing a little thank you letter in her mind, but . . . to whom? She rolled her head back, and laughed out loud for the very first time, looking up to the deliciously noisy sky.

"Hey," Bobby announced, "we're way off, man. I think we're going to Missouri or something. Swing us around to a heading of 180 degrees, and we should catch Highway 75 and be on our way to Oooooklahoma."

Tommy's eyes scanned the instrument panel, checked the dials, and zeroed in on the compass mounted on the windshield frame. One instrument that all the boys were familiar with was the compass. Besides using them all the time on Boy Scout hikes, most of their parent's cars had one, mounted up there on the dashboard. Kansas was still Out West, and most people here still had a dollop of pioneer blood in them. Tommy thought it was a little silly sometimes. If you felt an urge to head due W (270 degrees) to do a little prospecting or see what's over the next rise, you still had to stay on the durned road, even if it was WNW (292 degrees). Still, the boys were used to the slow, laborious searching of the compass, always lagging after a turn, taking its own sweet time to sort things out. The Rileys were lucky, their station wagon had a compass *and* a Saint Christopher statue. They had a bunch of guidance!

Following his navigator's instructions, Tommy swung the bomber to a heading of 180 and nailed it. Satisfied with their compass heading, Bobby spun his seat around and started reviewing his notes on his tail cannon. He didn't think he'd need them, but you could never be too sure. Not in this day and age.

The alert young pilot noticed the view below didn't look much like the maps on his ceiling. There were no yellow lines to follow, so he would have to trust Bobby and the AAA maps he had swiped from his parent's glove compartment, plus the atlas for the overwater leg. He was pretty sure they were under the radar like they planned, from having to pull up to miss some of the taller trees and barns. And they almost took out a Conoco station back there when Tommy had to scratch his, you know, privates. Those ejection seat straps were *itchy.*

Eddie sat in the old Ford, leaning up against the door, sort of sleepy, but bouncing way too much to get comfortable and take a nap. He looked to his left and saw his father's silhouette in the early morning sunrise. Eddie could sight straight down the right fender of the dirty red truck and line up the edge of the road with the big, yellow blinker light mounted on the top of it. His dad was doing okay with it, the light staying reasonably close to the stripe painted on the edge of the highway. The big side mirror was further out, tracking down the fenceline. There was constant movement to his left, out the corner of his eye. His dad, struggling with the sloppy steering of the old truck, occasionally reached for the big shifter, jamming the clutch to the floor with his left foot, then carefully selecting a new gear (with a minimum of grinding), his face grimacing at every shift, feeling, knowing each gear, each bushing, seeing the old parts in his mind sliding and spinning around down there, doing what they had to do. He and his dad had rebuilt the old truck so many times they both had it just about memorized. Rebuilt the other littler truck, too, the blue pick-up. And the tractor. Each piece of equipment had its own personality, and Eddie was getting pretty good with them.

His dad let him drive the blue truck around the farm: key in the ignition. Choke all the way out, then in two-thirds, unless it was summer, or had already been running lately. Accelerator to the floor, once and firmly. Let off. Back down one quarter, then off again. Wait four seconds, then down halfway, turn the ignition, and the instant it catches, full down immediately till it roars, maybe one second, then off again, and it's going. Wait ten seconds, then push the choke back in fully. Shifting it wasn't quite so easy, the second-to-third gear an especially interesting route, but he and his dad had that figured out pretty good, too. But whenever his mom tried to drive it, Old Blue would vapor lock. It smelled fear.

He liked the machinery, and spent a lot of time at the workbench, tinkering in the old, dark barn. Nice, heavy old tools, cool to the touch, hanging in order from pegs. Sawdust on the soft dirt floor, spongy underneath. Brittle tape on rows of rusty coffee cans lined up across the shelves announcing: Screws, wood; Screws, mtl; Nails; Washers; Hinges, sm; Hinges, big; Misc. And directly below the light, a big ol' vise, a *super* vise. A compressor. Torque wrench. The works.

Eddie loved taking things apart, and putting them back together. Anything to keep from having to mess with the dang chickens. He hated those smelly, stupid things. And the dang tomatoes, too. None of the other kids in class had to do this kind of crap, he bet. Everyday after homework: chores. All day Saturday: chores. And now on a sleepy Sunday morning, taking 144 crates of smelly chickens, four to a crate—more or less—tied down with ropes on the back of this smelly old flatbed truck.

Nothing exciting much ever happened to him. One day you looked up and *bam,* you're twelve years old and what have you got to show for it? What memories, what accomplishments? The other kids in class had exciting lives, went on vacations. And those Air Force kids, they had a lot of fun. Eddie liked 'em all all right, but they were spoiled. Baseball leagues, swimming around. *They* should try being a farmer once. *They* should get woke up at three in the morning to help cover two acres of tomatoes because your dad thinks it's gonna frost. And he knew when they finally got to the processor in Emporia, he'd have to crawl up on the back of the dang truck and hand the dang chicken crates down, all 144 of them. If he could wish anything, it'd be that when they got there, the chickens would be gone, the truckbed clean, and then they'd go and get some ice cream.

His dad was in a bad mood, the price of pullets having dropped eight cents last week, then four more at Friday's close. If they made it to the processor before the markets opened on Monday, his dad figured that they could get about $390 for chickens that were worth $565 the week before. The dang chickens were worth more dead than alive—insurance would cover them if they would just wreck. His dad had explained that as soon as they were tied down on the truck, they weren't chickens anymore. They were cargo. Insurance would pay for the old truck, too, in an accident. But his dad was careful and honest, and Eddie figured they'd probably keep fixing it forever. Some months were good on a farm, some not so good. They *did* do good on tomatoes last fall. Bumper.

He sighted down the fender again, and saw a silver glint in the side mirror. He frowned and leaned forward and scrunched his eyebrows. An *airplane!* It was getting bigger fast, and there was a bunch of smoke swirling around behind it, and what the heck was a jet doing flying down the row of telephone poles?!

He turned to yell at his dad, but he had seen it too, and was struggling with the steering wheel and hitting the brakes and looking in his side mirror at the thing. Eddie stared back out and had to crank his head up now, the thing almost on top of them, the impossibly loud shriek hurting his ears. He saw its shiny metal— black bumps on it someplaces—and as it got even louder the grass went flat and three dirty tornadoes were closing in on them.

"HOLY—!" yelled his dad at the top of his lungs as the roaring jet blotted out the sky through the windshield and both Eddie and his father instinctively raised their arms to cover their faces, screaming! At the same instant Ka*BAM!* and the thundering concussion smashed them like a dynamite explosion. 144 crates of cheap chickens exploded into frantic freedom as the jet and tornadoes ripped over the truck. They drove down into the ditch, then back up, through the fence, one last swerve, then up on two wheels, teetering, and over on one side in slow motion in the cool dirt. The motor died, and some wheat stubble tickled Eddie's surprised cheek. His dad was lying heavily on his side, squashing him, covering him. He tasted dirt.

"You okay, son?"

"I think so. What the hell was that?"

"Don't say hell, son. We talked about that. But I'll be goldurned if I know what it was!" He pulled himself up by the shifter to crawl up and struggle out the driver's open window. After he'd grunted and shimmied his way out, his weathered hand reached back in to help pull his groggy son up.

Eddie grabbed it, then stood there on the passenger door, his head now up by the steering wheel. He wiped some dirt off his face, and looked up at his father through the window. His dad was crouched on the door, looking back up the highway, watching the dirty tornadoes speed south behind the roaring jet. Then he grinned. "Well . . . it looks like we won't be sellin' no forty cent pullets *this* day," he drawled, pulling Eddie gingerly up out the window. "Them birds was cargo, and they're insured. Time to call the Good Hands people. Hot damn!" He lifted his son by his armpits, then slid him gently down the windshield to the ground.

Wow! Eddie thought, looking at the white, squawking confetti getting small in the distance. And to think he was just worrying that nothin' much ever happened to him! Ha! Just wait'll the kids in class heard about *this* one.

"Yikes! What was that!?" announced Bobby, still facing backwards, fiddling with the tail gun.

"What was *what?*" answered Tommy.

"I don't know. White stuff, white things. Like a cloud back over there by that truck we just went over."

"White things? So what are the white things doing?"

"I dunno. Goin' up. Goin' away. Just *goin'!*"

Hmmm. Tommy had no idea. But he was enjoying the trip, a lot! Sometimes he'd go right down the highway, sometimes he'd move over a little and fly above the fields, keeping the road in sight. It just depended. The fields and barns and cows were zipping by fast—they were making pretty good time. Watching the nose of the jet slicing its way through the fields was fascinating. The early-morning landscape changed constantly in the black frame of the cockpit canopy. He was the artist, making the horizon tilt to the right, then to the left—at his will. He could paint a teensy white house growing larger and larger, and then, with a deft stroke, smear it into a white blur as it disappeared beneath him. This was totally cool!

The steering yoke fell easily to his hand, all the noises were just right for a bomber (he supposed), switches and instruments were in their proper positions, and the big Boeing responded to his slightest input with grace and ease. He kept his eyes focused on the far horizon, always alert to new windmills and power lines scrolling toward them, his fingers gently adjusting the track of the bomber, the sinuous ballet of a perfectly-functioning plane weaving its way through the surprised subjects of his ever-changing painting. The low morning sun sent its rays through the left side of the tinted canopy, warming him, and threw harsh shadows across the crowded display of instruments on the black panel in front of him. He was enjoying the artistic aspects of his flight, but knew it was time to get his head out of the clouds, or the wheat anyways, and focus on the mission.

Bobby then announced: "Co-pilot to peabrain . . . co-pilot to peabrain— "

Mike was struggling with a bucket down below, muddy water splooshing down his jeans and onto his squishing tennies. Then part of his bomb load hopped out of the darned bucket and disappeared behind a radarscope. Criminy! The young bombardier was in no mood to put up with any of his big brother's stupid taunts. "Whaddyawant!?" he crackled defensively.

"Not you, peabrain! *Riley* peabrain. Yoo hoo up there, Mister Pilot Peabrain, sir! Lookit how fast we're goin'."

As Tommy glanced down to find the airspeed indicator, the heavy jet tilted lower and very nearly took out Altoona, Kansas. Bobby yelled *"Lookout!"* and Tommy quickly jerked the bomber's nose up as the boys screamed down Quincy Street.

Every man, woman, child, dog, horse, cow, chicken and spider in town were instantly awakened—their senses simply dynamited from peaceful slumber to amazingly total wide-awakeness. No lolling around in bed this Sunday. No snooze alarm. No friendly pats on the rump, trying to get the other half to putter out to the kitchen to make coffee. Just UP.

Mrs. Lashton, over on River Street, had spent the entire night sitting in her favorite rocker, petting her beloved old cat. The orange tabby was lying still on her lap, purring fitfully. Just old, the vet had said. She'd had a good, long cat life, but now it was time. "Poor kitty," Mrs. Lashton murmured, petting her gently. "Poor, dear kitty." But right about the time the living room window exploded, Punkin suddenly decided to climb quickly up Mrs. Lashton's arm, off her shoulder and on to the top of the china cabinet and live a little while longer.

Tommy and Bobby both held their breaths as the low brick buildings turned to a brown blur that streamed down both sides of the aircraft. It was all happening so *fast*—hardly time to think! Right up ahead, the road led to a large building, so Tommy eased the control column back a little further. As soon as they cleared the Mercantile and were safely back over the flat fields, screaming their way south, the young pilot swallowed hard, murmured another quick "Glory Be," scanned his panel again, and found the speedometer.

"It says here we're makin' 280 knots. So?" He glanced back up at Bobby in the rear-view mirror.

Bobby had pretty much recovered from his quick trip through town, and was again leaning over his maps, scribbling furiously with his pencil. He then looked up at the mirror, and shook his pencil sternly at Tommy, a move he learned from Sister Alice Ann. "*Soooo* . . . I just figured that unless you want us to get there an hour and a half late and blow the whole shootin' match, you'd better give it some gas! 280 knots fer cryin' out loud! We've got a pretty tight schedule today. Let's get a move on, shall we?"

"Oh, yeah? Well, as you may recall, creepface, we just took off a few minutes ago, and I'm still learnin' how to steer this thing!

This was the first chance I had to check the speedometer, okay? This puppy just likes to go 280 knots is all."

"Well don't let it. We gotta pay attention to all these numbers, Riley, and make 'em do what we planned last night. Let's get this thing up to 360 or so, and as we burn off fuel and lighten her up, I think we can even go a little faster. Okey doke?"

After all the planning, the fears—everything—Tommy suddenly realized, *knew*, that they were actually going to pull this thing off! They were doing it! He took a deep breath and smiled to himself. "Okey dokey, smokey. 360 knots comin' right up." *Fly the airplane, don't let the airplane fly you.*

Tommy's right hand spread wide over the six throttle levers, and he pushed them forward firmly, conducting the increasing whine of the jet orchestra, watching the engine pressures and rpms increase as six needles spun clockwise in unison on his panel.

CHAPTER 9.

SUNDAY SURPRISE

The sky was showing a pink glow to the east, with small, grey clouds moving silently across the horizon. Out on the huge concrete ramp at Offutt, dozens of technicians and laborers and finger-snapping managers busied themselves in the cool morning air. Bleachers had been wheeled into position and unfolded, flags were raised, and a large carpeted stage was towed to the front. TV crews from all the networks scrambled for the best positions in front of the varnished podium. Their cameras and microphones were connected by snaking cables back to their control vans, little antennas on top, ready to send their messages through the sky to an anxious populace.

The Vice President was already there, with LeMay and a few other staff officers, going over the agenda One Last Time. When everything was timed just perfect, Lyndon moved it all up five minutes, just to watch those flyboys sweat and scribble and erase, and synchronize their watches all over again. Gahdamm, he thought. This was a *hoot!*

Suddenly, a lieutenant ran up to the circle of men, winded after a hurried scramble from a nearby communications van. "Sir," he said, snapping to attention in front of LeMay, catching his breath. "We . . . we just received a non-coded transmission from Forbes tower. It sounds serious, sir. He's on the eight-band."

LeMay looked up from his schedule, sizing up the bothersome intruder. "Who the hell are you?" he growled. "And what the hell is an eight-band!?"

"Follow me, sir. Please, sir," the young officer insisted.

LeMay grumbled and followed the trotting lieutenant to a blue panel van at the edge of the proceedings. There were banks of radios and communications equipment mounted just about everywhere on the side of the vehicle. All were under the shadow of a metal awning, hinged to the roof. Three nervous radio specialists sat at a fold-out console, earphones clamped to their heads, watching LeMay in awe.

"Th . . . this one, sir," said the lieutenant, gesturing toward a large microphone.

LeMay snarled at the young officer, and snatched the microphone up, keying the transmit button. "Who's this?" he demanded angrily. "Forbes, is it? This better be reeeeal important."

"Sir!" the speakers crackled loudly, startling LeMay. "Airman Smith here. We got us a situation, sir. A . . . an airplane just took off!" The voice was hesitant, almost pleading.

"What!?" barked LeMay. "Impossible! We're standing down."

"I . . . I know sir, but it just took off! And the hangar too and the truck *Ohgod* he just—"

"Settle down there, dammit, and knock off the blubbering!"

"Umm, *yessir.*"

"Now, I want some answers. Straight and fast."

"Yessir," the voice echoed across the ramp. "I'm okay now, sir."

"Now, what kind was it?"

"A Dodge, sir, I think."

"What!? No, son, the airplane. What kind of airplane was it?"

"A B-47, sir. It just took off. Nobody knew about it."

"Dammit! You're sure? How the hell can a jet bomber just take the hell off without any kind of clearance? Who's your C.O.?"

"Lieutenant Colonel Bainer, sir, but he's not here. Nobody is. There wasn't any scheduled flights because of the stand-down, so it was just me and Santini up here in the tower all night. *Ohgod!*"

"Now calm down, son. You say this plane just took off? No clearances? No radio messages?" LeMay signaled urgently to a hovering colonel and hissed, "Lou, get on the horn to NORAD—now!"

"Honest, sir," the speakers continued. "No clearances. No nothin'. It was in a hangar and it just blew it all to hell, and then the truck, too, and then it just went and took off."

"A B-47?"

"Yes, sir. One of the ones with the black noses—the reconnaissance kind."

"An RB, eh? How long ago and which way was he headed?"

"M . . . maybe five minutes. He used Runway 31, sir, so he was headed kind of west. But he was really low, sir. I lost him right after take-off."

"Okay, son, you just stay put. Keep this channel open, but call Bainer on his direct line and tell him to get his ass up there pronto. My orders." LeMay clicked the radio off, staring angrily at the sky.

Colonel Robbins looked up, joining him. "What do you think, Curtis?" he asked.

"I don't know," answered LeMay thoughtfully. "A recon bomber just up and decides to take off? I don't like this one little bit." He spun back around to the colonel. "Louie, what have we got from NORAD or local stations? Any radio contact or radar reports?"

"Don't know yet."

"Well, get on it, and get back to me as soon as you have word."

"Yes, sir." Colonel Robbins scurried away. LeMay was still looking at the sky, trying to size up the situation, when a minute later the colonel reported back, out of breath. "Our comm officer at The Bunker says he can't raise them on air-to-air, but he's still trying all channels. Up to J-band at last contact. There's no transponder squawk, and the ELT boys are coming up empty. And no radar contact. Nothing NORAD, nothing DEW line, nothing local or Kansas City Center."

"No radar contact at all?"

"No radar contact of any military bogie, Curt. Not in this sector or any others for that matter. He's just not there."

LeMay took his cigar from his mouth and studied the sky intently. "Not there?" He then put the cigar back in his mouth

and responded quietly, "Oh, he's there all right, colonel. He's there."
LeMay squinted hard toward the horizon. "He's just damned good."

The jet raced south through the morning coolness, weaving skill-
fully to follow the gently rolling terrain. "How's it going down
there, Mike?" radioed Bobby.

"Pretty good," crackled Mike on the intercom. "I'm not spilling too much."

"Just keep all that gunk away from the camera. You remember
how to load it?"

"Got my notes right here. I'll be ready to shoot a test strip in
a little while. *Ow!*"

"What's up?"

"Man, this one crawdad is really starting to tick me off. He's a
feisty bugger."

In a while, the scrub and square fields of southern Kansas began giving way to the rolling hills of eastern Oklahoma, and all of
the sudden the small clusters of trees crowding the curving lines of
creeks and ponds since Topeka became a solid green canopy. Trees!
Forests, almost! Lots of them, just like that! And lakes!

"Tulsa's coming up, and I'd rather not hit it," reported Bobby.

"Hit *what!?*" yelled Michael.

"Sheesh, hold it down!" answered Bobby. "We ain't hittin'
nothin', so just cool it down there. What I said was: let's *miss*
Tulsa. Turn left a scosh to 160, Riley, and we'll hit the Oklahoma-
Arkansas border. In a few minutes we'll swing back to 180 again
and shoot down to The Lone Star State. Tex-ass. Texas-T!

"Roger, dodger," replied Tommy.

On the ramp at Offutt, everyone was abuzz about the missing
plane. Position reports seemed to indicate it was headed south.
Messages were still coming in concerning the damage at Forbes,
and to all the podunk towns the jet had flown over so far. Interceptors had been sent up, to no avail. By the time a frantic report
came in from a stricken town and fighter jets raced to the scene,

the bomber was long gone. Box patterns were set up but no one could sight the low-flying jet in the morning grey. Radar was useless. Two F-89s had loosed their rockets at a bomber-shaped pond shimmering in the morning light near Olathe, and an F-101 excitedly tracked its own shadow across four counties, drawing a squadron of frenzied interceptors to help in the chase.

The Vice President was really enjoying himself, boy-howdy! Seeing LeMay so double-dog pissed about that damn plane was a riot! That fancy-pants flyboy had been spittin' and pissin' on the radio like a wet cat, and he couldn't find his own plane worth crap! Even had half the durned Air Force up a'lookin' for it all durned morning. Last anybody saw, it was heading south, and nobody could catch it! Couldn't even *find* it! Haw!

At 07:12, a long, black limousine pulled slowly up to the cluster of diplomats, and stopped. A chrome-helmeted airman hustled to the rear door, snapping it open. The Russian general, sporting four rows of jingly medals on a white uniform pulled himself ponderously out and stood frowning, looking left, then right, and then back into the limo as he snapped his fingers. From the darkness of the car, a white hat emerged, attached to the obedient hands of the general's adjutant, who followed the hat out into the morning sunlight. The Russian general was in a foul mood. The insolence of these Americans! Forcing him off his Aeroflot photo-bomber, er . . . transport in New York, and making him fly on an American plane as a common civilian, a tourist! The American plane had droned on throughout the night, carefully avoiding any restricted areas—as if he were a common spy! And then landing at the civilian airfield in Omaha, and taking this ridiculous limousine, this pitiful copy of a magnificent Soviet Zil, for the short drive to Offutt Air Force Base, not allowing him to see the American base from the air. He was furious. How dare they? Was this glasnost? He thought *not!* And to add insult to injury, he had angrily hurled his jacket into the closet of the American plane in New York at the news of his revised schedule, momentarily forgetting about the tiny camera hidden in the second button, rendering it useless. He was beyond angry!

He stood there, shifting, getting the kinks out after the long, all-night trip, his tired adjutant joining him in his groggy calisthenics. Quickly he recalled the transmissions foolishly broadcast over his escort's portable radio, frantic calls concerning a rogue American bomber. Useful information that he was, no doubt, not supposed to hear. So the games begin, he thought to himself. He would bide his time.

The American vice president let them stand there and blink, and look lost, and just a little bit stupid for exactly the right few seconds, and then began walking smartly toward them, his blue-suited ducklomats following close behind. He led his entourage to the commie duo, and as soon as the cameras were whirring, he beamed diplomatically at the Russian general. The veepster grasped his hand and driveled the usual, "So glad you're *here,* let us work *together* in *peace,* a *new day* is upon us, blah blah blah." The Russian, General Wodka Buttinski, Hero of the Supreme Soviet, lied right back and said in broken English the same usual things people say to someone they'd like to kill, but need to change it up a little because the cameras were rolling. Johnson smiled hugely, and motioned his team up to the front. He pulled the adversaries together, like a ref at a boxing match, and checked his program. Come on up, come up to the middle, rightchere, put those hands down.

"General LeMay, this is General Wodka Buttinski, representing the Soviet Union. And this here is Colonel Steveski Khunyin, aide to General Buttinski. Buttinski—LeMay. LeMay—Buttinski. LeMay—Khunyin. Khunyin—LeMay." So far, so good. No fighting or spitting or joy-buzzers or anything. Thank *god* they were professionals. Okay! Now then, back to your corners till we start the ceremonies. Wait for the bell. Good luck.

LeMay couldn't believe he was shaking hands with a Russian four-star. Two days ago, if he'd seen this fat, red-faced piece of commie shit, it would have been down the barrel of an Atlas missile. Now, here he was, actually standing here, shaking hands with it, in *Nebraska!* In front of all these stinking civilians, with their stupid cameras and pretty decorations. LeMay was seething.

Boy, the vice president was a'lovin' this whole scene! He especially enjoyed telling that short, smart-ass flyboy that he would be sitting next to that Russkie generalissimo at the special chow-down they were gonna have after the ceremony. Right plum smack-dab between that Russkie and the the wife of a gol-dang, high-falutin' senator whose hobbies were Siamese cats and world peace. Boy howdy! This was gonna be some fun, lemme *tell* ya!

Then LeMay found himself shaking hands with Buttinski's disgusting lackey, Col. Khunyin. He looked a little like a pilot, but since he was a commie, Curtis knew he couldn't fly the broad side of a barn. All this ridiculous, pathetic, pansy-ass hand shaking was not what Curtis was hired to do. At the interview for Air Force Chief Of Staff, CEO of about a zillion megatons of assets, his job description was pretty specific: to use big, dangerous airplanes and missiles to keep those slimeball commies cowering in their pitiful, pathetic little corner. And, if they ever *did* get out of their corner, to grind them into a quivering, sniveling, piece of slimy, radioactive, commie pulp. *It never said nothin' 'bout shakin' no hands.*

Back behind the stage, skilled workers strung up a huge banner that had been hurriedly made last night at the Base Sign Shop. Requests for the sign had been made the day before in quadruplicate, and were approved and stamped in twelve different buildings by sixty-eight highly-trained personnel throughout the busy base. By the time the papers got back to the Sign Shop, the project had already cost taxpayers over $6,000. Then, in that wild and whacky (and highly lucrative!) tapestry of contractors, civil servants, and military personnel found on military installations throughout the world, seven supervisors had a hurried three-hour meeting, called in for Chinese food, and volunteered to see this vitally important project through. The brave septuplet, ranging from GS-8s to one grizzled GS-42, worked tirelessly throughout the night (at triple-time-and-a-half) to help the Airman Third Class with his brush, advising him when to put some more paint on it. After many hours of skilled supervision, the banner was finished. It read, in big red letters five feet tall: OPERATION TRUSTING GIANTS: A NEW ERA IN SOVIET/U.S. RELATIONSHIPS

LeMay eyed the huge banner, and seethed some more. He knew *exactly* what kind of relationship this was going to be, and America was on the bottom! He hated this whole, pathetic, civilian circus. And plus that renegade plane from Forbes. What else could possibly screw his day up any more?

Buttinsky swelled his chest—it was now time. "Ve understand one of your aircraft has seen to disobey you, general. And that you possibly do not know even where it is. Perhaps you do not intend to actually honor this stand-down after all?"

Now how the hell did this mother-lovin' commie know *that?* LeMay thought. Crap! "We'll honor it, General," he snapped.

General Buttinsky looked at the large map propped against the communications van, noting with a bemused smile the black line connecting the grease-penciled x's following the plane's route. "Your vaunted interceptor fleet cannot contain one lone aircraft? Tsk, tsk, general. Even with radar that can see 'a fly in the sky' I believe the claim was?"

LeMay fumed at the general, saying nothing.

"I am afraid that I must report ze stand-down violation of this errant bomber, general. Although the pursuing fighter craft can be excused, of course, due to the . . . um . . . *extreme* circumstances. This aircraft is obviously flyink below radar, of that I can be sure. The problem is—"

"The problem is," bellowed LeMay, "that my government sees fit to let your sorry ass be here at all. You ain't reporting squat, you commie bastard." Detente was wearing a little thin out there on the ramp.

General Buttinsky smiled, unfrazzled by LeMay's threats. "One of your reconnaissance bombers, a most valued asset, seems intent on escaping your country." His forefinger gently traced along the black line, going from Kansas to Oklahoma to Texas. " I believe

you have a defector, general. Someone wise to the evils of imperial-
ism, no doubt. Their obvious destination is Mexico," he cooed, his
thick digit stabbing the map on the sleepy country. "Our embassy
there would be most happy to offer refuge to such a . . . skilled
crew."

LeMay wondered furiously what kind of a SAC crew would
defect. Impossible! Absolutely no chance—all were hand-picked.
And yet it seemed . . . But why now, dammit!? Today of all days?
You wouldn't plan to defect on a day when you're the only target
up there. You'd likely sneak off during a regular ops mission, not
this ridiculous grandstanding nonsense. Something wasn't adding
up. His eyes followed the black line south to the Gulf of Mexico.
Heading to the Gulf, no doubt about it. But then where would he
go? *And who the hell was it?* And why Mexico, for God's sake?

"If we don't get that loose cannon before he hits the Gulf,
we'll never get him," LeMay muttered angrily to no one in particular. No, there's *got* to be something else, he thought. Something. His eyes scrutinized the Texas coastline, southeast to the
Yucatan Peninsula, then swiveled slowly to the right. Damn! He
zeroed in on the outline of Cuba through widening eyes, and
caught his breath. "Sonofa*bitch!*" he whispered.

Tommy felt pretty comfortable with the controls by now, and the
boys were snaking their way down the valleys and climbing over
the wooded ridges, progressing according to schedule. Bobby gave
position reports whenever he could recognize the name on a water
tower, and marked their position off on his map, giving small course
corrections to the front cockpit. A while later, Michael said the
camera was ready to power up and test. Permission was granted,
and soon a strip of very surprised just plain folks were caught forever on film, looking up through windshields with eyes wide and
mouths open, recorded forever as their pick-up trucks left the road
among the swirling tops of the pine trees. The jet raced south
through the still morning air.

"Fifteen minutes to the Gulf," reported Bobby, leaning over

his map. He was marching his compass in twelve mile steps down a penciled line drawn to Port Arthur, Texas, like a stiff soldier: pencil, point, pencil, point. " If ya' pull up, we could probably see the ocean."

"Nah," Tommy replied, "let's stay low still. They know we took off, but they don't know where we are, and I'd rather they didn't. I'd hate to blow it now. Let's keep it safe."

Thousands of angry and frightened calls had now been collected and disseminated from the heartland to the Gulf of Mexico. An airplane. Low. FAST! Ain't never seen nothin' like it. What about all my windows!? *Somebody's gonna pay fer my chickens!* The messages had filtered through local police, to state agencies, then the military, feeding eventually to Offutt. A plane was on the loose. A big one.

Tommy saw a city to his right. "What's that?"

"Beaumont, I hope. Keep goin'."

Tommy saw white smoke in the distance—a forest fire? He was thinking about turning when the trees below disappeared in an instant, an ocean of dark green pines surrendering to the straight-line edge of a white shell road, then to flat grey fields and fences, a hundred huge, upside-down tuna cans, and then they were over the outer edges of a huge, smoking refinery that zipped past beneath them. Suddenly, invisible waves of heat reached up—shaking them—causing the bomber to shudder in the abrupt updrafts. Yikes! The boiling white smoke was coming from a line of smokestacks and towers, lots of them, *big* ones, coming up fast with blinking red lights around the top, and Tommy yanked back on the wheel.

"Eeek!" squeaked Bobby, as the bomber shot skyward, his eyes wide. "Let's miss this stuff!"

"Let's miss *what* stuff!? radioed Michael from his dark compartment, struggling with his balance against the sudden g-forces.

And just like that, they were over and past it. Bobby twisted around sharply to watch the forest of stacks get small in the distance. "They're gone now, Mike. It was smokestacks, but Riley missed 'em. Way to go, Riley!"

"Uh—" answered Tommy. His throat was dry, his hands sweaty. *Too fast!* He'd hardly known they were there, and now they were *gone!*

He lowered the nose back down to follow the contour of the flat land. Some houses flashed by, then some buildings and the colored dots of cars, and now a muddy brown bay. The bay was big, about thirty seconds worth, then they were back over some marshy land that was cut into patterns by thin lines of curving water. The snaky tributaries were sprinkled with the white dots of pole houses and birds and edged in black grass, all connecting to a sudden, huge, brown canal.

Tommy and Bobby both watched in amazement as spindly, Electra-Set oil rigs flashed beneath them, somehow floating on the water, small boats nudging them like worried water spiders. Then bigger rigs—big as skyscrapers!—lying on their sides in the brown dirt at the edge of the canal. The flash of welders at work popped like little camera flashes going off all over the huge pipes. Then barges and ships, huge and black and not moving—all sitting in the murky water feeding out to a wide jetty. Two parallel lines of pink rocks about 200 yards apart guided the dirty water out to the Gulf, with red and green markers lined up with each jetty that continued the wet highway out to the horizon. And then the boys were over the ocean, just like that! A thin line of cream-colored surf divided the brown beach from the brown water. The Gulf of Mexico. The ocean!

Bobby smiled as he congratulated himself on his navigation. This was an A+ in geography *easy,* he thought, if he survived.

He put his clear course plotter over the straight line drawn from Sabine Pass to Havana. "Turn left to 110 degrees now," he said, looking back down to the sea, "and we'll be on our way to Havana-banana! Sheesh! This water looks like crap!" He craned his neck to watch as they rocketed over the caramel trail of a boat wake leading to a greasy black vessel churning through the ugly water.

A few seconds later, the boys watched in amazement as a stark silhouette of metal pipes and boxes grew out of the sunlight, piercing the far horizon ahead of them. What!? The vision grew and grew, then became a rusty, metal *city!* Cylindrical towers, in clusters of three, connected by metal rooms and walkways, brown and yellow, each standing resolute—dozens of them brooding over the water, their huge dark shadows covering the busy black and white boats that scurried beneath them.

"Oil rigs, I guess," gulped Bobby, looking up at a huge tower to his right. "Let's not hit one."

"Let's not hit one *what!?* radioed Mike from his windowless compartment. This let's-not-hit-stuff was really starting to get on his nerves.

"Yeah, let's not," agreed Tommy, weaving through the stilt city. Heck! He thought it would be smooth sailing once they hit the water—he was amazed at all the crap they had to dodge! How long did this dang stuff go on?

Bobby waved up at a man in a cook's white apron, flashing past, framed in a black door. His up-turned can of garbage was loosing a colorful waterfall of bottles and packaging, a fluttering, sparkling movement against the solid grey of the platform and the dirty water below.

"Litterbug," mumbled Bobby, spinning around once again to watch the city of rigs disappear behind them. He spun forward to a sharp, clear, horizon dead ahead—straight as an arrow. "I guess that was it."

"I sure as heck hope so," exhaled Tommy. He never thought he'd have to worry about buildings and stuff out in the dang ocean! Sheesh! Soon, the brown water became a strip of milky green color, then suddenly it became absolute pure black-blue, deep and clear as anything he could imagine.

"Wow!" exclaimed Bobby. "That water just got blue, just like that! It was like a line in a coloring book back there. This side brown, this side blue!"

Tommy agreed, nodding, looking over the side. Crazy how

the scenes below could change with such suddenness. In a car, things blended slowly from this to that. But in an airplane, a carpet of trees would sometimes stop in a line—just like that! He was amazed at the stuff he'd seen: rolling fields of green brush and cows nestled for miles and miles along one side of a road, with solid ochre-colored fields on the other side—the road a straight, black line separating two worlds. Miles of grey scrub could be undulating to the horizon, and suddenly bright green or brown squares would just be there, perfectly cut, placed at random by a giant hand making a checker-board. Powerlines charging across the landscape, a perfectly straight line, oblivious to the twisted, roiling terrain beneath it. And Bobby was right about the water, too. Brown. Green. Blue. Just like that! Amazing sights from this airplane, he thought. This flying thing was really pretty, he couldn't believe he'd waited so long to try it!

The warming sun had risen well above the horizon, and Tommy experimented again with the thick visor, up and down. He preferred up, but had to squint a little. He flew on for awhile into the sun, checking gauges, course 110, listening to the sounds of the jet. Alert, but hardly moving for the most part. He turned his neck from side to side and shifted in his seat. They had a long ways to go, and he was getting a little stiff, and hungry, too. He radioed back to Bobby, "I think we're out of radar range now, I'm gonna climb a little." He looked in the rear-view mirror at his co-pilot. "You wanna steer? Just don't crash it."

"Just don't what!?" Mike again.

Bobby wasn't sure if he wanted to, mumbling, "Well, I—"

"Don't worry, Mike," radioed Tommy. "We're not gonna crash. I was just talkin'. C'mon, Bobby. It's easy. Just keep your horizon steady on the nose and calm down, fer cryin' out loud. Remember what you told me?"

"Hey, I'll come up and steer!" radioed Mike, excitedly.

"Nope. Bobby's gotta learn. We've got a lot of flying to do, and I'm gonna need a little help. Now put your hand on the wheel, and just barely move it back. Follow me."

Bobby did, and Tommy felt his pressure on the column. He looked up at him in the mirror, and watched Bobby's eyes grow wide as the jet began a shallow climb. "See? It's easy. Now follow me down. Good, now let's level off at 200 feet. Small corrections. There." He showed him how the trim worked, and the yaw damper. "Okay, you got it."

A few minutes later Tommy was chewing on a sandwich, watching Bobby in the rear-view mirror, and thought it was kind of funny. Looking ahead to the east, to *Cuba* for pete's sakes. In an Air Force bomber! A display of black instruments below, a white horizon ahead, ocean swells to the sides, and here was Bobby, *his* Bobby, framed in a small, curved mirror ahead of him, guiding them, flying them. Through the sky! His co-pilot was smiling, sitting tall, and weaving his body from the left to the right to see around the headrest of Tommy's ejection seat.

"Hey, this is a cinch," Bobby shouted. "Easy! And the less ya' do, the easier it is!"

"Yeah, well, just keep us out of the water, bozo. And watch that trim." Tommy ate the last of his peanut-butter and jelly sandwich that Michael had fetched up from below.

The young bombardier crawled up the treehouse steps to look out the canopy for a little bit. Gosh, cool, the ocean! but there was hardly room to even poke his head up there, so he soon went back to his duties below.

Tommy then had his apple, two carrot slices, and his Twinkie. It felt funny eating lunch in the morning, but they hadn't known what exactly to take along for breakfast. (Milk and Wheaties? Bowls? *Spoons?*) But they all knew how to pack a lunch, so . . . He finished eating, took a swig of water from his canteen, and pulled the mask back across his face. "Good job, Bobby. I'll take it. Why don't you eat now, and then check on our ETA to Cuba. We're probably about an hour out still."

Tommy felt Bobby's pressure on the control column ease, so he took over and made a few shallow turns to get back in the loop. The feeling was free and magnificent, the wingtips carving invisible, joyous paths through the sky. He shifted in his seat, wondering what Michelle would think of him up here. She'd probably go steady with him. He wasn't exactly sure of the costs or benefits of going steady, or even what it was, but the high school kids seemed to base their entire existence on attaining it, so it must be something good. He squirmed in his seat again, his belly full, his little loins warming to the thought, the sun beating down on him—heading helplessly toward IDLE, as his small brain, you know, *took off* again. Below he saw the sparkling ocean swells racing beneath them, and tried to find a more comfortable position. His back was acting up.

He had hurt it on one of his trips to Hawaii. He and his beautiful fiance, Michelle Vanderbuilt, always tried to head out to those exciting, tropical islands whenever they could get their busy schedules to jibe. They'd load up Rex Riley's Piper Cub seaplane, and soar out toward the sunset. He had fixed up the trusty little plane with extra-long-range tanks, some ice-coolers in the floats, and attachments for hammocks under the wings. The two lovebirds really enjoyed their Pacific excursions, but Michelle's parents never ceased to worry, of course. The Rexster knew that Mr. Vanderbuilt had his speedy 400' yacht follow them each time (staying discreetly behind the horizon.) Mr. Vanderbuilt was a good man. He was a kind, brilliant, military-industrialist, and despite his self-made fortune, a regular guy. He liked a beer with the fellas, and there were a few wealthy toe-nails back there behind the ol' couch (a Louie XIV.)

After a long day of flying, Rex would set the little plane down on the long, rolling swells, drop the sea anchor, and amble out onto the pontoons. The two frequent-flyers would sit on the floats and generally get all the kinks out, then go for a little swim. "Last one in is a rotten egg!" Michelle laughed as she jumped into the clear water, splashing her boyfriend with a picture-perfect cannonball. He followed, and soon they were in a giggling embrace.

He treaded water, looking into her fresh-scrubbed face, fascinated by the droplets of water that accentuated her shiny, alert eyes. He reached toward her and gently grasped one of her wrists while she raised a sculpted leg, offering her ankle to his other hand as they began the tender, romantic ritual that they had consummated so many times before. Rex's heart beat a little faster as Michelle raised her whole body to the surface of the water. He began slowly spinning her around him, his arms outstretched.

"Motor boat, motor boat," he whispered eagerly, "go so slow." She looked at him slyly out of the corner of her eye, grinning in anticipation as she continued the seductive circling. "Motor boat, motor boat, go so medium," he said breathlessly, spinning her faster around him, watching her body carve graceful wakes through the sparkling water. Then, in unison, the two lovers sang out in rapturous urgency while Riley's legs kicked furiously, "Motor boat, motor boat, go so fast, motor boat, motor boat, *step on the gas!* Wheeeeeee!"

The frenzied love-circle subsided in a pool of briny foam and sweat, the two water dancers heaving and collecting their breaths. They gazed at each other in spent silence, then began a formation side-stroke back to the little plane, sharing an intimacy that required no words. They pulled themselves back onto the pontoon to enjoy a nice, leisurely dinner. Their favorite was pate on crackers with an ice-cold orange Nehi. They would toss crumbs into the deep, dark water to attract a few fish so to have some around the next morning. Rex and Michelle *loved* sashimi for breakfast! For the trip, everything had to either be fresh, on ice, or in a can. Rule #1 on a Piper in the middle of *any* ocean: No Open Fires.

After a brilliant sunset, they'd share yet another lingering kiss, and then the two love-birds each got into their own separate hammocks, one strung lengthwise under each wing. They weren't married yet, so there was no question about the sleeping arrangements. Plus, if they ever *did* try to share a hammock, their little yellow steed would tip over—Piper Cubs simply weren't meant for some things! At night, they would gaze out to the dazzling stars, and hear the gentle lapping of the water against the little aluminum floats. They'd talk about their dreams, names for their children, stuff like that. Sometimes they would make up these wild, crazy adventures to have together, and giggle themselves to sleep in the balmy night. Michelle giggled, anyway. Rex chuckled manly.

On the third day out, they'd spot the familiar profile of Diamond Head, and Rex would bring the little craft down expertly in the crystal waters off Waikiki. Michelle would whoop, and pop open the champagne, then they'd putter the little plane up toward the beach to The Royal Hawaiian Hotel. Sammy, their good friend and concierge of the luxurious pink hotel, would be waiting for them, and paddle his bright red outrigger canoe out to greet them. There were always some pretty girls in it (oh, that Sammy!), and usually a photographer from the Honolulu paper. The pretty, waving girls would throw scented leis into the water, and then place one around the tired little propeller as the paparazzi clicked away.

"Howzit, Mistah Riley! Howzit, Miss Michelle!" greeted their smiling buddy.

"Hey, Sammy, long time no see!" Rex yelled back. "Where'd ya' get such a pretty crew?" Sammy blushed, the girls giggled, and then jumped into the clear, green, water to begin pulling the travelers the last few yards to the beach.

"So what's up, Sammy?" asked Michelle, placing a scented plumeria behind her ear.

"Eh, *surf's* up," answered Sammy excitedly. "Let's hit it!"

After the adventuresome young couple unloaded the Cub, and answered all the questions from the admiring crowd, Sammy helped them get set up in the Presidential Suite. When their clothes were all unpacked, and the Ming dynasty room-divider was set up between the two, huge, four-poster beds, they all hopped excitedly into Sammy's woodie, surfboards poking out the back, and headed to the other side of the island, legendary for its huge, dangerous surf. They were on a surfin' surfari to Waimea Bay!

After a leisurely tour through the pineapple and cane fields, the classy little wagon pulled up to the cliff overlooking The Bay. They all got out, the fresh ocean breeze disheveling their young hair, and they gazed, awe-struck, at the scene.

The waves were huge that fateful day, and Sammy—knowing his limits—wisely decided he would just watch from the cliff. Michelle had the car radio on, and was dancing a slow hula to the music, looking gorgeous in her grass skirt. Her milky thigh showed teasingly through the fronds as the smooth movements swayed her young body to and fro.

"Too beeg for me!" exclaimed Sammy. "Tink I stay up heah, watch dis lovely lady!"

Rex smiled, roughening the surface of his board with a scented bar of coconut wax, then headed down the cliff on a narrow trail— his huge board held tight under one arm. From the trailhead, he looked back up at the smiling couple. "Hands off, Sammy," he scolded mockingly. "Look, but don't touch!" They waved back, laughing.

Rex launched his board through the foaming shorebreak, felt the water splash coolly on his face, and pulled his muscled arms down through the brine, paddling swiftly to the deepness of the channel. He stroked out past the edge of the reef, white and churning with the huge, smashing rollers to the deep ocean water beyond. The waves *were* big that day, forty or fifty feet, and the only other person out was Kimo. The two watermen greeted each other warmly, and discussed the best way to line up for the huge, cresting waves. Surging from the blue-black ocean, a monstrous wave swept toward the surfers, getting bigger and steeper as it sped toward the reef.

"This one has your name on it, brah," yelled Kimo, as he scrambled for the safety of the channel.

Rex spun his board around and began stroking deeply, trying to match the speed of the hurtling blue mountain, to be in perfect position when the rogue wave broke. The huge wave lifted him up, up, to the sky, and soon his board was pointed straight down, fifty feet above the surging ocean. He rose to his feet in a smooth, practiced motion, and began hurtling down the face of the huge wave, angling toward the channel at the edge of control, water spray stinging his happy face, his board bouncing and charging its way down the surface of the mountainous wall of water.

He had nearly made it to the bottom of the huge wave and was racing into the relative safety of the channel, when suddenly, a small, cute porpoise popped up, right in his path! The little mammal saw the bronzed surfer racing toward him and *froze!* Right in front of his hurtling, sharp surfboard! Oh, drat! The porpoise—just a child, really—sat there, bobbing away, treading water with eyes wide, unable to move. Double drat!

Rex had one choice, the Suicide Turn! No one had ever tried it on a wave this big, but it was the only chance for the young mammal. Rex grunted as he flexed his knees and cranked the speeding foil into a sharp turn to narrowly miss the youngster and back up the face of the wave. He had almost made it to the top, when the thick, watery lip pitched over and smashed into him, ripping him from his board. Triple drat! Rex quit being a surfer for a little while, and became a kind of a skydiver, but without the parachute part. The hissing lip of the wave was following him down, down, just inches behind him as he hurtled, spinning, toward the roiling abyss below. He had a second to take a last breath before impact, and noticed the small youth he had barely missed was scurrying to the safety of the channel. Good!

Rex spun helplessly one last time as his back struck the surface—Ka*BAM!*—the stunning impact knocking the wind from his lungs. A split second later, the leading edge of the thick lip exploded through the surface, smashing and following Rex down into the dark, turbulent wipeout zone. His arms flailed frantically for purchase in the frothy water. There was no up, no down, only a gray darkness in the maddening currents, coral ripping at his flesh. After a minute more of battling the frenzied surf, Rex finally rose and burst through the surface—his lungs bursting. Air! *Life!* He looked up at the sparkling sky, breathing deeply, happy to be alive.

Moments later, the young porpoise and his grateful mother nudged Rex's surfboard over to him, rolled their flippers out of the water and nattered a little "thank you" to the tired waterman. He heaved himself up on his board and gently shook the fins of his new friends. "Danka," he murmured, bleeding and exhausted. Rex then saw Michelle stroking out toward him through the smoking breakers, oblivious to the danger, intent on rescuing her man. Bless her heart, he thought tiredly. He then remembered that he'd promised her they'd go out hula dancing tonight. He wanted to mention that his back was likely broken and maybe they could do something less strenuous, but . . . it was her vacation, too. He'd manage somehow.

"I saw what you did, my darling," she said lovingly, treading water beside him. Her eyes gazed up at him, sparkling like jewels. "You saved it's little dolphin life."

"Porpoise, actually. And anyone would have done it," he answered tiredly, holding out his hand. "Anyone caring and strong. Come."

She took his wrist, Injun-grip style, and pulled herself up onto the board, sighing, forming herself against his hard body. "Take me in," she cooed.

The rest of the trip seemed to go a little better. They even named a new dance in his honor at The Royal Hawaiian Ballroom: the Sexy-Rexy, Band-Aid Hula. But the three-day ride home in the cramped little Piper didn't help his back any. During the trip, he thought of exercises to help it. Oddly enough, despite his protestations, his back felt a little better after a good hula. The smooth, massaging motions seemed to relax and strengthen the ol' spine-aroo. And then, *Whammo,* he had an idea!

As soon as they got back, Rex headed for his workshop. Heck, some ideas were so simple, you could hardly see the palms for the coconuts! He took his thin, plastic invention out onto the rear lot and tried it out. By doing a vigorous hula, the hoop would stay at waist-level, spinning and massaging his aching back. Kids on bikes stopped, and wanted to try it. He told them it wasn't a toy, but their excited little faces said otherwise. Hmmm . . . maybe he *had* something here! Perhaps he'd show it to a toy manufacturer. Rex needed to come up with a name. Hula Something. Hula Wiggler? Hula Loop? He thought that wh—

"You gonna hit that ship or what?"

Tommy snapped out of his vacation and saw the huge slab-sided hulk towering solidly before him *Holy smokes!* He yanked the wheel back furiously, the sudden g-forces crushing their helmets down on their heads. The bomber surged skyward, clipping the topmost mast, hurtling pieces of the radar dish and girders through the sky.

"Christ!" screamed Bobby, instinctively covering his face with his arms. "Where'd ya learn to drive—Sears!?"

Tommy hurtled skyward, staring, wide-eyed, hands gripped tight on the yoke. The vision was burned into his brain—the grey ship, a white 53 on the bow, the radar on the top of the tall metal framework spinning steadily in front of the black smokestack, growing impossibly large in his windshield. Even the little figures jumping from the high walkway to the water below were still clear to him. Vivid.

"We hit something, we *hit* something!" screamed Michael. "What's happening up there!?"

"Snap out of it," came a far-away voice in Tommy's ears. "We're too high, and it's a mile back there already," scolded Bobby. "Jeesh."

Tommy shook his head, and began breathing again. He squeaked something compliant, and moved the wheel forward to get them back down on the deck.

"Somebody just better tell me what the heck is going on!" yelled Michael.

"We're okay, it's okay, I think," radioed Bobby. "Any damage down there?"

"Heck, yeah there's damage! My stuff is spilling all over the dang place down here!"

"No. I mean *damage* damage. Any . . . you know . . . holes or maybe pieces of a boat in there with you?"

"Pieces of a what? We hit a *what!?* Dad-blast it all to heck, Bobby, if you and Tommy are gonna keep runnin' into stuff, you can just find yourself a new dad-blasted bombardier because if you think I'm just gonna sit down here in the dark and—"

"Oh, cool it, Michael. So there's no holes down there, right?"

"Well, no, not exactly, but—"

"So then shut up. It's gonna be all right. Riley's okay now, aren't you, Riley?" Bobby asked, watching Tommy carefully through the small mirror.

"Nnnnhh," answered Tommy groggily. He shook his head from side to side and blinked his eyes deliberately. "I . . . I guess so."

"See, Mike? Everything's hunky-dory. Now let's all just calm down, and get back to work, whaddyasay?" Bobby squirmed in his seat, and jiggled the oxygen mask across his face, squinting out to the bright sky. What would coach say, thought Bobby? He rattled off a confident, "Shake it off, babe, shake it off. Lots of innings left in this game." Then his elbow accidentally hit a button labeled Remote Transmit as he sang out: "Hey, batterbatter!"

CHAPTER 10.

RECON STRIKE

Colonel Robbins ran across the ramp from the radio van, tripping over and cursing the heavy black cables snaking their way from assorted generators and vehicles to the growing forest of television cameras. He stopped breathlessly in front of LeMay. "Curt! A radar picket ship reports contact with an aircraft, sir. Could be the Forbes plane, sir. It's got to be."

"Which ship?"

"Our western Cuba ship, sir." He pointed to a yellow dot on the map.

"Hot damn!" yelled LeMay, snatching his cigar from his mouth and looking up at the sky. "I knew it! That crazy mother-loving sonofabitch is going to Havana!"

"Seems like it, sir. Plus we have a transmission."

"What!? A transmission? What did he say?"

"Umm . . . 'Hey, batterbatter,' sir. Should we scramble interceptors?"

"Hey batter*what!?* Is that in our Code Book?"

"We're checking, sir. But what about the interceptors?"

"Hell, Louie," LeMay answered, scrutinizing the map. "The closest fighters we've got is Homestead in Florida. That plane will be in Cuban airspace before they even get their gear up."

"So what can we do?"

"There's nothing we can do," LeMay said quietly. "They're on their own and they're not talking. Listen, Louie, we've got to make it look good in front of the cameras. We've got to scream and yell bloody murder at that crazy bastard. But if he's doing what I think he's doing, he's one brave son of a gun. Or a loonie. Either way, we've got to do what we can to help them. *Hey, batterbatter.* He's telling us we're on the same team. That he's going to bat for us, comprende?"

"Um, got it," answered Colonel Robbins, nervously. He looked over at Johnson and General Buttinsky, standing in the distance, discussing the god-knew-what that high-rankers usually discussed. Rich food or polling data, probably. "Should we notify the Vice President, sir?" he asked, gesturing at the duo. The Vice President saw him, and he and Buttinsky began walking toward the officers, wondering what this latest ruckus was all about.

"Oh, he'll learn soon enough, don't you worry. That prick." LeMay put the cigar back in his mouth at a jaunty angle, and looked up to the sky. "Where does radar paint that crafty son of a biscuit-eater now?" Buttinski and the Vice President joined the group, quizzical looks on their faces.

"Umm, that's another thing, sir. Their, umm, radar doesn't really paint them anywhere." Colonel Robbins looked down, fidgeting. "They don't actually have radar contact."

"What?"

"You see, Curt, the radar contact was the, uh, the aircraft actually contacted the radar, sir. It hit it. The radar."

"Hit it?!"

"Busted it off or shot it or something. The boat's pretty excited. Plane could be anywhere."

"What the —?" LeMay looked to the Vice President, then up at the sky, smiling. "Colonel, do you mean to tell me that airplane took out our only radar ship off the west coast of Cuba?"

"Yes, sir. That's about it, sir."

"And we can't track them?"

"No, sir. Not until they decide to climb."

"And they're going in?"

"It looks that way, sir. Couldn't be anything else. They can pop up and get their photos long before any Cuban MiGs could get to them now. They're just minutes out."

LeMay turned to Buttinski and grinned. "My, my. A rogue Air Force bomber with a bellyful of cameras sneaks up on Havana harbor." He looked back up to the sky, squinting in the morning light. "I just wonder what it will see?"

General Buttinsky's eyes grew large as he looked to the sky, muttering angrily.

Cuba's western tip showed up on schedule, and the boys prepared for their run. Bobby finished his sandwich, keeping a pretty sharp eye on the daydreaming pilot up there, then went back to his charts and guesstimated they'd see Havana in about four minutes. They had gone dead-reckoning and turned northeast, keeping the coast of Cuba off their right wing till they hit their climbing spot, forty miles from Havana. Gas was good, speed was good. The windshield wiper kept pace pretty well with the salt spray they were picking up. Mike had been busy down below with the K-14, and reported that he now had new film loaded in the camera, with shutter speeds and aperture set for their planned high-speed pass at 12,000 feet. Low enough for crystal-clear photos, but high enough to stay out of small-arms fire. But SAMs, flak and fighters they'd just have to handle—some risks you just had to take.

"All set, boys?" asked Tommy. *Set.* "Okay then, mi amigos. Oxygen on, seat belts tight." He pushed the throttles to the stop and began a zoom climb, feeling the g forces crush him down into his seat as the horizon disappeared. "Could get busy soon—watch out for MiGs," he warned his crew. "Ready to make a phone call?"

"Ohmygod!" There was frantic activity around the communications van. The lieutenant scurried from it to the ring of high-ranking brass and blurted, "Key West radar now reports an unidentified target thirty miles west of Havana, sir. Heading oh-nine-five, speed 460 knots. We're painting him good, NORAD confirms. And the Cubans are on Guard Channel and they're angry, sir. They insist it isn't one of theirs. It just popped up."

"No shit," chuckled LeMay.

A captain ran up, wide-eyed, and saluted to the circle of men. "Sir! We have radio contact, sir. They just called us. It . . . it's the aircraft from Forbes, sir."

"What the—" stammered Johnson.

"The aircraft is on SAC link, and they can patch him through to us using the radio and television set-ups right here." The captain turned ever so slightly toward the Vice President, tucked in his chin and announced, "The aircraft commander wants to talk to a . . . grown-up, sir." He looked directly at the Vice President, eyes bright and senses alert, swelling up his chest, feeling a spot promotion coming on. "And you, sir, are definitely our *biggest* grown-up! SIR!"

Johnson stepped forward. He liked that captain. He'd make a good dog, a good licker. He started to ask it how to talk to that plane, but then LeMay lost it! He shoved the vice president aside and put his raging face inches from the messenger's nose. "Dammit captain! How do I talk to that plane?"

"Oh, through the microphone right here at the podium," the captain replied neatly, saluting and switching allegiances brilliantly.

LeMay shot back, "This is the stupidest . . . how the hell can I *hear* him, you twit?"

"Oh, his voice will come out all these speakers, General." The captain swept his hand across the ceremonial area. There were four clusters of speakers—big ones—high on posts, for the large crowd they were expecting later for the ceremony. "See, your Chief of Staffness?"

LeMay shot him a seething glance, and knew his dog-licking butt was headed to Greenland for a long, fun tour, but he had a runaway bomber to attend to right now. Everyone was watching, and he had to make it look good. The general leaned up to the podium, squinted fiercely at the microphone like it was the enemy, and yelled: "FORBES B-47 DO YOU READ ME?"

"Yes, SIR!" boomed back the errant bomber.

The voice sounded strange, LeMay thought. Kind of . . . high. Must be a 2nd looie. He then announced, slowly and angrily, "Do you know what the heck you're doing?"

"Yes, sir. So do you and the commies by now."

"The hell you say!" he shot back. "This is a court-martial offense. You are leading a totally unauthorized mission, specifically against the direct orders of your superior."

"We have different superiors, sir."

"*What!?* What squadron are you with!? Who's in on this with you?"

"Our squadron is Troop 26, sir. That's all I can say just now."

There was general bedlam as dozens of reporters scurried to transmit the strange proceedings to their affiliates.

Troop 26? Well, good grief, thought LeMay. That ought to keep those busy-body reporters busy. Every 30 seconds of this nonsense gets that plane three or four miles closer to target. Go, man, *go* you crafty sonofagun, he said to himself. Get a good run.

He looked at Colonel Robbins, smiled slyly, then turned back to the microphone. "Mister," he barked angrily, "You are currently busting just about every reg we've GOT! Unauthorized use of government property! Failure to file a flight plan! Destruction of government property! Plus, and most importantly, you are disobeying a direct order to stand-down your aircraft! *Do you read me, mister!?* Who are you, anyway!?"

"Thomas, sir!" boomed the reply. Tommy always used his given name for formal occasions, and his parents used it when he was in trouble. Both reasons seemed appropriate now.

Damn! thought the general, witnessing the uproar that the radio transmission were causing. So this crew wanted to buy a little more time—fine with him. Captain Thomas? Major Thomas? He knew a lot of the SAC crews, but the name didn't ring a bell. Well, enough of these pleasantries, people were watching. The bomber had just made two more miles. *Go!*

"What's your rank, Thomas!?" he shouted, sputtering into the microphone.

"Tenderfoot, sir!" Tenderfoot Thomas H. Riley had almost made Scout, Second Class, but was having a little trouble with his knots. Mike was helping him with them, though. That Mike was a knot-natural! Tommy didn't have any Eagle goals or anything, and he felt kind of bad about it, but he'd really joined up just for the camping privileges, and the always popular snipe hunts. He figured he'd get his Second Class, then level off. When a kid went for First Class, they started grooming you for management, and you had to start ironing you uniform. No thanks!

LeMay screamed, "Slam-dang it, whoever you are. Get that airplane down. Right now! First airstrip you get to—Key West or Homestead! That's an order!"

Curt glared out into the empty sky, trying to look fierce to the whirring cameras. The crew must be at their IP about now, he thought. Cuban MiGs would just be lifting off. And if they were the new MiG-21s, the SAC bomber had two, maybe three minutes tops. *Good luck, gentlemen.*

"General LeMay, sir," the speakers announced, "I know you're the big SAC guy and all, but we don't have to do what you say. I mean, we could, if we wanted to, just to be good, but we don't really have to, sir."

"That's about enough of this!" spat Johnson, his face turning livid. He bumped LeMay aside with his shoulder and leaned into the microphone, sputtering, "What the godda—"

"My lawyer says I don't have to say anything more to you just now," Tommy said, *"sooooooo,* over and out I guess." He added thoughtfully, "Please don't be mad."

Johnson yelled, "What the hell are you doing, dangnabit!? You're gonna start a war!"

"Nope, we're gonna stop one," came the young voice. "I can't tell you exactly what we're doing, but you might want to tell them Cubans and Russkies to say 'cheese.' See you when we get back."

"I order you to—"

Up in the cockpit, Tommy switched off the radio.

Johnson sputtered, staring up at the static from the speakers. "He turned off his dang radio to me! Can he *do* that? LeMay looked at Col. Robbins and smiled knowingly. The colonel nodded back silently, hands at parade rest, barely showing his crossed fingers.

Ignoring both of them, Johnson snapped his fingers at the

captain and signaled him into a quick huddle. "Git me some fighter jets up there and as soon as that crazy idiot gets out of Cuban airspace, I want his ass shot down. IF he gets out, that is."

"But, sir, the stand-down—"

"I'll worry about the stand-down, son. You just whomp me up some fighters."

"But General Le—"

"I'll worry about that pretty boy, too, dammit," he hissed. "Now do as I say!"

The speeding jet had levelled off at 12,000 feet, and Tommy could see the white city of Havana directly ahead, carved out of the surrounding jungle, nestled peacefully up against the turquoise water. A highway paralleled the beach, and other roads spread out like a spider web from the center of the city. Compared to the towns and water he'd seen so far in America this was beautiful! Being a godless, repressive, totalitarian state with no industry to speak of certainly did wonders for the water quality! The harbor was crowded with the grey and white dots of ships, and he could make out their shadows sitting beneath them on the bottom of the bay, each vessel a formation of two. Some bigger ships—Russians, no doubt—were tied up at a wharf, cranes hovering over them. El target-o! "We're headed right up the middle, boys. Over target in 20 seconds. Mike, get that camera ready."

"Hearts." Captain Ciranni had his cigarette clenched in his teeth and smiled like a riverboat gambler. He tossed the winning card down on the folding table.

"Christ," grumbled his opponent. Major Kirk leaned his chair back from the table, sighing. He surveyed the Ready Room. Some silly-ass embroidered curtains and a horrible print of some lily-pads on a pond were pitiful camouflage for the austere room. He saw the silhouette of his new F-106 through the yellowed curtains. It was like the trusty 102 he'd had back in Bitburg, except bigger. Bigger engine, bigger radar, and fast as hell. He loved it, all the pilots did. In other corners of the day room, flight-suited men made small talk or pretended to sleep in worn vinyl chairs—all amid the churning hum of the air conditioner bracketed to the window. Cuba was hot right now, and they were all pulling a 36-hour alert. Despite the stand-down coming up, all the men were on edge as they were the closest base to—BRAAAOOO-BRAAAOOO-BRAAAOOO!

The maddening claxon literally lifted the occupants of the room into the air as they tried to cage their eyeballs. All recovered almost immediately, cinching chest belts and g-suits, and stabbing out cigarettes. They ran out of the room as a well-practiced herd, scrambling nimbly over upturned chairs and toppled ashtray stands.

Bobby leaned to his right and peered down to have a look-see. "Hola, Cuba. Como estas?" he sang, kind of remembering his Spanish lessons. "Donde es la biblioteca, senor Fidel?" Ha!

He looked back to his map and reported smugly, "Our ETA over target is still 9:45 exactamundo. Right on the button, mutton! Right on the money, hon—"

The first barrage of flak was four immediate, orange-black smudges off their right wing. The plane rocked violently, and Michael screamed from below.

"Jeesh!" yelled Bobby. "I thought they'd still be asleep! It's not even 10 yet!" Another barrage of flak bracketed them to the left, slightly low, but each burst tracking closer. *"Turn! Turn, you bozo, turn right hard and climb!"*

"What?" Tommy screamed.

"I said turn! Turn hard! Turn right *HARD!*"

"I can't turn! The pictures—"

Another barrage burst above them with a blinding flash, causing the crew to instinctively duck, and sprinkled the plane with deadly flak. It made a remarkably soothing sound, like a gust of rain on a metal roof.

Bobby knew he had to get away from the black puffs, the ones that wanted to kill him. More burst ahead in the distance, waiting for him. *Ohlord!* "Dive, you moron! Dive! Dive! Dive HARD!"

"What's that? I can't hear you," yelled Tommy over the roar of the explosions.

"I said dive, DIVE!" Bobby felt life draining from him, help-less.

"What?"

"Dive, dive," he sobbed. *"Dive—"*

"What!?"

"Turn," he choked.

The plane continued its steady course, more clusters of flack reaching up to them. *Oh, no,* moaned Bobby. He'd never been shot at before—he didn't like it. Angry black puffs all around the jet, looking for him—*him!* Bobby Kontovan. He was useless, a passenger. The plane continued over the harbor, Michael dutifully clicking away below. Then the flak was behind them, falling away.

"What?" It was Tommy.

"Never mind," Bobby sobbed. "Never mind, never mind. Let's get outta here."

"What?"

New bursts suddenly appeared to their right, slightly above them. Bobby shrieked, "Turn left, you bastard! Turn left hard and dive!"

"What'd you say!?" Tommy couldn't believe his earphones.

"I said turn left hard and dive, you bastard, NOW!"

Tommy believed his earphones now, you better know it! "Okay!" he yelled, shoving the wheel forward and cranking it to the left.

By the time the angry MiGs were cleaning up their gear and climbing in full afterburner to their intercept altitude, the Ameri-can plane was shuddering at mach speed, screaming down in a wide turn back to the north at full power, down, down, putting the largest possible distance between them and the enemy coast. The control column bucked and the entire bomber shook as the boys sped down, through 10,000 feet, 8,000, then 5,000, now 1,000, Tommy pulling firmly on the control column to try to level the shrieking bomber out before they impacted the ocean, watching with airman concern as the glistening blue swells rushed up to meet them. The boys grunted against the savage g-forces as the plane leveled off at the relative safety of 30 feet, heading toward Key West, their first checkpoint on the way back.

The F-106 taxied quickly through the Florida heat toward the end of the runway. The air conditioner emitted a distracting white smoke from the vents in the humid air, but Kirk was used to it and knew it would stop as the cockpit cooled. He breathed noisily in his oxygen mask, securing switches and monitoring instruments. Was this the big one? No, it's *got* to be practice, he reasoned. But I thought we were standing down. I thought this hair-trigger stuff was what we were supposed to stop! Before we blew ourselves all to hell and gone! Enough of that, he told himself. Calm down. Fly the mission one hundred percent.

He maneuvered his mount to the end of the runway, the sharply-pointed black nose dipping slightly at the squeal of the brakes. He turned to his right and saw Ciranni looking back at him, nodding through the fearsome whine of jet engines. Ready. He sighted two more fighters in his rear-view mirror, shimmering in the heat waves. Ready. Two more would be cocked on the ramp as reserves.

"Dagger Flight," came a crackling noise in his headset, startling him—another layer of noise to comprehend.

"Uh, Dagger Flight reads, tower," responded Kirk. "Ready on sixteen."

"Dagger Flight, cleared for take-off on runway sixteen. Altimeter three-oh-oh-one. Turn right immediate heading two-seven-oh and contact Key West on one-two-one-eight for intercept instructions. Tower out."

Intercept instructions? Christ, this really *was* the big one, thought Kirk, as he adjusted his altimeter. He looked to Ciranni once more and got thumbs up from his wingman. "One-two-one-point-eight, roger. Dagger Flight rolling." He moved his throttle smoothly forward into the afterburner detent, feeling his body get pushed firmly and evenly back into his seat, and watched the scruffy grass to his sides turn to a blur. They hurtled forward into the shimmering heat mirage, trusting that the runway was still there in the liquid vision, then lifted into the opaque sky at 170 knots in a practiced motion.

"Holy cats!" yelled Tommy. "That flak was murder. How come they were waiting for us? I thought you said it'd be okay this early in the morning." He was breathing hard.

Bobby had calmed down some, and looked at his charts again. His eyes grew wide as he noticed the line they had flown through south of Louisiana, way back there. He'd been flying along like a durn fool, so impressed with himself, unaware of it. "Oh, man. What a dumb bunny navigator!" he moaned.

"Why do you say that?"

"'Cause we flew into the Eastern Time Zone way back there, and I missed it. It wasn't 9:45 over Havana, it was 10:45! Some of them were awake!"

Ching-gow, thought Tommy. Let's not make *that* mistake again.

The Russian general's voice boomed from the speakers of the Cuban radar unit as if he could kill his subjects by radio waves. "You will intercept this aircraft! I do not CARE where he is or how fast he is going!"

The meek voice from the dark bunker at Mirala Air Base promised, 'Si, si,' but was actually thinking of which village he could escape to and hide. Miami came to mind. His prison sentence was increasing by the second as the squadrons of MiGs floundered around all over the sky, blind, hopelessly chasing the vanished intruder. He didn't notice two tiny targets blips on his screen, turning.

At the edge of his assigned search sector, the pilot of a pursuing MiG thought he saw a glint amid the shimmering waves below, heading north. He signaled to his wingman, and they descended, gathering speed.

LeMay snatched the radio from Buttinsky. "Dammit, we sure as heck ain't gonna let you give orders to attack one of our ships!"

"General, I must protest!" Buttinski replied, sputtering and turning red. "An American bombing aircraft has deliberately crossed the border of our brave allies in Cuba."

"This aircraft caused no harm. Nothing was bombed, general."

"Mines may have been dropped. We don't know the extent of the damage yet."

"That was a photo plane, Buttinsky. You know it as well as I do. And we'll know the damage when that film is developed. But you don't have anything to worry about, of course," he spat out. "Just a bunch of boats loading up your goddam medium-range ballistic missiles to take back to Russia! Right, Ivan?"

The Soviet general scowled and backed away, drilling the American with his eyes, and signaling for his adjutant to join him.

"*What!?* Curt!" Colonel Robbins announced breathlessly, holding an earphone to one ear. "Interceptors have just been scrambled from Homestead."

"On whose damn orders?"

"Umm—" He looked off in the distance toward the Vice President. "His, according to TAC. We've got four alert birds from Homestead on their way, eight more ready at MacDill, and eight at Tyndall."

"Whose radar control?"

"Uh, Homestead with a pass off to Key West as primary. And they were painting three targets initially coming from Cuba, but now only two."

"Three? Someone's on their ass. Either that bomber got splashed, or he's down on the deck again. Get me patched through to Key West Control." The colonel saluted and spun around toward the van with LeMay following. Within twenty seconds, the general was on line.

A new voice crackled over Kirk's headset from the Key West channel. Christ! He had heard that growl before, only once or twice, but there was no mistaking it. How the hell had LeMay been plugged into Key West?

"That is correct, major, my orders," the general said. "You are no longer on an intercept mission—you are on an escort mission. Follow intercept instructions from Key West, but identify targets visually. Bust up the chase, do whatever you have to, but protect the lead target. Shoot only as a last resort, I don't want to start a war just yet. Believe the lead plane is an American. I repeat, an American."

"Yessir. Dagger Flight copies new orders," replied Major Kirk.

The four interceptors hurtled to the west at mach speed. "Got three targets painted, major," announced Ciranni. His Hughes radar was blasting effectively through the muggy air, trying to separate the targets from the low altitude clutter. "ETA ninety seconds. Head two-eight-five."

"Got it," answered Kirk. "Okay boys, ready to split formation on my command. Dagger Three and Four go angels five for high cover. Dagger Two and myself are going to stay on the deck and try to break off pursuit."

"Hell's *bells!*" yelled Bobby. He had his seat spun back around and watched the pulsing dots on his gun radarscope with terror. "Now I've got four more coming in from the left—I mean right. Plus those two from Cuba and they're still gaining! We're getting surrounded or something. Can't you go any faster!?" he pleaded.

"I just can't!" yelled Tommy. He occasionally looked back over his shoulder, unable to see the relentless pursuers but knowing from Bobby's frantic reports that they were gaining in the distance. "Can't you shoot 'em yet?" cried Tommy.

"I . . . I don't know, Riley!" Bobby stammered. He watched in panic as a column of numbers flashed and changed continuously on the edge of his gunsight scope. "There's too many numbers on this thing," he cried hysterically. "I don't know what it's saying or what their dang range is. Plus this azimuth thingy is—"

"Well, just aim at some radar dots and shoot!" blurted Tommy. "It can't hurt, dang-nab it, just shoot!"

"Yeah, I vote shoot, too!" panted Michael in a high-voiced squeak from below.

Bobby gulped, aimed the guns slightly left, and punched the GUNSFIRE button.

"They're engaged!" yelled Major Kirk. "Christ, they're engaged!" He had just made out the low-flying bomber when puffs of smoke chattered rhythmically from its tail cannon. "Break left!" he snapped to his wingman—he wasn't too keen on flying through the cone of twenty millimeter spewing from the bomber. As he and Ciranni careened left, they saw the glint of two MiGs speeding directly at them from out of the haze.

Bobby watched wide-eyed as two grey fighters with USAF painted on the bottom of their wings arced through the sky. Air Force! He saw two more planes glint above him in a turning climb. "It's . . . it's Americans! They just showed up!" he yelled jubilantly, watching the delta-winged fighter jets smoke their way into the middle of the fight.

"Well, quit shootin' then!" cautioned Michael. "If you shoot down an American, dad'll kill us."

"W-*what?* Oh, yeah." Bobby's trembling fingers flicked the yellow and black striped switch-guard down to the SAFE position as he watched the chasing dots converge in the distance.

The lead MiG had first seen the yellow tracers growing from the tail of the bomber, arcing away to his right, then the impossible vision of two American fighters screaming in from that same direction in a pursuit curve directly toward him—their wings instantly disappearing beneath triangular clouds of condensation.

Major Kirk grunted from the g-forces, slapping the throttle back with a gloved fist, praying not to cause a flameout, but willing his speeding fighter to tighten its turn nonetheless. Come on, baby, GO! I mean *STOP* you slippery . . . The two enemy fighters grew huge out his left windscreen at an impossible rate, then flashed below and behind him in a split second. He racked the plane hard, hoping Ciranni could follow his maneuver without smashing into the glistening swells only a few feet below them. *Christ!*

"Dagger Three here," came the excited report in Major Kirk's headset, "the MiGs are scattering to the right, you busted 'em up! They almost hit each other—I'm following!"

"Affirm," shouted Kirk over the shuddering vibrations of his machine. "Key West, Dagger Flight has broken interception and top flight is in pursuit. Permission to lock on and fire."

"Dagger Flight—where are those MiGs?" demanded LeMay.

"Dag One to Dagger Three," rasped Kirk, scanning the sky in a frenzy. "Maintain weapons lock and report."

"Sir! Dagger Three and Four have two MiG-21s trail-behind, heading one-seven-oh at about 500 feet," came an excited voice. "We've got 'em dead on. Ready to—"

"Dagger Three do not, I repeat, do not fire," barked LeMay. "As long as they continue south, you are to stay on their six. And do not lock on. I don't want to spook anyone into escalating this thing any further until I'm good and goddam ready. Understand?"

"Uh, yessir. Dagger Three copies. Missiles off LOCK, radar to passive search."

"That's good, Three. Dagger One and Two," commanded the general, "do you have the good guy in sight?"

Kirk and Ciranni had continued their turn till they saw the bomber charging off in the distance. "We're overtaking the target now, but we don't want to get behind him in his gun range. He's probably still jittery."

"Copy that, Dagger One. Just pull up nice and easy and tell me what you've got."

The two interceptors held formation as they stayed carefully out of the scope of the bomber's tail cannon, sliding smoothly up the right side of the bomber. "It's a B-47. What was he doing coming from Cuba?"

"Never mind that. See any damage?"

Kirk scrutinized the airplane. There was no major damage that he could see. He looked at its cockpit and saw the helmeted crew staring back at him, the pilot waving shyly. Somehow, the plane seemed . . . *larger* than he remembered. Then he saw the tiny holes. "Some damage ahead and starboard of the cockpit," answered Kirk, "small holes. But no leaks or fires that I can see." He was concerned about having to formate on a plane with the ocean rushing by below at such a dizzying speed. "They're just so . . . low. And there's no response on air-to-air, either."

"Okay, Dagger One, don't worry. You won't get that bird on air-to-air. Three and Four stay with the MiGs, One and Two escort that bomber. Good job, boys. Stay with assigned targets till bingo fuel, then head for the nearest base. Report in then."

Tommy and Bobby were staring, wide-eyed, at the fighters off their wing-tip. "Think they'll shoot us?" asked Tommy nervously.

"No way," answered Bobby, nodding toward their sleek escorts. "Somebody just saved our butts." A few minutes later, the thirsty fighters broke off with a salute and wing-over that made them two small dots on the bomber's windscreen within seconds. "Good-bye, little friends," said Bobby quietly.

CHAPTER 11.

FLYOVER COUNTRY

The ceremony was bedlam. Reports of the plane over Havana and the chasing MiGs were fueling gossip at an alarming rate. Then the uncensored messages of the intercept and the fleeing MiGs blared out the speakers to the unbelieving crowd.

Within minutes, Kennedy was briefed by LeMay on the entire episode. His orders: all planes down. No pursuits, no escorts, no screw-ups. When that outlaw plane lands, we'll just handle it from there, he said. But in the meantime, all planes *down.*

Buttinski snarled at the whole fiasco, his veins bulging from the sides of his neck and head. He motioned to his adjutant to join him at the edge of the crowd. "Colonel Khunyin," hissed the general. "Find a map immediately, and scribe a line from Havana to here. We must find a way to stop that plane before it arrives." He turned his head urgently and eyed an aircraft parked in the distance—a fighter, seemingly poised at alert status. "Do you see the interceptor, colonel?"

"Yes, general. I am familiar with that craft from many briefings."

"Excellent. The film must not arrive."

"Yes, general," he replied, swelling his chest. "I estimate he will be in range within the hour. Allow me now to gather information from our . . . partners in peace."

Buttinsky's eyes narrowed as he smiled, "Very good, colonel."

Khunyin saluted, clicked his heels together, and headed for the communications van.

Dozens of military personnel were huddled around radios and maps, trying to estimate what had happened and where the bomber was headed. Was he coming here? It sounded like it. Or Pensacola? Or back to Forbes? A grease pencil line was drawn on a large plastic overlay from Havana to Omaha. Unnoticed in the confusion, Khunyin leaned over the back of the crowd, taking in the messages and reports. He began scribbling with a pen on the back of his hand: Havana to Omaha, 315 degrees. Reciprocal of that would be 135 degrees, his route. He made notes of the states the fighter would fly through if he had the chance: Al-a-*bam*-a, Miss-i-*ssip*-pi, Ar-*kan*-sas, Mis-sour-*i*. He struggled to write them down— hard names indeed for a boy from Nizhnly Tagil. He looked for landmarks along the route, something that he could recognize and wait nearby in ambush. No one was making note of him, he was just another uniform in the raucous crowd. Good. One capitalist official after another was spitting red-faced into the microphone, trying to raise the errant plane.

Minutes later, a lieutenant rushed up to the knot of officers at the podium and reported, "The plane has made landfall in Pensacola, sir. The Navy base just confirmed it. They say it destroyed most of their Officer's Club, and want to know if they could chase it down for us, sir. Said they'd be more than glad too, sir."

"No," snapped Johnson. "No more interceptions. We're standing down, remember?" he added slyly. "They'll be here soon enough. Their ass is mine."

Colonel Robbins then rushed up. "Sir, the aircraft is reporting in, sir. I've put him through on the speakers again." LeMay scowled, signaling the colonel away with a flip of his hand, and looked up at the nearest loudspeakers.

"Hello, down there, General LeMay, sir," boomed the voice. The crowd fell silent, and also stared up at the speakers. "Sorry about all the radio silence and all, but there was MiGs and stuff chasing us back there. And some friendlies—thanks. Say, we were hoping you wouldn't start the ceremonies till we got there. It won't be too long, my nav is guesstimating one o'clock. CENTRAL time. We have something to show you that might be pretty important."

LeMay looked to the sky, smiling silently, and began to answer into the microphone when Johnson saw an opening. He shoved the general aside again, smiled demonically, and grabbed onto the podium with both hands. This had gone far enough! It was time to act vice presidential. He leaned up to the microphone, and started gently, like with everyone he was about to fire. Or kill. "Colonel Thomas, is that you?" he purred.

"Colonel?" interrupted Bobby.

Then Mike added from below, "Hey, way to go, Riley. Ya' made colonel. Wait till Michelle hears about this. Smoochie-smoochie!"

Lyndon jerked back from the microphone, trying to make sense of the strange banter. He collected himself, then barked angrily, "Gol-durnitall to hell! Do you know who this is?"

Tommy wasn't sure, but whoever it was, it had shoved LeMay off the air, and had given him a substantial promotion to boot! Must be a biggie! Wowie-*zowie!* Tenderfoot to colonel in one day! He didn't even care if it was lieutenant colonel or full bird—man, he'd *take* it! Now, who was it exactly? Hmmm. Tommy was pretty good at tests, and this one seemed like a multiple choice, so he figured he'd start with the most obvious, start at the top. "The President, sir?" he asked nervously.

Johnson smiled, good answer. "No, son, this is the *Vice* President. Of these Yewnited States."

"Oh yeah," someone else replied, "the one with the big ears!"

Tommy spun around and yelled angrily, "Bobby, get off the phone! *I'm* on it!"

"O.K., sheesh!," Bobby muttered, cringing a little. "Have a cow why doncha', I'm off, I'm off—"

Johnson ripped the microphone from the podium and jumped off the stage, the cord following him out to the concrete. He spun around in circles, looking up at the sky, getting tripped by the cord. "Lissen you! You gol-durn slimy little shi—"

Colonel Thomas wasn't going to listen to any more of that type of language. *"POTTYMOUTH!"* boomed the speakers, like from God or Charlton Heston or something.

Johnson was jumping up and down and yelling, "Get that gol-durn flyboy down right gol-durn *now!* I . . . I want . . ." Lyndon couldn't complete a sentence, he was starting to get plugged up. Back at the White House he could clobber a servant or chunk one his dogs, but with all the ding-danged, gol-durn cameras around . . . he wasn't too smart, but he understood the cameras part.

"You little turkey," he driveled, looking up at the sky and going around backwards in tight little circles, whimpering now. "You get your skinny little ass down here, you peckerwooded sack of horse slop. I'm gonna personally beat you to a pulp. I'm gonna box your gol-durn ears till they're so big you'll be *seeing* through 'em. I'm gonna dock your pay. Then I'm gonna have you *shot,* you high-falootin' piece of flyboy fish poop!"

The captain tried to match his vice president's little tango and straighten his master's clothes at the same time, and sensed that his owner was starting to get angry. Johnson sensed this sensing, turned, and grabbed the gol-durn captain's gol-durn ears and the gol-durn *hell* with the gol-durned cameras, and spun him around, two complete 360s, and threw it, yelping, as far as he could.

Immediately, Lyndon felt a little bit better. He grabbed the microphone, his voice coming out of his mouth slowly and dangerously: "You. Will. Land yore. Airplane. Here. And report. DahRECKLY. To ME!"

"Yes, sir! We're on our way, sir! Please don't start the stand-down till we get there. And for pete's sake, don't sign anything."

Lyndon looked up to the sky, cringing. "Let me tell you WHAT. I don't give a flying fig what you men is up to. At one o' clock this afternoon, we're gonna have us a stand-down ceremony. There's some mighty big wheels in motion, and some little piss-ants like you all ain't a' gonna stop it! When I put my John Henry on it at one o'clock it's a done deal, and all you danged flyboys will be shovelin' shit for two weeks. Ain't nothing you can do! *Unnerstand!?"*

"Um, kind of, sir. Hope we can change your mind. We'll be there at one o'clock sharp."

Johnson rushed back over to LeMay, who was still smiling up at the sky, his cigar clenched in his teeth at a jaunty angle. "I don't trust that flyboy varmint!" spat Johnson. "GO GIT THAT PLANE!"

LeMay took his cigar from his mouth and chuckled quietly. "No, Lyndon." Then he turned to the vice president and said, "We're standing down, remember?"

Col. Khunyin cursed under his breath. He could not believe this pitiful spectacle before him. So *this* is what rich, plentiful food and the freedom to move from state to state accomplished! But it was also his chance. He glanced again at the waiting F-100. It was unguarded, and seemed ready for flight. He knew much of this particular aircraft. It was very similar to the MiG-19 that he had helped to develop. If it had fuel, he could fly it!

Khunyin checked the coordinates inked on his hand, then sprinted through the chattering, capitalist crowd toward the silver fighter. Something had to be done about this marauding American. Their entire plan of world conquest was centered on this two week stand-down. A first step that must not fail! By salvaging this operation, perhaps he would attain Hero Of The Soviet Union status. He knew that this would surely translate into many medals and hopefully, that special Hero-Grade cabbage for his family. Yes! Perhaps they would even move that other family out of his living room—but then he felt ashamed, thinking only of personal gain. How decadent! He must do this for his glorious Motherland! Or was it Fatherland? He had forgotten the gender of their latest five-year plan. Vhatever! He would escort this renegade airman down. Or kill him.

Up the ladder now and into the familiar cockpit. All the gauges and switches seemed similar. To accomplish this risky subterfuge, speed was of the essence—as was absolute confidence. He put on the waiting helmet and gloves, hit the starter, and the engine began its piercing, whistling wind-up.

A startled line crewman came running out, arms wide as if to say: what the holy heck is going on, sir? Col. Khunyin glared down at the confused young airman, gesturing angrily at the ladder. Since the lineman couldn't yell his questions above the roar of the jet, and didn't want to get in trouble what with all this brass around, he quickly pulled the ladder back from the side of the sleek fighter, then scurried underneath to yank the dirty, yellow chocks from the wheels.

All the crowd heard the jet winding up, and they turned to watch. What was this? *Another* pilot, disobeying the stand-down?!

Col. Khunyin taxied out, the silver jet responding easily to his practiced commands. He plugged in the radio jack while the canopy whined down to the closed position. By now he was taxiing past the podium, and the crowd stared up at him, jaws slack, *what's going on now!?* Khunyin smiled to himself as he watched LeMay gesture wildly, barking orders to scurrying officers, then saw him running over to the communications van. The vice president was just staring up at him in disbelief. Khunyin chuckled, then snapped a salute down to his beaming general, and maneuvered out toward the end of the runway.

General Buttinski walked cautiously up to the American vice president, hands over his ears to protect them from the shrill scream of the jet. "Ahem."

Johnson spun around and yelled, "What the hell do *you* want, ya' gol-durn commie?! And what the hell is yore gol-durn lapdog doin' in one of our planes!?"

Wodka answered slowly, "Mister Vice President, sir, I assure you that the glorious People's Party have no . . . 'lapdogs.' We prefer to call them, er, umm, how you say . . . 'salivation engineers.'"

Johnson cocked his big head. Hmmm, that sounded purty good. He just might use stuff like that in his great society. But still, "What the sam-hill is yore boy tryin' to *do?*" he demanded angrily.

Buttinski cautiously put his hand on the ticked-off shoulder.

"Your eminence, what Col. Khunyin is trying to *accomplish,* is to safely escort this bomber to the ground, so that all of this . . . considerable ceremony can be salvaged." He made a sweeping gesture with his arm, turning them both slowly around, showing him the many hundreds of people gathered to watch the highly-skilled diplomats. The crowd had become very quiet now, and all the television cameras had their little red lights on.

The Vice President gathered his thoughts. He smiled warmly, grasped the shoulder of the Russian with one hand and shook his hand with the other. Then they both looked up at the cameras in the distance, smiling. They were *pros.*

"So. What d'yall need?" asked Johnson quietly, out of the corner of his mouth, still smiling at the cameras, still shaking the commie's hand.

"Ve vill need his position and altitude," hissed Buttinski.

"And then yore boy will . . . *escort* him?"

"Da! To Davey Joneski's locker!" hissed the general.

"Guuud . . . "

They quit shaking hands to wave to the crowd. Johnson spotted his dog, and snapped his fingers. The captain scrambled up from the tarmac and scurried over. He reached his master, then lowered his head, covering his bruised ears.

"Go get mah microphone, boy! Fetch!" The officer spun obediently around, ran to the mike, scooped it up, and brought it back. Johnson reached over to pat it on it's head. "Good boy. Sit. *Stay.*"

Lyndon had a call to make.

Bobby thought hard. So . . . where *was* he? The Vice President of the United States wanted to know, and he was curious too. Tommy was busy not hitting the ridgetops, so he'd asked Bobby to handle communications for awhile. They were in the southeastern United States, he knew, but let's narrow it down a little. Let's see . . .there were a bunch of brown and green fields, and little clusters of trees looking like small green and grey explosions zipping by underneath them. Look, here came a sign now: Memphis . . . 38. Then a yellow one: Stuckeys . . . 4.8. Hmmm.

He checked his map. Memphis was in in the southwest corner of Tennessee, and he wasn't to Memphis yet. Therefore, he was still in Mississippi. Hey, this was a cinch! If he ever got a C in math and didn't make it to astronaut school, he knew he could be a SAC navigator.

Bobby reported back, "We're still over Mississippi, sir."

The Vice President wanted altitude, too.

"I'll handle this one, Bobby," said Col. Riley. "You make sure there's no fighters on our tail. Keep alert." That Johnson's kind of a nosy guy, thought Col. Riley, wonder what's up? He must know we're low and that we've been dodging stuff all morning. Still, he wanted their altitude. Hmmmm.

The altimeter was a jumble of numbers. It looked like a clock, except it only went to 10, and with two needles moving around, often backwards, at different speeds. Plus, there was *another* tee-nier window where the 3 o' clock should have been, but wasn't, with another set of numbers inside *that.* A guy could crash looking at this one too much! Col. Riley felt sure he wasn't too high, from having to pull up to miss some windmills, and from being able to read the signs on the highway. He hadn't actually ever flown in a plane before this morning, so he wasn't real sure how high high was. He knew the plane *could* go to 40,000 feet, from pages 8 thru 11, and he'd enjoyed the run over Havana (except for the flak part). But basically he kept it pretty low, like they'd planned. Everything felt comfortable where they were—safe—down there on the deck. It had pretty much saved their you-know-whats so far. Flying this low took a lot of attention, plus his arms were tense and tired from the constant corrections he had to give the racing jet. Tommy didn't want to crash, though. Not crashing and turning them all into a roaring ball of exploding fuel and hot, sharp metal was a *huge* incentive to pay attention and fly good, so he did.

Bobby had his seat turned around backwards, watching for fighters, and reported that a lot of cars seemed to be spinning out or going into ditches. He added that they were making these real neat little dirt tornados behind them and almost all the signs were blowing over. At any rate, the Vice President still wanted to know how high.

Tommy figured, what? Twenty feet? Thirty? Forty? Did he mean the altitude from, say, his head to the ground? Or his seat to the tops of these trees coming up? What about from the very bottom of the plane down there where Michael was to the roofs of the barns? That wasn't much. Or maybe the tippy-top of the rudder down to the fenceposts?

"Ya' better say something to him," cautioned Bobby. "He sounded a little ticked. Just pick a number, for cryin' out loud."

Tommy had a little catch in his throat, and was a little nervous. A "Thirty, sir," squeaked out.

Col. Khunyin had taken off and cleaned up the powerful American fighter jet. When he heard this transmission, he streaked south. He would kill this man. All the other men in the Air Force were obeying the stand-down orders, and were so obedient of their superiors that it sickened him. He had been on the American base since sunup and had not witnessed one food riot! These Americans were *weak!* But . . . what of this pilot? Then he shuddered. This one was different. This one had to be stopped. This one *knew.*

On the ground, LeMay stared up to the sky.

"So what do we do now?" asked a worried Col. Robbins. The whole crowd was looking up to the sky, as if they could somehow make out the unfolding drama.

"I've got my orders, Lou. I hate it as much as you. But I'm putting my money on the good guys. If they made it through all this stuff so far, I think they may be able to shake one commie in an F-100. Let's pray to God that they can."

Col. Riley was admiring the hills and trees of northeastern Arkansas, and found a pretty little valley to fly up. The plane responded real nicely, especially on the ailerons. It was getting *terrible* gas mileage at thirty feet, really using up the ol' JP-4, and was getting lighter by the second. Despite the exterior shrapnel damage off to the right of the canopy, Tommy thought the jet was doing pretty good. The damage had to be contained in the air conditioning ducts of Station 12 because there didn't seem to be any leaks into the cockpit. There were some hydraulic runs right about there, he knew, but everything else felt okay so far. He stared at the small holes, trying envision the schematics on page 44 of the manual and what to do to isolate—

"You gonna hit that grain silo or what?"

Tommy snapped his head quickly ahead and saw the huge concrete cylinders towering solidly before him. *Criminy!* He whisked the bomber up to miss the imposing structure, the sudden g-forces crushing their helmets down on their heads. Sheesh-o-rama! They should be more careful where they put those things, he thought, releasing his frenzied tug on the wheel that had shot them skyward in a split second. Thank the Big Kahuna for co-pilots!

William Robert Evans sat cross-legged and balanced precariously in the huge grain scoop at the top of the silo, three shiny chains reaching from the edges of the scoop to connect to the big, green hook a few inches from his face. He always hated this part of his job, getting hauled up sixteen stories in a stupid damn bucket scoop. Like flyin' around up in the goddam air on the hood of your goddam Chevy. A few minutes ago, Elroy was leaning over him, helping him get situated down there in the cold scoop with his tools and junk. Then the old coot looked down at Billy Bob with a leering grin and always said the same stupid things: "You comfortable down there, Billy Bob? Ready?" "Ready." Elroy tossed his end of the rope weakly around the winch, looked back and asked, "One wrap okay?" "No, four please." "Two, maybe?" "No, four." "Well . . . okay, four. Seems two would do it, though. Sure hope this old rope don't break. Looks kinda frazzly every now 'n again. Y'know, I recollect it broke once, not six, seven years ago, full load up at the top. Took out the ass-end of Wilson's new truck. Did I ever mention that?"

Yes you did, fumed BB silently. Every damn time. Elroy could go to hell. Then four wraps on the winch and a press on the foot pedal to start the motor, and the rope drew tight as BB watched it disappear straight above him into the dark gloom at the top of the shaft. From up there came a small, piercing beam of yellow light from the tiny window. He closed his eyes and gripped tight on the chain as he was lifted slowly up off the dirty floor, spinning slightly. "See ya' later," said Elroy, "and don't be looking down now. Hell, we could charge money for a ride like this."

Billy Bob went higher, higher, turning slowly, eyes and fists shut tight, listening to Elroy's cackling comments. Shut up, shut up, shut *up!* After what seemed forever, he reached the top and stopped, swaying gently. He breathed slowly and evenly for awhile, careful not to upset his balance with too much lung movement. Then he opened his eyes and reached ever so carefully beside him for the grease gun and went to work.

As always, the anticipation was worse than the event, and in a little while he was more or less comfortably going through his routine. Pretty soon he was sort of thinking about replacing that old 5/16" fitting nipple, but also about why did he have to lube the damn rafter pulley on a damn Sunday? Then he thought a little about his new Browning twelve gauge, then what should he get his wife for her birthday coming up (no sports equipment this year, or ever, if he understood her correctly), and then a little more about their daughter's new puppy. They gave 'em all away, except the one. He had forgotten how sharp their little teeth were at that age, the little rascal. Yeah, good name. Rascal. 'Cept this one was gonna probably turn out to be ugly. He had chased the father out of their fenced backyard a few months ago, and *he* was ugly. Good fence climber, though. Ugly, horny and determined. He chuckled to himself. His wife had said something like that about *him* on about their fifth date, that time she slapped him, parked out by the reservoir. But he got in there, eventually.

A weird, strange whistle coming from behind him quickly became a shrill scream, then a thundering roar Ka*BAM!* He screamed and dropped his spinning grease gun into the bottomless void beneath him and watched in confused horror as the dirty little window a few feet in front of him exploded and disappeared out into the mid-day sky. The explosion blasted a storm of dust from the walls of the shaft, as if every square inch of surface blew out a puff of smoke at the same instant. Little motes of wheat dust swirled thickly in the beam of light, choking Billy Bob with each fresh, new scream. He grabbed both sides of the shallow, swaying scoop with his trembling hands, his fingers digging into the cold metal. He swayed and spun and creaked up there, praying. He held on tight, wide-eyed, ears bleeding—trying not to die—and blubbered out some immediate and fervent and extravagant promises to his Maker, most of which he kept, except for the one about becoming a missionary in the Amazon.

He *did* become a deacon in his church, however, as did Elroy. William Robert Evans never again took the name of the Lord his God in vain, and he spent a lot more time with his precious little family. They decided to name Rascal Thaddeus. He turned out to be a good one.

Back in the jet, Michael screamed, "What the holy heck is going on up there?! How come we're climbing!? You're doing it again, so knock it off! I'm spilling stuff!"

Bobby yelled back something to the effect that the spasmo Aircraft Commander obviously had his head up his butt, and that you surely didn't have to be *too* danged smart to miss the only ding-danged thing higher than a tree in the last three counties. What the hell!? "Are you blind or something up there, Riley? Or just stupid?"

Col. Riley's mouth was dry as Kansas dirt, and a shudder shot down his little spine-aroo, from his neck hairs to his tailbone. That was *too* close. "I, uh . . . I saw it all right," he chirped nervously. "Just seeing if you were paying attention." He gently pushed the wheel forward, to get them back down on the highway.

"Suuuuure you were. Swear to God, Riley, if you crash this

thing, I'll be ticked!

"All right, all right. Lighten up, willya'? I didn't hit the darn thing, did I?" Criminy. What a worrywart! He scrunched up his face under his oxygen mask, and whined very softly, in his most smart-alecky voice, "Swear-to-God-Riley-if-you-crash-this-thing-I'll-be-ticked."

"What was that?"

"Nothing, nothing," he sighed. Eighth graders! "So where are we now, anyway?"

Bobby had all his maps and rulers and stuff out on his plotting board. Tommy could see their weird reflections above him in the curving glass of the canopy. His nav was busy! Bobby looked outside intently, his brows furrowed, then checked his map, looking for clues like any good navigator. He estimated they were still right next to Highway 63, because he could see it. Then he figured they were, oh, what? an hour out or so, because he was starting to get a little hungry. He looked out again, this time to his right, and saw a big sign just before it disintegrated. Dutifully he reported this find to the crew.

Mike quickly called from below, *"What?!"*

"What I said was: 'Welcome to Missouri. The Show-Me State.' You heard me, peabrain. Pay attention."

"Oh, nooooooooooo," came a slow, sad wail from below. Michael dropped his head down, the helmet suddenly feeling very heavy. He shook his head sadly from side to side, and clenched his little fists. He wanted to raise his arms and scream and jump up and down and kick himself in his big, dumb, butt, but there wasn't enough room.

"So what's eatin' you?" radioed his big brother.

"Oh, maaaaan. We just had that big geography test on Friday is all," Mike replied.

Yep, Tommy remembered that one. He thought he did good on it.

"I remember one of the questions now," Mike groaned. "I put down Missouri. The Nutmeg State."

The other two crewmen said nothing, caught up in their own thoughts. They knew how it felt. It wasn't funny. A test could be going pretty good, and then one slip-up, *one!* and a B became a C, a C became a D. It happened all the time. Futures and lives were determined by tests, a good report card, a note from the teacher. Tests were so serious. But hey! Tommy decided, and thought for a second. Why sure! They might get some Extra Credit for this mission—but in what? Social studies? Math? He perked up. Of course! How about geography? Why *not* geography? They were sure going over some! It would help Mike pull that grade up, too.

Tommy liked geography. It wasn't at *all* abstract, it was real as dirt. You could really sink your teeth into geography. He knew all the states and all their capitols. The only part he didn't like was all that stuff about major exports that they had to memorize, so dumb! I mean, who cared? Michigan: steel, autos. Kansas: wheat, cattle. Persia: petroleum, rugs. Now there was an interesting mix! How's about, St. Luke's: dumb girls, nuns. Texas: cow poop. Lithuania: dipshits. Some countries' main export was: flax. *Flax!* Man, they had a long way to go, buddy boy! How'd you like to grow up knowing you'd be in some phase of flax production after struggling diligently through high school? Anyone with half a brain would high-tail it out of there. Even Lithuanians. Maybe an extra report on their trip would help them all a little. He certainly hoped so. They flew on in silence, headed into Missouri: The Show-Me State. Capitol: Jefferson City. Population: 4,387,000. Major exports: transportation equipment, beer, hogs, Mark Twain.

Besides saving democracy, the boys' journey was about to change the eating habits of America. All the way out—Kansas, Oklahoma, Texas—and now coming back in through the southeast, a tremendous number of cows were being affected. With the exception of the piney woods of the deep south, immediately below the plane's route was one of the highest concentrations of beef cattle in the nation. Well, the effect of 110 feet of nuclear bomber screaming fence-high over a cow was immediate! The large, easily-impressed bovine brains gave the big muscle groups that were attached to it one simple message: Run! Thousands, tens of thousands, then hundreds of thousands of cows obeyed this order as the plane sped north over Cattle Alley. Herefords, Charolais, St. Germains, those sturdy Holsteins, plus a few Red Romains, they all took off. They *ran!* The sight and sound of the bomber made such an impression on their juicy, soft brains in fact, that it stayed branded in there, stuck. Hundreds of thousands of cows, stuck on run, from Kansas to Oklahoma to Texas, then from the Florida panhandle up through Alabama, Mississippi, Arkansas, then Missouri and onto Nebraska. All running! Some right through fences and out into the heartland, but most were more polite, being Southern and Middle American cows. They ran up to a fence, turned, ran to the next fence, turned, and ran again. Always counterclockwise. Scientists later determined that this phenomenon was due to the rotation of the earth, that cows in the southern hemisphere would probably go clockwise. They would certainly be willing to do some research on it, if there were some government grants involved.

The frenzied scramble of the cows on the first few days turned to a steady, practiced gait. After a few weeks, their lungs were strong, and their leg and flank muscles (those tasty, versatile briskets!) were bulging. The rest of the meat, the steaks and chops part, was less fatty, too. The cows learned to eat on the run. They could lean down and grab a bite, usually on the corners. They learned to drink on the run, too. They would slow up a little and take a long, straight slurp at the trough, but would keep on going. For months after the event, dusty cattle trucks pulled up to the huge stockyards scattered throughout the south. The gate foreman, with his clipboard and scuffed boots, would saunter out to the cattle trailer, peer through the holes, and see the thin, muscled cows, eyes wide, running in place, trying to turn left. He'd walk back up to the driver and spit and say, "Them's more of them *aero*plane cows, ain't they?"

"Yep. 26 head this load. From Miller's place, uppit Benton county. Hard by the highway."

"Welp. Okay then. Bring 'em on in."

Meat merchandisers from the supermarkets weren't sure at first what to do with the meat. It was red, not pink, and *lean,* so was immediately suspect. It looked pretty good on the shelf, but the public knew what meat looked like, and this wasn't it. As an entirely different product the lean, red, meat needed to be introduced carefully. The fluoride fiasco was fresh in everyone's minds and no one wanted a repeat of that brou-ha-ha. Most merchandisers wanted to go with a cautious, informative approach. Experts were brought in, and marketing specialists from across America had long, productive meetings, made up some charts, looked at the numbers. It became apparent that America's best advertising minds would be required to determine the best ways to promote the product. Word went out, and agencies made their pitch. Some brilliant presentations were made. Some young careers took off, while others began a slow decline. It all began to gel, and then the campaign was approved.

A logo was selected from many entries. The winner, by Faber-Collins-Drudgeman of Chicago, showed a healthy, happy cow, running on its back legs, little cow tennies and cow running shorts, and a chest and arms like a boxer's, except with hooves. A simple farm scene background, with the slogan at the bottom: "Eat Lean, Stay Lean." Clean, simple, elegant. A steal at $12,500.

The campaign would break with the TV ads on Sunday. Sponsors bought time on Ed Sullivan, two spots. Media buyers made sure one spot was up at the front of the program, by the "Reeeallly big shewww" part, with the second commercial preceding the fourth act, always a favorite. It was almost certain to be either spinning plates or Topo Gigo—both a top draw. The network wouldn't guarantee advertisers which acts went in which slot, due to the unfortunate Sammy the Seal vs. Tony Bennett backstage incident of 1959, so the two time slots were selected for the best probable demographic coverage. The best estimated bang for the buck.

The major dailies would break the following day, and that blitz would go for two weeks, full page ads. The advertisements

were created to extol the benefits of the new meats and the re-
duced fat. A particularly bright young copywriter invented "cho-
lesterol," which was used aggressively. Color inserts would go in
the Sunday papers in all the majors—from New York to California. At point-of-purchase, flyers would be available, 4" x 11", three
fold, full color, with the same message. Included would be dis-
count coupons, 15% off with the purchase of $2.50 or more. (Void
where prohibited). 9 out of 10 advertising people agreed: a careful, systematic and expensive campaign would eventually convince
Mr. and Mrs. John Q. Public that the product was safe, and good,
and deserved a try.

But before any of this could happen, a young Assistant Man-
ager at a Piggly Wiggly in Fort Worth, who had one semester of
advertising theory at community college, rolled out a big roll of
butcher paper, and had the stockboys tape it up to the front glass.
Then he painted in red letters, five feet high: NEW LEAN MEAT.
MOVIE STARS EAT IT. They sold out in 40 minutes. Other
stores followed suit, and hungry citizens fought for the new, improved product. The huge, now-unnecessary campaign was shelved,
and America started eating itself to better health.

CHAPTER 12.

LAKE OF THE OZARKS

Bobby watched Sedalia, Missouri streak beneath them, wrenched from a peaceful Sunday afternoon. He marked their position off on his map, took out his ruler and compass, and checked his watch. Speed x time = distance. He found the airspeed indicator.

Yikes!

"Check your speed again, moron," he shouted. "420! We're *way* too fast! We're gonna blow it by . . ." he checked his whiz-wheel. "Twenty minutes, I reckon. Slow us down to 360 again! You're making all my equations go off."

"I don't wanna slow down, now," Tommy replied. "This puppy likes 420 knots!"

"Well, tough titty," snapped Bobby.

"Huh?"

"You heard me, dinglebrains. Just slow us down or else."

"Or else what?"

"Or else we blow it, comprende? Sometimes it's good to be early, but not today, ya' bonzatrope. So slow the heck down or else let's go somewhere's and chew up a little time. We need to get there at one o'clock exactly. That's when the cameras start rolling, remember?"

"Well, *you're* the nav. *You* got the maps. Figure something out!" scolded Tommy.

Bobby drew a long line northeast, squirmed in his seat, and did another calculation. "Hey," he suggested, excited now, "if you floor it, we could hit 500 knots indicated and make Chicago." He had always wanted to see the ol' Windy City. Lots of sophisticated girls there, he bet. Smokers.

"Nah, too far, that'd be pushing it. Let's stay around here."

"Can we go to Kansas City?" radioed up Mike, hopefully.

"Nope. We've been," answered his brother.

"Well I haven't," Michael snapped back. He had missed Troop 26's excursion to Kansas City because of the chicken pox, and had to stay home.

"Well, I seen it once already, and I ain't goin' back," announced Bobby. All the the troop had seen was roads, and bridges, and brown buildings, and trains, and then the stockyards. Phew! "It's just a bunch of big buildings and sirens and it stank. Plus, most of it's in Missouri anyway."

"Can we go to Dodge City then?"

Bobby checked his map. "Too far. We'd have to go supersonic, and that's against the law, I think. Plus *you* can't see anything anyway, ya' moron. See any windows down there?"

"I could come up and sit with you."

"No, you can't. There ain't enough room. What are you gonna do—sit in my lap? Look, you're a crow and a bombardier. You knew you'd have to sit in the dark when you signed up. Riley explained it."

"Well, how about Tuttle Creek then?" suggested Michael. They'd had Scout camp there. It was a funny name for a 40 mile long lake in the middle of the prairie. He thought it should've been called Tuttle Ocean. Or the part where their camp was might have been named The Smelly Green Scum Tuttle Sea Mosquito Factory. Still, it was something.

Bobby checked his map, drawing a long line to the northwest. "Sorry, Charlie. Too far. But I like the lake idea, they're easy to find."

"Hey!" sparked Tommy, "then how's about going back to Lake Of The Ozarks?"

Bobby checked his maps and twirled his little compass. "It's within my circle, easy. Heck, it's right behind us. Wanna go?"

Col. Riley had gone on vacation there with his family and all his cousins two years ago, and had a blast. He caught a 2 lb., 3 oz. bass, and his older cousins taught him how to bonk the Coke machine at their tent camp and get free Cokes. "Yeah, let's go!"

"Oh, sure," grumbled Michael, carefully strapping a 3/8" manila up and over two fully-loaded buckets. "It'll probably look as good as Kansas City from down here. Oh, boy. Thank you so much. I'm *very* excited. Hooray."

"Oh, pipe down" radioed Bobby. "If ya quitcher gripin', maybe I'll let you come up for a minute when we get there. So just cool it down there. Okay Riley, let's whip a quick 180 back to Highway 50. Then head east till we hit Tipton. That'll be Highway 5. Hang a right and we'll shoot down to the lake."

"Okey-dokey, smokey!" Tommy felt excited, but also worried. It was getting hard to see. When the sun came out in America, so did the bugs. Ever since they visited Altoona hours ago he'd had to hit the windshield wiper every so often. It was a big, heavy job that worked okay for a while, but by now the fluid was almost out. Planet Earth, especially central Missouri had a couple kazillion bugs flying around out there. Little baby bugs, twirling and swirling, trying out their new wings, seeing how high they could go. Adolescent bugs flitting around, checking things out, pestering the older ones and chasing the littler ones, trying out some simple maneuvers—loops, stalls, slow rolls. And the older bugs; checking each *other* out, fighting a little, flexing the ol' exoskeleton. Plus some even . . . you know. The Mile-High Club was in full swing eons before the Wright Brothers ever got their act together. And the oldest bugs, heavier, sadder, were down low, dodging birds. Trying to find a place in the shade where they could just talk and rest.

And moving briskly through this rich, bug soup was big, hard B-47. It was *pea*-bug soup for the six water-injected J47-GE-25 engines. Insects were no match for 12 rows of stainless steel compressor blades. Easy meat! But the angled plexiglas windscreen directly in front of Tommy was getting severely carapaced. The glycol-alcohol-water mixture of washer fluid was meant to loosen up a little grime, but mainly ice, and at considerably higher altitude. But not this many bugs, this low, this *long!* A B-47 stayed spic and span at 30,000 feet, but not at thirty. The front plexiglas panel was turning to grey sludge, and the huge wiper was just smearing the stuff back and forth now.

Tommy leaned to his left, to the curved back part of the canopy. That made things a little better, but an ever-increasing family of yellow and red and greeny lines of bug juice was still streaming away into the slipstream.

"Hey! This wiper ain't hardly workin' no more, Bob-o. I mean, it's bug-city up here!"

Bobby leaned up and and sighted over his pilot's right shoulder. "Yeesh! Ick-o-rama! Hey look! Let's fly over to that rain over there, and wash this sucker off!" He pointed north at a big cloud that sat heavily over the fields. It went way up there. Its edges were flecked with a soft orange, and it occasionally lit up from within. It was really pretty!

"Good idea, spas-mo! Fill 'er up, and wash the windshield, please," Tommy chuckled into his mask.

"Plus, if we fly fast enough, we'll be using hydraulics!" reported Bobby. "We just started learning about it in science."

Hey, thought Tommy. Maybe they could get Extra Credit in geography *and* science!

Col. Khunyin was weaving back and forth along his prescribed route, searching frantically. The controls of the American craft were so balanced and harmonious, he thought. So superior to the planes that he was used to. Enough of that! Pay attention—keep scanning. They must be near by now, they *must!* Suddenly he saw a sparkling movement to his left. Water? The glint disappeared, then flashed again as it raced over the crest of some wooded hills. *There they are!* Khunyin racked his plane hard to the left, struggling to keep his quarry in sight. The sleek jet buffeted slightly as its nose raced across the horizon, gathering speed.

The boys raced toward the huge cloud and saw the rain beneath, grey and slanted. As they got closer, the cloud looked a lot, *lot* bigger. Tommy and Bobby were both looking up now, their necks craned back, staring at the edge of the swirling mass.

Col. Khunyin saw the bomber smoking steadily toward the base of the huge cloud, seemingly unperturbed. No—! This crew was not only dangerous, but deranged! *No* airplane could survive such a storm! He racked his plane in a hard turn to skirt the forward edges of the towering cloud, watching in disbelief as the American flew headlong into its center.

Tommy swallowed hard and remembered his dad joking nervously with Major Connor at a bridge party about flying in storms: Don't. But if you have to, do it with your eyes closed tight, one hand on the ejection seat and the other on a rosary, praying to the wing gods. Tommy knew that when Captain Macklin was still a lieutenant, he'd hitched a ride on a KC-97 that accidentally flew into a thunderstorm one night near Guam. When he got back, he didn't drink anymore, not even beer, and he liked kittens and kids.

Was *this* a thunderstorm? It only looked like a big cloud when they were way back there. Real big, now. Under it. Hmmm, shady under here—not so bad. They weren't in the rain yet, but it was darker ahead, and it smelled a little funny. Real funny, now. He checked the panel. No fire warnings, but he smelled something electric. He pulled the mask an inch from his face and sniffed. Frowned, and sniffed again. Something electric or metallic.

Bobby radioed up, "Let's turn around, I don't like the feel of this. These clouds are looking green up there, and it's *dark* up ahead!"

Tommy agreed instantly. Little hairs shot up on the back of his neck. "Hey Mike, tie your stuff down and hold on," he ordered. "I'm gonna turn around real sharp here."

"I'm tyin', I'm tyin!" Michael radioed back, confused. "Why are we turning around? What's goin' on?!"

Ka*BAM!* Light blinded the crew and they screamed and Tommy instinctively pulled back on the yoke. *"Holy BATS!"* screamed

Bobby, as his helmet cracked hard against the plexiglas canopy. The bomber careened to one side, uncontrollable, bending, shrieking. Another sizzling crack of thunder, a savage GZZZZZZZZZ filled their heads with fear and then more light! Eyes closed tight, hold on!

Bobby's eyelid veins looked like little purple rivers, with a white-hot dot floating around among them. Still blinded, crying, he opened his eyes, blinking, seeing nothing, smashing his shoulders against the sides of the cockpit, smelling the ozone stink, only seconds had gone by. Going up again . . . he blinked hard, eyes straining . . . slowly, slowly making something out. Impossible! It wasn't raining . . . they were *UNDERWATER!* Unbelievable amounts of water streamed back, exploding off the canopy in a white, foamy, savage torrent.

"*What's happening?!*" screamed Michael, his voice barely audible to Tommy and Bobby over the whistling blast ripping by their heads only inches away. The clear thinness of the canopy seemed incapable of protecting them from the fury of the storm.

Despite pulling the bomber up, Tommy was aware of his body lifting off the seat, the jet hurtling down, shoulders straining at the straps. *Ohgod!* Then the runaway jet suddenly charged up again, slamming his head down to his chest, so he hunched over painfully. A fist of impossibly cold air smashed and leaked in on the jet, slamming all of them sideways again through the roiling grey-green muck. They couldn't see the fields, the horizon, ANYthing. They were going down! His ears were a flurry of sounds and messages . . . screams . . . his crew was dying. The storm shrieked, a hurricane blast of noise mixed in with the other sounds, jets, metal and instruments shuddering and banging. His body pulled back on the yoke, then slammed forward, straining, his eyes wide open but still blinded, grey and black shapes—forms—starting to emerge and flash by, his neck aching from the shaking of his head, smashing the headrest, the side of the canopy, stick still back.

"*Oh-God-Jesus-Riley-are-we-gonna-die?*" sobbed someone distantly, only a crackle. Static attacked Tommy's headset. The violence subsided somewhat, but everything was still dark. Then they were slammed again harder! Felt cold. His vision began coming back, he could only see spray exploding off his windshield out of the corner of his eye. So loud, torrents, he felt so heavy. The sky around him was lighter, he thought. Was it? Was he dead? He was heavy in his seat. Now darker, the noise still deafening. What's going on? *Oh, sweet Jesus!* He blinked and tried to lift his helmet up. He couldn't. G-forces were crushing him down, down. He sensed it was getting lighter again, but he couldn't look up. He saw his knees, the blue jeans wet. Wet! He didn't know SAC bombers *leaked!* Oh, the flak holes, he thought dreamily. He rolled his eyes up, saw his own little hands on the black yoke, knuckles white. The base of the steering yoke rose to a circular hub, just inches from his face. In the center of the hub was a black button, with red lettering: *Boeing B-47,* it said.

Wow! What was he doing in a Boeing B-47? Not right. Should get out. He squeezed his eyes shut and opened them again. Some blurred instruments slowly came into focus: the vertical speed indicator had a little, white needle that wasn't moving. It was pegged at 6. So, they were going over 6,000 feet a minute, up. Well, up was better than down, he thought dreamily. The g-meter wasn't moving either—pegged—but all the other instruments seemed to be spinning around okay, fast! He thought he might nap. It was getting lighter. The altimeter seemed to be going around especially fast. Getting lighter still, less stinky. Maybe a little nap.

A sudden burst of hot white light slammed Tommy and Bobby's eyes fully shut as they rocketed through the top of the cloud into the blinding sun. Bobby screamed, clenching his eyes closed against the painful light. "God *jeesh!* Riley! What's goin' ON!?

Tommy snapped his eyes open, blinked, and saw another dot of white light dance before him, then shut his aching eyes again. *Where was he? Who said 'God jeesh?'* He blinked some more, and looked out to his left and slowly focused on the prettiest, fluffiest cloud he had ever seen—revolving slowly, standing on its side! Well, I'll be. A magic cloud!

He chuckled dreamily, and leaned back hard on his seat. He

was still pulling back on the wheel, going straight up, and it felt good. Soooo good. WHOA! He snapped alert immediately. Not good! Bomber, going to Omaha, over on its back! His bomber! HIS back! Tommy jerked his head up and shook his helmet. They were going up-side down! *NOT* good!

Bobby realized what was happening at the same instant and cried, "We're gonna fall, Riley! We're gonna fall *OUT!*"

Tommy shook his head again, and sighted out to his left. The horizon kept a steady motion, turning, straight up and down now, they were a rocket, going straight up, flat grey below, the clouds impossibly vertical.

"God DAMMIT, Riley, we're going to *DIE!*"

For some stupid reason, Tommy felt good. Man, he had never heard so much cussing! They'd *all* better get to confession when they got back! After the jerking, savage storm, rolling over on your back in the clean, warm sky felt good. Great! He even checked his instruments, calmly. The artificial horizon was . . . oh, forget that mess. Check something else. Altitude: 10,600 and slowing. G-meter heading down, ball centered nicely, V.S.I. near zero. Ha! They were at the top of a ding-danged loop, their very first! He knew that in a loop, the pilot should try to keep positive gs all the way through. He had heard that a good pilot could even loop with a glass of water on the floor, and nothing would spill out.

Tommy couldn't imagine anyone actually flying that good, though. He figured he could continue the loop and zoom back down into the storm at about 700 miles per hour, and pull back to 6 or 7 gs, or until the wings pulled off or they hit Missouri. Or they could just stay up here in the cool, smooth air and roll it out. Better to do that, probably. He knew from pages 166-172 that B-47s were stressed for the Low Altitude Bombing System maneuver: head for Moscow, low on the deck, and a few miles from the Kremlin, haul back on the stick, the Strato-Jet heading for the strato, and at the top of your maneuver, release your little "special weapon" and let it tumble on ahead toward its doomed target, while you continued up, up and over, on your back, and when you're completely, absolutely, upside-down and heading in the other direction, you turned the wheel hard left (or right, for south-paws), and aileron-rolled the airplane and skedaddled the heck on out of there before you blew yourself up with those poor Russkies. The Immellman maneuver. Not many jet bombers were designed to loop or Immellman, and neither was the B-47, really. All planes *could* loop, but it wasn't usually recommended.

Yet Col. Riley knew that the Air Force had put all its B-47s through a wing strengthening overhaul (called Milk Bottle, of all things!) to allow this hairy maneuver. Oh, oh. He wasn't in a *bomber* bomber, he was in a *reconnaissance* bomber. Blast! Had they strengthened this one? He sure hoped to heck that they did! The boys were about to find out, big time!

He looked straight up (down) at rolling Missouri, that durn cloud flashing right below them, made a quick Sign Of The Cross and cranked the wheel hard left. His left shoulder went down (up) and the right wing lifted up (down) and Bobby screamed and they kept going . . . over . . . over . . . then Tommy rolled the wheel back sharply to the right and then, there they were! Level, straight. Flying around perfectly good! In the other direction, of course. He glanced back at the wings—still there! Good ol' Boeing! Good ol' *Milk Bottle!*

"Ya-hoo, pea-brain!" exulted Bobby. "We're alive! Where'd ya' learn *that?!*

"Oh, books and stuff," said Tommy modestly. But under his oxygen mask he was grinning so hard his face hurt. And the windshield was spotless!

They flew on in silence for awhile, basking in life. After a while, Tommy reported, "Well, I'd better get us back down where we belong. Looks like we won't make Lake Of The Ozarks."

"Nope. Looks like we won't," agreed Bobby. "Hey, Mike, ya' didn't miss much up here, Lake Of The Ozarks-wise."

"Sir, radar reports a target over Missouri," said a major, nervously. "We thought it was a missile launch at first. It went about straight up to 12,000, stayed there a minute, then dove and disappeared."

"Whaddya think, Lou?" LeMay asked.

"Normally, I'd think a busted radar," the colonel said. "But with this crew—"

"What have we got on the commie?" asked LeMay, searching the horizon through binoculars.

"Well, he's in their general vicinity and pops up every once in awhile, but it's erratic. He's got to be lost."

Khunyin skirted the edge of the storm, smelling its dangerous stink the whole while, rain peppering his windscreen. *Those fools,* he thought. *Maniacs.* He kept looking up to the roiling mass as he finished his circuit, weaving around the hilltops and power lines. He reached the other side of the storm and circled slowly, waiting for them to emerge. Minutes passed. Nothing.

"Hey, Mike, how'd you like that little ride?" radioed his big brother. "Didja puke?"

"Yeah," snickered Tommy. "No extra charge for the loop-de-loop. Wanna come up here and look out? We went up to about 12,000 feet, but we're going back down now. Still, if ya' hurry, you can see *everything.* "

"Oh, Mikey-poo?" Bobby waited, no answer. They were carefully weaving through the little thunderbumpers ahead of them. Bobby looked up at Tommy in the mirror and saw his concerned face. The strange, muted roar of the jet engines was all they heard. "Mike? Michael?" Bobby asked again. Then he screamed, *"Answer me, Michael!"* looking down, fumbling at his safety latches, the belts becoming an impossible tangle of webbing in his haste.

"Mike, do you read me?" yelled Tommy. He looked up and watched his co-pilot struggle feverishly with his belts. "MICHAEL?!—"

"Oh holy, oh no, please God not Mikey," pleaded Bobby. "Oh please don't be dead or bailed out, Mikey. Dad's gonna just kill us if you die!"

Tommy saw his co-pilot rip the helmet from his head and toss it down, then disappear from his sight in a red blur. He heard a bang from behind and to his left as his co-pilot scrambled down the hatch.

Bobby swung open the door and crawled on his hand and knees through the tunnel. *Oh Michael,* he sobbed. He burst through the small door into the dark crow's compartment, and launched into thin air, scrambling for traction on nothing—confused—then dropped and slammed painfully, shoulder first, into the hard, wet floor. Mike was lying there, the bottom of his sneakers by Bobby's face. He reached to grab —OW!—his shoulder! Still he reached, grabbed the tennie and tugged it toward him. Nothing. A little, wet, inert leg. Oh, God! Not Michael. *Not Mikey!*

He raised his head a little, and saw the back of his brother's helmet wedged into the dark corner between the ejection seat and the green, metal wall. Black, evil, water—moving like mercury—thick and together, flowed toward the front, hesitated, then rushed back and to the left corner. Michael's head was face down in the violent water—it surrounded his shoulders, clung to his face. Bobby shoved himself up furiously and smashed his head into the PRF Discriminator rack. He cried, closed his eyes and dropped heavily to the cold, wet floor, his cowlick smeared with blood. Not fair. Not Mikey.

Bobby felt himself going to sleep. So tired. Say g'night. Night, Michael.

NO!

He pushed himself up to a sitting position, groggy and confused. Look! Think! Grab Mike's legs, pull, pull up, out of . . . water. No room, drag, keep dragging, grab his belt. Turn him over. Turn him!

Bobby had to twist his little brother's legs around like pretzels. Up on his side, over, more over. "Michael!" he screamed. "MICHAEL!" Nothing. He grabbed his brother's jaw, shaking it furiously, looking into the pale, wet, motionless face. What . . . what should he DO? Why was Michael dead? What the hell was he doing in the hold of a B-47, watching his little, dead, wet brother? No! Stop! StopstopSTOP! First Aid, from Scouts. Oh, the

HELL with First Aid! Do something *NOW!* Slug him? It worked on Bonanza. No, they splashed Hoss! SPLASH HIM!

He jumped up, not too high this time. Buckets! Buckets of water! Amazingly, the top ones still had most of their water in them, the bottom ones looked full—they were all tied in. Of course they were tied in! Michael was good! *Ohgod,* he sobbed, struggling with a textbook sheepshank, drawn tight. Don't let him die, God. God durnit, God, don't let him die. Let him see Kansas City. *They should have gone to Kansas City.*

Finally Bobby unknotted the knot, fingers bleeding, and grabbed one bucket by the rim. He ripped it over and down and the rancid water sprayed onto Michael's face and helmet in a waterfall—his little pink nose splitting the filthy water to the sides like the bow of a ship charging through an ocean swell. Bobby watched his little brother's face grimace and frown—eyes still closed tight—then suddenly and violently spray water out of his mouth with a choking cough.

"Heckhhh . . . Chhhfl*poooft!*" Michael spat, his head shaking back and forth, the helmet cracking against the seat railing. He looked up but couldn't see anything. Now something, something red; a shirt, then a face. Bobby? What the—? "Hey, cut it out!" Michael screamed. "What the holy heck do you think you're DOIN'?"

"You were drownin', knucklehead."

Michael lay there on his back, choking and gurgling, soaked, water up in his helmet, in his hair. Everything was dark green and black and sort of out of focus. Except for his brother's goofy face, and his red shirt, shiny, stupid, hovering over him. He forced his eyes open wide, now feeling the wet, hard floor pushing painfully—unyielding—into his backbone, everything wet and surreal. "I was . . . *drowning?*"

"Yep."

Michael was wet and angry. Confused. "So . . . so you go an' pour *water* on me, ya' turdbucket?"

Bobby looked down at him and sort of shrugged and smiled

one of those stupid, embarrassing smiles. "Uh, well, kinda beca—"

"Help me up."

Bobby grabbed his outstretched arms, and pulled. He wanted to tell his little brother that he was glad he was alive, and loved him dearly, but of course he couldn't, being a guy and all. So he just said, "Well . . . we never made Lake Of The Ozarks. Ya' didn't miss much. Anyhoo, better scoop some of this water back up— we'll be in Nebraska in a few minutes. And there's some frogs and crawdads and junk hiding over in the corner."

Michael was sitting up now in the dirty liquid, the last small rivulets of water flowing out from under his helmet and down his shirt. A small frog hopped from his lap to the welcome darkness beneath the AM-1250 Mixer-Amplifier. "Okay, yeah. I'll get 'em." He shook his head and blinked hard, squeezing the last of the water from his eyelids. "And thanks for . . . you know, saving my life and all."

Bobby smiled and rolled his shoulders casually, reached up to tap the brim of an imaginary cowboy hat, and did his best John Wayne. "Walllll . . . you're welcome there, little fella." He quickly grabbed the side of an ejection seat to steady himself as the jet flew through a little blip of turbulence, then drawled, "And let's try to be a little more careful down here, pilgrim, wah-hah." He flashed his brother a casual Duke salute, spun around, and headed purposefully through the dark hatches, back up to his station.

CHAPTER 13.

THE GREAT BIG AIRSHOW OF '62

When the boys hit their last checkpoint—La Platte, Nebraska—they were still about two minutes ahead of schedule. Col. Riley throttled back a little more and started to perform a few low-level 360s to chew up some time. They were all still a little shook, Bobby especially, but his head had stopped bleeding. Mike also needed a little more time to get his bomb load back in the buckets. Some of them were still hiding.

The sturdy folk of La Platte (pop. 1,106) were treated to a scene that they still talk about to this day. Ask anyone in town about the Great Big Airshow Of '62, and most of the citizens that had been there would put a cupped hand to their good ear and say, "Huh? . . . speak *up!*"

Tommy found the water tower, and started circling it. The newly minted colonel was worried that they had only reached SENIORS 58, Joey Loves Debbie XXX000, Nebraska, but Bobby assured the crew that it was actually La Platte. Only 7 miles to Offutt!

Time to get everything ready. No one had to go to the bathroom or anything, which was good, 'cause they couldn't see a runway down there, and most of the roads looked curvy. The small town was used to seeing airplanes, being so close to Offutt, but no jet had tried to steal Mrs. Langstrom's laundry before! Tommy cursed a little—a venial—and got the wing-tip up some, vowing to pay a little better attention. They were so close to Offutt that he was thinking too far ahead, acting a little nonchalant with the task at hand. He waggled the wings a little bit to get the sheets and underwear off, and made a mental note to write A Letter To The Editor, to explain their transgressions, and offer to pay for the quick-dried linen.

The people down there seemed friendly enough. Most everybody in town was lying on their backs in their yards or out in the streets, hands over their ears, eyes wide, sizing up their new visitors. The town looked clean and neat to Tommy, except that all the signs were blown over, and lots of cows seemed to be running loose. They really should have a leash law down there! He'd mention that in his letter, too.

But they were nearly back on schedule now, so Tommy completed his last circle and waggled his wings a little bit to say a proper, airmanly "bye" and felt a bump. He spun around quickly to look behind him. Dangit! Too low! Now he'd have to cough up for some laundry and a street light. Man, he'd be mowing lawns for two *years* to pay all this off! Hell*s bells!*

He followed the road signs up the highway out of La Platte, took the Offutt exit, and guided their plane in low over the Main Gate. On his left he saw that Offutt's sign was lots bigger than the one at Forbes, and with some neatly-trimmed hedges around it, too. Everybody below looked up for a second in disbelief, then hit the deck.

"Whoah, Nelly!" radioed Bobby. "Hey! All those APs flat on their backs down there have *chrome helmets!* Man-o-man! Now *this* is some *Air Base!*"

Tommy had to agree. Throttles way back now, flaps coming down, the boys were slowing down, having a little look-see. Col. Riley had always wanted to see Offutt, Headquarters of SAC. El Base*ooooo* Grand*ooooo*. It looked like most bases, just a heck of a lot more of it! Back there was the gate, and straight ahead a huge, sprawling headquarters complex. The church steeples were right over there with so many other buildings that it looked like a city. More barracks all over the place, and long, white warehouses by the train tracks, way off to his left. Wow! They even had an Atlas missile down there, standing next to an office building! Now that was some serious decorating!

Tommy pulled up a little to miss it, but it blew over anyway. This place was much bigger than Forbes. There were thousands of people down there, falling down.

He missed a few big trees, and then they were flying over the hangars. There were lots of them, 15 or 20 maybe, and the ramp was just plain huge! A few planes, mostly transports and a couple of B-52s were parked in front of some of the hangars. He saw Air Force One just ahead by the tower, but most of Offutt's planes had scrambled like everybody else. Farther out, runways were all over the place, actually crisscrossing themselves, there were so many! He pulled up a tad to miss the control tower, and saw the crowd for the ceremony over to his right, the bleachers all set up, with lots of red, white and blue bunting and flags and stuff. There was the podium and stage, with a bunch of TV cameras, their black cables snaking away to TV vans behind the stage. The whole set-up was right in the middle of an empty part of the huge ramp, 300 yards at least from the tower. Perfect!

Tommy gave them a little wing-waggle, chuckling in his mask. He felt great, like Rowdy Gates on "Rawhide," just before he opened up on the bad guys, all huddled up and stupid by the campfire. Feeling really confident with the airplane now, he started a sweeping turn that would take him out past the base boundary where he could hang a 180, and come back and aim for the biggest runway, farthest out, that paralleled the festivities.

Colonel Riley hit TRANSMIT, and his voice boomed through the loudspeakers. "Hi! We're here! Just flew in from Havana, and boy are our arms tired! Heh-heh-heh!" Down below, Michael heard his cue, and hit a trash can lid with a hammer, making a neat cymbal-crash noise into his microphone. Ka*Wham!* The boys figured a joke right about now might lighten things up down there, disarm them. They weren't serious all the time, y'know.

"I'll just turn it around over here, and then we'll be comin' around for a landing." Bobby had told him to say, comin' around *for* a landing, not that they *were* landing. Keeping it honest, keeping it legal. "You folks down there wait up! We'll be back in a jif."

There was not much need for the announcement. Everybody at the ceremony area had heard the piercing whistle of the plane coming low over the base, combined with honking horns and little tire screeches and crunches of metal and glass. Their eyes all followed the noisy trail of the jet they couldn't see, hidden behind the row of hulking hangars, followed by the snapping noises of trees and poles, *there!*, now *there!*, now over *there!*, closer and closer, and then the shrieking bomber popped into view from behind the shattering glass of the huge control tower. It had left behind a scene of bedlam, and screaming, sobbing, deafened humanity. Windows were broken, cars wrecked, signs and trees blown over, and thousands of government employees lay dazed and crying, many now starting to think very seriously about early retirement.

Khunyin was headed back to the northwest, searching for the base in the unfamiliar surroundings. He would have to report that, despite his escort efforts to help, the American was sadly destroyed by the savage storm. "Fools," he chuckled.

Walter stood studiously out on the ramp, an earphone in place, the microphone up to his mouth, saying, "and *that's* the way it is . . . and that's the way it *is*". . . over and over. Practice made perfect, even for the pros. The program director had decided to make the errant plane a part of the newscast, to turn this whole, crazy episode into a plus, to use the event! Heck, if it's gonna be here, *write it into the script!* He had spent three years in L.A., learning to "go with the flow," and to "emote." He was in touch with his feelings, years ahead of everybody else. That's why he earned the big bucks!

"Ten seconds, Mr. Cronkite," he announced.

Walt put down the headset, straightened his tie, and when the little red camera light came on he announced professionally, "Good afternoon. CBS News comes to you now, live from Offutt Air Force Base in Omaha, in this Special Report. In just a few seconds, the airplane you will soon see behind me will land, the last United States Air Force plane still in the air, and will officially begin this unprecedented stand-down for the next two weeks, as the United States and the Soviet Union struggle to de-fuse this dangerous Cuban Missile Crisis . . .”

A far-off speck grew larger as Walter and the crowd turned, pointing. Cameras zoomed in on the silver jet as the landing gear doors snapped open, the black gear swiveling slowly down. The roar became more of a high-pitched whistle as the power came back, and the flaps shoved deeper into the slipstream. From the stands, the plane was steadily lowering on its final approach. Nearing the end of the runway, the jet's slender fuselage was barely visible, level with the low, rolling hills and the trees of the cluttered horizon behind it. Almost at touchdown, only the huge, swept tail clearly poked above the horizon, silhouetted against the sky like the fin of a shark, slicing its way through the prairie sky.

Then . . . *what?* Gen. Buttinski caught his breath. The roar began increasing as the engines spooled up, starting to roar like it was taking off, not landing, and heavy black smoke was now being churned out by the engines.

Tommy moved the throttles forward, and slapped the gear and flaps handle up.

“Gear up, and *innnn the greeeeeeeeeen,*” reported Bobby, airmanly.

Tommy smiled and chuckled to himself. They were getting pretty good at this stuff, acting like a SAC crew. Maybe they'd split a brewski after the flight, catch a game on the tube at the O Club. Sneak a peek at those Esquires they always had lying around.

Slowly, the fin of the shark began turning towards its prey— the huge rudder skewing itself until it was aimed directly at the stunned crowd. Now the serious black snout of the bomber was head-on to Wodka and the podium. By the time the crowd could make sense of the fast-changing scene, the B-47 was all silver and flexing and alive, gear doors snapping shut, flaps hanging menacingly, all framed by the sooty black smoke that its engines spewed out, swirling behind it. So low, it was no longer a plane but a locomotive with wings, chugging deafeningly down an invisible track that led right through the middle of the wide-eyed crowd. They stood there, frozen, like deer in a spotlight. The shrill maniacal whistle grew louder and louder and LOUDER, and then it was *ON* them, and the crowd screamed and cried and bellowed as the huge thing completely blocked out the sky—Ka*BAM!*

The pressure and noise of the thundering jet *slammed* the unbelieving Gen. Buttinski down to the concrete, and sent its crushing roar over and under and through every molecule of every person there, all of them now on the ground, faces covered, screaming, ears bleeding, each body in overload as the sight and sound of what had just happened stayed . . . burning in their eyes and ears and brains, unable to turn the scene off, even when the plane was a quarter mile away . . . turning . . . the flaps retracted, the wings thin and silver, bending gracefully like a gliding hawks from the force of the turn. Crawling cautiously up from their hands and knees, clothing torn, handkerchiefs patting bloodied elbows and knees, crying, the stunned crowd saw the plane arcing . . . heading out low over the grassy stubble, continuing its sweeping circuit. Oh, my God! *Was it coming back!?*

Col. Khunyin, now within miles of the base, heard the screams of the crowd through his headset. He transmitted urgently, a sickening knot beginning to form in his stomach. "W . . . what is happening? Report, please. *What is wrong?*"

Buttinski cursed, crawled over two or three whimpering capitalists, and found the microphone. "He is down here, *on the ground,*" he spat. "Coming right at us, you fool! He almost hit us! He is a *madman!*"

Col. Khunyin cursed. On the ground? No, he is dead! *Who is on the ground?* But of course he knew: the American. What manner of man *was* this? No matter! He armed his Sidewinder missile and began a screaming dive toward the base.

"Got those crow's seats ready, Mike?" radioed Col. Tommy.

"Roger!" Michael crackled back professionally, busily finishing up his duties up in the navigator's station.

Tommy expertly swung the black nose of the bomber toward the wrecked podium off in the distance, his sweeping turn nearly completed. Michael had the safety pins all pulled, the seats armed, and one end of the ropes tied to the three ejection-seats, the others tied to the companionway handle. The Scout book had a knot for every reason he could think of, but nothing about ejection-seat triggerings—he'd checked—so he used a double half-hitch on the seats, one of his favorites. The three seats in the belly, normally occupied by the highly trained electronic warfare officers, most of whom had completed four years of college, now contained two large buckets each of Forbes Air Force Base ditch water, some crawdads, a little solvent, and some thoroughly ticked-off frogs. There was also a little mud in them, and some cigarette butts. It was a mix worthy of those filthy, cheating Russians. Some Americans would get messy too, but hey, it was a messy world. And they were *collaborators*.

Mike fastened, prepared, and loaded the navigator's ejection seat up in the nose in the same expert fashion. Tommy saw his white helmet struggle out of the darkness of the nav tunnel, onto the narrow catwalk to his left, and carefully hand the rope up and back to his big brother. Bobby would be in charge of yanking the nose rope, Mike would be in charge back in the belly. The last step on Mike's lengthy checklist, the Nav-Seat-To-Co-Pilot-Rope-Transfer, was done and he hurried back to his position. Reaching the companionway handle, he plugged in his intercom, un-slipped his slip-knots, and waited.

From the ramp, the sleek bomber continued its steep turn, wings perpendicular to the ground and showing its handsome top view to the stunned crowd. It was about half a mile out, and moving! Its slender wings swept back, engines slung neatly beneath— the right wingtip near the ground, stirring dust and startling small animals—the left wingtip 120 feet higher, scribing a path through the sky. The smaller horizontal stabilizers at the tail matched the sweep of the wings. The teardrop canopy was glistening in the sunlight. Inside, two white dots, the helmets of the pilot and co-

pilot, turning, looking around, grunting from the g-forces, measuring the turn, the speed, the distance to their quarry, hands on
the throttle, gripping the wheel . . . gently . . . gently . . . *eeeeeeasssy*
now, small corrections. Turns this steep, this low, took co-ordina-
tion. And Guts. With a capital G!

The slender plane was a brilliant silver-blue, then a dark grey
flash, then silver again as its thundering path took it in and out of
the shadows of the scudding prairie clouds above. The stunned
crowd stood mesmerized as the jet screamed in completing its
steady circle to come around, and aim at them once again.

"*MahgawdsweetmotherJesus* can he bomb us!?" cried Johnson,
still struggling to get up.

"No, it's a reconnaissance aircraft, you idiot!" snapped Gen.
Buttinski. How he hated those black nosed B-47s, the very ones
that teased and prodded the defenses of his country, besting them
always. And here was yet another one, signifying the very power
and arrogance of the United States Air Force. That would soon
change. Still, what was this young pilot trying to do? Another
buzz job? The second could not have the impact of the first! Then
a wry smile crossed his Cossack lips. High in the sky, but still
miles out, he saw a small flash.

The F-100 glistened, hurtling across the horizon at the bomber,
the dangerous speck curving toward the base with savage determi-
nation. Pompous dolts, Khunyin fumed to himself—expecting
correct altitude and position reports from this marauding aircraft.
They were such fools! This American was very, very clever. He must
kill them now, before they spilled the beanskis. The slender shape
of the American bomber, slightly below and in front of him, led a
brown trail of dust and debris. Khunyin's face had the grim, determined look of a pilot about to do battle, but only in Russian.

Up top, Tommy could see the taut rope that Bobby was holding, snaking down past his foot and through the crawlway, then
disappearing into the nose station. He just hoped it wouldn't catch
on any of those darned knobs and switches which cluttered the
side of the cockpit. He just might have to write to Boeing about all

those. With a tug on the ropes, powerful rockets attached to the seats would blast them straight through the bottom of the jet. Although designed to propel their human cargo to safety from a stricken jet, their use today would now be as powered, guided bombs—a smoking symbol of defiance from the boys from Forbes.

Gen. Buttinski watched, hypnotized, jaws agape—still trembling from the last pass—as the American headed directly for him again! He fumbled with his binoculars, cursing, trying to focus on the image of the fast-moving jet. *Lenin's ghost!*

Hurtling across the midwestern sky, Col. Khunyin had the enemy plane clearly in his sights. He did not worry any longer about the politics of shooting down an American over an American base, or showing it on TV. Screwski it! It was now mano a mano, one of them would live, and the other would die. The American had surely shown prodigious amounts of aviating skill and savvy, but Steveski was going to shoot his ass down anyway.

The huge bomber barreled down on the podium, its racing shadow flashing across the short grass and runways at the far end of the Flight Line. "ATTENTION EVERYBODY DOWN THERE!" boomed the voice through the toppled stage speakers. "HERE'S WHAT THE FIGHTIN' FIFTY-FIFTH THINKS OF YOUR CRUMMY OLD STAND-DOWN! VIDEMUS OMNIA, BUB. *WE SEE ALL!*" Tommy grinned. This was gonna be *sooooo* good!

On the ground, those still conscious saw a numbing scene: the bomber blotting out the sky two hundred yards away . . . one hundred . . . eighty . . . the shrill scream of six jet engines sucking the atmosphere from their frightened lungs and bludgeoning their senses. People still stunned and confused from the first pass tried to prepare again for the unprepareable.

"NOW!" ordered Tommy Riley. Immediately, both Konto brothers yanked their ropes as one, and the bottom of the jet instantly erupted in four blinding, orange-white explosions. *KaBAM!* People on the ramp gasped as the rockets smoked their unbelievable cargo onto the tarmac just yards in front of them, where it enveloped them in a steaming mass of dirty water, crustaceans, cigarette filters and seat parts.

Col. Khunyin could scarcely believe what his eyes were telling him. The unarmed reconnaissance aircraft fixed in his sights and making another buzz job, an impressive but futile gesture, and then, in the next instant, the ramp *exploded,* covering the crowd in a mixture of smoke and steam and . . . what? What *was* all that?

The B-47 began a sweeping turn to the right, leaving behind a scene of swirling, smoky confusion as diplomats and officers scurried like squawking, flapping, headless chickens, bumping in to each other or just lying there, spread-eagle, in the slowly expanding puddle. But Khunyin could not worry about those pitiful groundlings. Nyet! This American was about to be a disappearnik!

The Sidewinder tracking signal warbled insistently in his earphones, like a spastic, growling dog straining at its leash. The dog-warhead's sensors wanted to follow the hot exhaust of the bomber like a bloodhound, to bite it, to kill it! Khunyin gritted his teeth and furiously punched the yellow, blinking MISSILE FIRE button. The missile bolted from the wing of the fighter and hurtled toward its quarry.

Bobby had just spun his seat around backwards to look for the plane that he knew was chasing them from the claxon blare of the MD-4 Homing Threat Indicator. "Holy Moly! A Sidewinder!" he screamed, sighting the small, deadly missile glinting in the morning sun. "Its gonna *cream* us!" His frightened voice could barely be heard through the tornado-like wind whipping through the cockpit from all the jagged, new openings. The maps had all disappeared in an instant, and #2 pencils and specs of dirt and checklists and grocery lists and who-knew-what swirled, and spun, and stung their eyes. Bobby thought he was in one of those darned, shaky, snow-things for a second, and it smelled like a couple of zillion firecrackers had gone off.

"Quick! Visors down!" coughed Tommy. He twisted his head around, and saw the tiny, dangerous dot of a missile hauling ass toward them. "Hang on guys . . . *reeeeal tight!*" His calmness surprised him. He knew the airplane now, knew what this baby could do. Throttles full forward, a little right rudder leading into the turn, watching the growing dot in his rear-view mirror, a little more right rudder, keep that ball centered, the chasing dot growing larger, larger, easy . . . eeeeeeeasy . . . NOW! Full back on the wheel *HARD!* At the same moment, his right hand, which seemed a little stronger and more rugged now, slammed the flap lever to FULL DOWN in a practiced motion.

Sixty-eight feet of cold metal flaps shoved themselves relentlessly into the slipstream, the wings shuddered, and then immediately flexed upward, straining to haul the shaking fuselage up with them. The engines, howling in protest, bounced and twisted so much that Tommy was afraid they might tear off their mounts. They *had* to hold, they just *had* to! "Hang on!" he yelled as the huge, shuddering bomber shot skyward, the g-forces pulling the masks from their faces, their vision growing cloudy as the blood drained from their heads.

And poor Mike, down below! Jiminy Crickets! Despite all the planning and getting everything just right, he was totally unprepared for the fierceness of the blast of three ejection seats just a few feet away. The dark green interior of the crow's bay flashed bright as the sun. He screamed, blinded, acrid smoke stinging his eyes and nose as the terrifying blasts pounded into his body, like being clobbered with a 2x4. His head slammed back, and his ears rang and bled, and he was *blind!* Oh no, not that! He had only learned to you-know-what a few months ago! Everyone warned that something like this could happen, the going blind part, but what were the odds of it happening to him now, what with all this other stuff going on? The timing so crazy, so unfair! Plus, he went to confession each time, and if you confess it, it wasn't supposed to count! Those were the rules! He went by the rules! The *Pope's* rules! This just plain wasn't fair!

Then suddenly, he raised a trembling hand to his sooty face and felt his eyes. Well heck, *there's* some of the problem. Sheesh! After he picked loose the little molten blobs of eyelashes, tops and bottoms fused together, his eyes opened to reveal a totally wrecked compartment. It was a mess, and looking pretty empty now, without those three big seats. Most of the instruments and stuff had been ripped out by the blasts, and dials and broken radar screens were hanging, jerking from the low ceiling, with wiring and twisted braces shaking and swaying in the vibrating hell that was the hold of the jet. The startling vision was even more surreal as it was all happening in complete silence. He couldn't hear a thing! And now a new motion, a sickening lurch skyward, what the heck-o-rama was going on up there!? He was going to die, he just knew it! What a gyp! His tears left a clean, pink trail down his gunpowdered grey face as he thought of his mom. Suddenly he was tired, very tired. There was so much he would never be able to do. He had never had a woman. Never eaten Hawaiian food. Never been to Kansas City.

As the bomber elevated, the Sidewinder missile came within yards of the trusty #4 engine and fulfilling its odious mission, as it punched out a sharply-curving exhaust trail into the clear midwestern sky. Its sensors searched frantically for the target, but they were now blind and lost. Almost immediately the missile found another hot trail. It wasn't as juicy as a B-47, but would have to do. It locked onto it and followed unerringly, like a bloodhound, to a chimney and then through the roof of the Officer's Club. The huge industrial oven—full of hot, bubbling borscht for the brunch reception to follow—was blown to smithereens.

At the apex of the zoom climb, the plane shuddered and bucked, and the stall warning blared just as Tommy knew it would from page 67, paragraph 2. His eyes were closed from the g-forces of the climb and sting of debris, but no matter—the plane was a part of him now. He slammed the flap lever to the UP position and shoved the wheel and throttles full forward, to the stops. Full blast! This sent the nose of the bomber hurtling down toward the ground, against all instincts. He opened one eye to see some Nebraskan geography coming up to meet him and knew he needed speed, precious speed, to stay in the air and survive, and escape that pesky F-100. Who was that guy back there, anyhow? And why did he have it in for him so bad?

Col. Khunyin saw all the brilliant maneuvers that the slippery bomber had performed in foiling his missile. The plane now flashed across a stream and a farm, only feet from the ground. How could anyone fly that well, and after all *that?* The American pressed his plane to the very folds of the earth! Khunyin was closing from behind, but still way up there, safely above the trees and power lines, afraid to go as low as the bomber at such speeds. The sight of the silver B-47 hypnotized him, flying smoothly . . . so smoothly . . . adjusting altitude continuously to compensate for the rolling terrain. He couldn't stop staring or make himself do anything except watch the huge bomber flash across the landscape, with him following, following . . . drawing him in . . . mesmerized . . . trying to keep up.

Suddenly, it seemed as if the bomber was completely still. *Stopped!* He shook his head sharply. The silver bomber *was* motionless, as was *his* plane, the brown earth streaking by underneath them, only a blur. Khunyin focused on the dark shadow of the bomber . . . racing . . . chasing its silver mate across the square fields, rushing up the low hills to nearly touch itself, and then dropping away at the valleys. It disappeared at a cliff near a river, only to magically re-appear and charge up the other side of the river bank to continue the chase. It flashed across roads, wrapped itself instantly over lines of trees, flattened itself over the stubbled fields, so close to itself, never stopping. Khunyin felt drawn to the scene, falling into it. The F-100 was lowering . . . lowering . . . no, wait! He banged his heavy helmet with his gloved fist. Vertigo! He had almost succumbed to the sense-numbing chase. What was he, a sightseer? A pathetic cadet? Nyet! He would have this pilot in battle. There was a terrific man behind the wheel of that bomber, and the American had bested him so far, but no more. Now he was close enough to kill him with his cannon.

Maneuvering closer to his target, Khunyin saw the sleek jet hurtling toward a farm house, lower than the house, small dirty tornados ripping behind it, tearing through the fields, the barn a red streak to his left. The American bomber snapped its right wing up, then down, surgically missing the small, white, capitalist dwelling—but slicing off the television antenna. A shower of glass and curtains exploded out of the rear of the house, spraying through the backyard sky. Glorioyski! Khunyin glimpsed a cat, back arched, feet straight out, spinning, never to doze on a warm windowsill again. *Poor kitty!* Enough! It was now time to finish this! It would be so easy, like gunnery practice back in the Parentland.

The bomber filled his sights, and he closed one eye to draw the perfect bead when rhythmic puffs of smoke appeared suddenly from the tail of his fleeing imperialistic target.

"*Yeeee haaaaaaaa!*" yelled Bobby. "Bullseye!" The tail cannon had worked as advertised. "Cowabunga! *Gotcha,* ya' crummy old RAT FINK!" That was the very first airplane he'd ever shot down, and an F-100 to boot! A toughie! It felt great! Only four more and he'd be an *ace.* A guy could really get the girls if he was an ace. Maybe he'd be an astronaut, *and* a tail gunner!

Col. Khunyin was aware only of the sensation of his surroundings disappearing in a violent spasm of noise and jerking metal. He yanked the stick back for precious altitude as the canopy turned opaque, shattered, and disappeared in a stinging spray of plexiglass. The wings twisted sharply and flew off, then the whole right side of the airplane peeled back, banged once, and was gone, exposing the clear midwestern sky. The instrument panel smashed down against his knees and disappeared, until it was just him, belched from his disintegrating mount in a dizzying, unstoppable, brutally final apogee. Khunyin hurtled forward through the sky— end over end—still chasing the American. A fierce wind slashed at his face, his bloodied legs, then his face again. The helmet whipped off his head and a vision of fields, sky, fields and sky rotated before him. He felt strangely at peace. There was no more struggle, no more chasing. An alert little dog looked up at him and barked— two quick ones. He then knew it was all over, and a thin smile came across his lips. He managed a groggy salute in the direction of his American victor, then closed his eyes and thought of Hero-Grade cabbage and his sturdy Natasha as he plunged towards the rich, free soil below.

CHAPTER 14.

AT THE BRINK

Across America, the whole unbelievable scene was captured and broadcast live, the cameras shaking, dropping, scanning and re-focusing through the flying muck. The bomber was shown from its first thundering pass to the circle back, the message from the jet, then the bomb run, and finally the speeding blur of a white missile following the plane, rocketing over the crowd's cowering, unbelieving heads, starting the chase across the sky.

And what a bomb run! The CBS camera had captured a big, brown, aviating crawdad just as it impacted the pompous Russian general squarely on his forehead. The water bug sent Buttinski stunned to the ground, eyes wide and arms flailing, like a miserable commie turtle on its miserable commie back. The whole world saw it, and at that second, despite the pomp and bull-poop of the stand-down proceedings, everyone knew that *that* airplane was providing the *real* answer of the American people.

TVs were also turned on at SAC alert bases across the world to see the stand-down ceremony, and all the crewmen had been sad and de-moralized by all of it. They'd followed the drama and radio reports with keen interest all morning, then tuned in to the live broadcast. *Shazaam!* The men were stunned as they watched one of their own turn this gutless farce to a shambles! Who *were* those guys!? This little airshow got their attention, and cheers rang out on bases throughout the free world. A thousand highly-polished flight boots bolted down a hundred hallways, unstoppable now, and out the doors to their waiting aircraft. Stand-down, my butt!

That B-47 on TV had just shown what Peace Is Our Profession was all about, and by God, they were going to shove some Peace down some commie throats! Within minutes, hundreds of angry bombers and tankers were screaming to their Fail-Safe stations at the doorstep of Mother Russia. Just say the word, buddy boy, and they would finish it! They were psyched, they had some *hustle!*

Everything had been going pretty good for the boys since Bobby shot down the F-100, until the #6 engine ingested a haystack and caught fire. Moments earlier, Tommy was wondering if the President was gonna have him killed or decorated, and if there were any more darned fighters back there that Bobby had missed. Fierce wind howled through the cockpit, and debris peppered his visor and neck and arms. Mike was still screaming back there in the crow's compartment, still deafened by the explosions, crying like a darned sissy. No matter how much he and Bobby radioed at him to shut up, he kept on screaming, "What's happening, what's *happening?* Us crows got a right to know! I can't hear nothin!" over and over. And after Bobby finally shot down that pesky F-100, then *he* started screaming and yelling like he was at a football game or something, and his yahoos and yabadabadoos were starting to tick Tommy off.

The jet handled differently with all the new holes in it, and he struggled with the vibrating control column, trying to keep them out of the trees and windmills. So when his noisy co-pilot leaned forward over the instrument panel and jubilantly smacked Tommy on the back of his helmet with his ruler, Col. Riley just about ejected. He was yelling at Bobby to put his seat belt back on and plot a course back to Offutt when the right wingtip engine flew through the huge haystack.

"Wow, Riley," Bobby said, wide-eyed and concerned, watching fodder spray through the sky. "Whadjya go an' do *that* for!?"

"Because you were bugging the crap out of me!"

"Sure, blame me! You're the one steering this stupid thing."

"Just shut up and tell me how bad it is! That's your job. I got some hills coming up!"

Bobby muttered and cranked his head back to the right to assess the damage. The powerful jet engine, used to a diet of oxygen and fuel and the occasional butterfly, wasn't sure what to do with this much straw. The thin sticks were shredded and spun by the spinning compressor blades okay, but once saturated with fuel and passed on to the ignition chamber—

"Holy moly! Five churnin' and one burnin'!"

"Oh, this is great! *Juuuust* great!" snapped Tommy.

"No it ain't great—the danged motor's on fire!"

"Very observant! So whaddawe do *now*, Mister Hot Shot Co-pilot?"

"How the heck should I know!? We're ON FIRE!"

"Just like I thought. Sure, you co-pilots get to shoot the guns and criticize every little teensy thing, but when it's time to do some serious stuff, you haven't even studied."

"What are you talking about? The number six engine's about to blow!"

Tommy turned left to miss a small town. *"That's riiiiight,"* he replied, using a particular, grating, sarcastic tone that grown-ups used so often. "It seems we have an engine fire. So what do we do next, *hmmmm?* We went over all this last night. Weren't we paying attention?"

Bobby snorted, having to listen to a seventh grader talk to him like that, and made a pledge to beat him up when they got back to Topeka. But the fire was growing, and he knew he'd have to swallow his anger this once and try to remember all that stupid checklist stuff. "Fire, ummm, means Exit Aircraft, right?"

"Nope. *Ground* Fire means Exit Aircraft. *In-Flight* Fire means—"

"Wait, don't tell me. Inflight Fire means Emergency Bold-Face List, right?"

"Correct. So get out your Bold-Face List and look under Engine Fire. We don't got all day!" Tommy looked up in his mirror at Bobby's frightened face, then breathed deeply and slowly. He lowered his voice and said calmly, "Listen up. This is big-time, Konto, let's do it fast and do it right. And for pete's sake, make sure you shut down the right engine!"

Bobby stammered, looking around, almost crying, "I . . . I can't find my checklist! It's not . . ." He searched frantically at the sides of his seat, the floor, looked out to the burning engine, then back to the chart storage slot and up at the mirror, pleading and confused. His eyes were wide, his breath short. "It was here, honest! It musta' blew out! It blew *out,* Riley!"

Tommy saw his co-pilot was losing it. Dang! He radioed back forcefully, "Okay then, hot shot. I sure as heck hope you were payin' attention last night at the briefing, or Mike's gonna *die.* Get it? We can eject, but something's wrong down there and Mike can't hear us. He won't hear the bail-out order. So shut that fuel off first thing— NOW!—and then do the rest, darnit! Think! We went over this last night— if you don't put that fire out, it's gonna put *us* out!" He looked up at Bobby's paralyzed face in the mirror, and snarled, "So quit staring at me like a chickenshit spaz, and get to *work!*"

Bobby suddenly snapped out of it, blinked his eyes, and shook his helmet back and forth in quick, little jerks. Huh? Chickenshit *what!?* Man, he was gonna pound that freckle-faced twerp when they got back. But instantly, from way back in the old grey matter, he suddenly remembered the drill they'd practiced last night over hamburgers. Over and over and *over.* Got it! Suddenly, his brain and hands were communicating by themselves—fast. He almost felt like an observer.

He shut the fuel off to #6, confirmed the turbine pressure drop, shut down all electrics to the engine, then off-lined the generator. Next, he opened the inlet irises to block intake airflow, and pulled the fire extinguisher T-grip. He swiveled his head out toward #6 and watched anxiously as a puff of orange retardant blew out the tailpipe. The small, fierce flames shooting out of assorted engine panels and openings gave a few last flutters and surges and then went out. He took a deep, thankful breath and leaned back, relaxing a little. Sheesh! That was scareder than he'd been in a long time. "Okay, Riley. Fires out."

"'Bout time. Now that wasn't so hard, was it?"

Bobby narrowed his eyes and stared malevolently at the back of his Aircraft Commander's helmet, thinking dark, co-pilot thoughts. He ground his teeth and started counting to ten, slowly.

The boys flew on in silence except for the scream of the wind, and Michael's sobbing and constant queries about their current situation. Tommy had throttled back #1 to control a pesky yaw that started as soon as they lost #6, but still had to use a lot of left rudder to compensate for the drag of the dead engine. So he cranked the rudder trim control knob to the right. There. Much better.

Tommy then asked Bobby how to get back to Offutt.

Bobby was still mad, but tried to figure a reciprocal heading from the overall direction they had been going. He took a deep breath, looked up from his one remaining, torn, map—taped hastily to his plotting board—then radioed up in his most professional voice, "Try 230 degrees, you retard!"

"Oh, yeah?" Col. Riley shot back. He'd just about had it with that goofball shavetail. "Whyncha' try plastic surgery, ya' ugly puke-headed goonface!" He horsed the big jet around to the revised heading but was so mad he actually aimed for a flock of birds at 205 degrees, then settled down and quickly got back on course. He knew they couldn't afford a break-down of crew morale and discipline now—they had to be back on civil speaking terms before landing. Puke-headed goonface may have been a little much. They were all tired. Funny thing, he thought dreamily, even the airplane felt tired. What a day. His helmet weighed a ton, and he closed his eyes in the warm sun for just a second. There was less wind as he went up, up, just a little more up. Mmm. Quieter, it felt good. He leaned his head back against the headrest. Just another second or two, a little rest, he thought, just another sec—

"Hey, don't stall us, ya' moron!" Bobby shrieked in alarm as he watched the airspeed decay with the climb. "Snap out of it, Riley! If you crash this thing now, I'll be double *triple* ticked! Now pay attention up there and get your dang nose down!" he yelled as he hurled his protractor at the front cockpit.

Tommy felt a *thwack* on the back of his helmet which startled him awake. *Huh?* He opened his eyes, and slowly focused on the altimeter. Climbing? How come? Sleepy. He blinked hard, shaking his head from side to side and squirmed in his seat. Cripes! Climbing? No! Snap out of it, he told himself angrily. Fly the airplane. Get that nose down and pay attention. *Fly!*

Pretty soon, Council Bluffs and Omaha were a cluster of far-off white and grey squares poking delicately through the trees and hills. The sun was high and a little ahead of them, so Tommy knew they were approaching from the east. That meant Offutt was below and to their left somewhere, and the skilled pilot continued his descent down to where he was more trained—where they could read the road signs—and navigated them in the general direction of the base.

Bobby crackled, "Oughta be there soon. Hope we're not in too much trouble. Let's hang a right."

Michael's ears were starting to pick up a little sound, finally, and he heard the preparations for landing going on up in the cockpit. "So what do I do?" he radioed up, nervously.

"Hey, good to have you back, spasmo. Strap in. we're landing soon."

"But my seat's gone."

"Oh yeah. Well, just hold on tight, I guess. Riley's gonna land this thing smooth as a baby's butt, aintcha' Riley?"

"Plus I gotta pee," added Michael.

"Well, just hold it in. We're almost there."

"I can't. I gotta go bad!"

"Dangitall Michael!" yelled Bobby. " We're trying to land an airplane up here! Pee if ya want. Jump if ya want! Just quit yer dang moanin'. Moan, moan, moan, that's all we've heard for the last ten minutes! Just knock it the heck off!"

Michael made a silent face at his big brother, then crooked his arm around the handle, steadied himself above the howling void, and began fumbling for his zipper.

Tommy watched some fishermen jump out of their little boat,

pulled the roaring jet up a nudge to cross the river bank, and aimed across the scrubby fields toward the huge red and white checkered water tower standing guard over Offutt. "Flaps 10," he requested.

They flew over the base boundary again, and he saw that their downwind approach would take them right over the ramp where the ceremony had almost taken place. They had been gone fifteen or twenty minutes, but it was still really crowded down there, plus there were lots of ambulances and cops now, and flashing lights and TV cameras everywhere.

Tommy drew a deep breath. He knew that landing this battle-damaged B-47 would really separate the men from the sixth graders. It was Heads-Up Time in Omaha.

"Flaps 20. Gear down," he ordered his co-pilot, in a grave yet controlled tone.

"Flaps 20 is a big roger dodger, and gear is showing down *aaaaaand* locked."

Col. Riley rolled his eyes and barked, "Hey! Sterile cockpit! No unnecessary chatter back there!"

"Aaaaand a wilco on the unnecessary chatter. Reading you five by five, skipper-dipper. Over and out."

A shrill, thundering roar brought Gen. Buttinsky back to groggy consciousness. He opened his eyes and saw the bomber smoking toward him yet again, and knew that he was in hell. A nurse, removing the small bomblet from his forehead with tweezers screamed at the sight of the approaching jet and jumped up. Wodka's head left her comforting lap and struck a jarring bounce on the wet concrete. So there really is a God, he thought painfully. And as such, there is surely a hell. And this was his hell: an American bomber flying above him again and again, over and over—for eternity—smashing his senses, pummeling him, ridiculing him, showering him with filth and vermin, and he would never know the sweet release of death. A true hell. From a true God.

As the sky turned dark with the image of this craft from Hades shrieking at Buttinski with a never-ending fury, he blinked up at the belly of the beast and thought he saw a small figure looking down at him through a jagged opening. The little demon had grey skin, a fire-streaked helmet, and no eyebrows. It also had a little pink pecker which began emitting a sparkling, wavering stream that glistened from the darkness of the beast on a perfect trajectory towards the general's unbelieving eyes. He opened his mouth to scream, and immediately realized his mistake, but it was too late.

The jet finished its base turn and lined up for final approach. "Flaps 30 and call the numbers," commanded Col. Riley.

"Flaps 30 and call *what* numbers?" Bobby asked.

"The altitude numbers, ya' ditz. Whad'ya think? I'm watching the VASI." Tommy had read that the VASI lights would help him keep correct altitude on landing. If he saw two rows of white lights, he was too high. If he saw one red row and one white row, he was okay. Two red rows meant too low.

Bobby scanned his panel. "Well, according to my altimeter—"

There was a sudden, muffled whump in the cockpit as the VASIs disintegrated in a shower of support girders and shattered lenses, then a rumbling, bouncing, shuddering deceleration that threw Bobby forward into his seat belt. His instrument panel was vibrating so hard that he could barely make out his gauges. "A-a-altitude is low" he reported, his voice quavering as he shook against his seat and straps. "P-p-possibly zero."

The bomber charged across the flat, grassy field, then bounced up onto the end of the runway. Sure that they had the runway made, Tommy pulled the throttles back. He yanked the CHUTE handle, and felt another little braking surge as the huge parachute bit into the slipstream behind the bomber. He guided it with the rudder until it had slowed to about 70 knots, then kept them on the centerline of the runway by steering with the forward mains—still shedding wiring and battered sockets.

The brakes squealed noisily and there was a vibration throughout the huge plane as Col. Riley brought the shuddering, heavy bomber to a stop. "Ya-hooo! How was that landing, huh? Did I make the numbers?"

"Oh, yeah, you made the numbers, all right," Bobby reported. "Ya' made the lights and the fence, too!"

Chasing them from all angles, dozens of AP trucks and cop cars and fire trucks came careening toward the bomber, lights flashing and sirens screaming. It took about 90 seconds for them to completely surround the jet. The tired young crew methodically went through the Shut-Down checklist—by the numbers. As the surviving engines wound down to a stop, the big plane made the typical clicking and pinging noises a hot jet makes as its systems cooled down after a flight.

Col. Riley tiredly slouched in his seat, his helmet pushed back hard against the headrest. His gaze swept down across the dozens of AP trucks and cop cars surrounding them, lights flashing, their occupants crouched behind doors and hoods, guns pointing nervously up at the cockpit, waiting for further orders. "Hell's bells, just look at 'em down there," he muttered to himself. He shook his head as he shut down the ARC-27 UHF Command Set, then switched off BATTERY BANKS 1 and 2, and sighed, "Some of them are just kids."

The hatch banged open and he heard a scrambling noise up the crew ladder. The pressure door clanked open, and Tommy looked down and to his left saw a large .45 pistol waving slowly back and forth between him and Bobby. The AP was standing on the ladder with his head and shoulders poking up out the hatch. He had a huge, mean grin and cold, black eyes.

"Well, well. What has we here? Looks like two guys who don't know they's up shit creek without a paddle. Ho, boy! I would truly hate to be in your ass right now." The sergeant leered at the boys. "Now, would you's gentlemens please accompany me to the outsides of this particular aircraft?" He made a 'get goin' motion with his pistol.

"We will if you moves out of this particular hatch," Bobby retorted.

The sergeant swung his pistol menacingly at the co-pilot position. "And you sir, is in a world of hurt. The jig is over!"

Bobby unsnapped his oxygen mask, and slid the helmet off his head. He rubbed his face, then looked back down at the AP. "And you, sir, are a moron."

The sergeant's eyes widened. "You . . . you're just a kid!"

"No shit, sherlock. But we're officer kids—you gotta salute us. Now get the hell out of the way! You deaf? Or just stupid?"

Tommy had never heard Bobby talk like that. Sheesh! He also unstrapped his oxygen mask and pulled off the heavy helmet. Leaning back against the headrest, he rubbed his scratchy eyes hard. When the feeling and blood came back across the ridges that the oxygen mask had carved into his face, he looked down at the crowd surrounding the bomber, then back at the AP.

Cold Eyes jerked when he saw Tommy. The AP's helmet clanged on the open hatch door, and he grimaced. Another damn *kid!* What the hell's goin' on here? Oh, well—he had his orders. Mine is not to reason, he thought. "Foller me, please," he sneered. "And don't try nothin' funny—you're on pretty damn thick ice as it is."

He began stepping back down the ladder, keeping his weapon pointed up at the cockpit. The gun looked like a nun's finger to Tommy, only smaller. "Time to face the music, I guess," he sighed. The boys crawled wearily out of their seats to the pressure hatch.

"You first," said Bobby gallantly, bowing toward the ladder.

Tommy looked down it and out the hatch to the bright square of concrete below. The muttering sergeant was a silhouette in the cramped tunnel, still signaling up with his gun. Tommy gulped as he spun around and began the long climb down. Each clanging, echoing step was a somber thought, a promising life about to end. Clang: bye bye, allowance. Clang: bye bye, new Huffy. Clang: bye bye, Mrs. Michelle Riley. Clang: bye bye, life!

He took a last jump off the bottom rung, steadied himself on the concrete, and quit counting guns at twelve. A few seconds later, his co-pilot joined him in the sunlight, surrounded by more cops and APs than they had ever seen, and Bobby instinctively put his hands up in the air. A second later, they heard a plop and an *oof!* as Michael exited the crow's compartment through one of the jagged holes. The young bombardier slowly straightened up and joined his crew, quietly surveying the circle of armed men surrounding him, which grew and reshaped itself to include the new perpetrator within its circle. Tommy watched as Michael walked stiffly toward them, grimacing. He looked like he had been on fire or something.

Bobby hissed out the corner of his mouth to Michael, "What happened to you? Ya' look burnt! Last I saw you, you were wet!"

Michael countered loudly, "Well, I *was* wet, and then I got blinded and burnt, and then I couldn't hear, and now I just HURT, and how come all these guns are aimed at us? Put your hands down, bozo—we're the good guys."

"SHUDDUP!" Cold Eyes ordered. "All a' you's. My orders is to appreHEND and deTAIN you's poipetrators until General Curtis E. LeMay can get his gold-plated ass over here and personally beat you to a ribbon. And I don't care if your hands is up OR down, one false move and I'll shoot your ass right between the heart! Now shuddup!"

Pleased with being in charge and his performance so far, the sergeant fished a Tareyton out of his shirt pocket, keeping his gun pointed at the crew with his other hand. He clenched the cigarette in his teeth, and without taking his gun or eyes off the intruders, told the nervous AP next to him, "Airman Benson, you may cease shaking your weapon now. I is in complete control of this particular situation." He squinted menacingly and shifted the cigarette to the opposite corner of his mouth. "Now could you's please be a gentleman, and lends me the loan of a match?"

Moments later, from way across the ramp, fresh sirens and screeching tires announced the arrival of LeMay and the Vice President. The two men angrily chiseled their way through the clutch of APs, making their way to the center of the circle. Going to Cuba was one thing, the general thought, bombing the ever-loving shit out of Offutt Air Force Base was quite another. Furiously, he brushed goopy mud and some slimy something from his lapel.

"*Where are they?*" he roared.

Cold Eyes ditched his cigarette and snapped a salute. "Sir, the perpetrators is ascertained and DEtained, sir."

"BULLSHIT! Search that airplane! Find that crew!"

"But this is them, sir," the sergeant said apologetically.

LeMay leaned over him, his roaring mouth inches from the wide-eyed sergeant. "You mean these dang kids? This is the crew?!"

"Yessir, sir. This is them, sir," he sputtered.

"And how do you know *that?*"

"'Cause I was the foist one in, and they was up in the pilot's seat when I got here, sir," he gulped. "Honest, sir."

LeMay spun around toward the boys. There were three of them. One had a helmet on, kind of charred from the looks of it. He and another one were in some sort of uniform. All had blue jeans, and one had on a ding-danged red shirt! A redshirt! A dirty, rotten commie? Three mother-lovin' infiltrating commie midgets! In cahoots with that other damn commie who stole the fighter, no doubt. *"Who are you!?"* he bellowed. *"And who do you work for?"*

The boys were looking down, a little nervous about all the attention, and maybe getting shot and all. Then Bobby said quietly, "We're the crew, sir. We flew it. And we don't work for anybody, I don't guess. The Boy Scouts, maybe."

"What!? Who the be-jesus are you?"

"Bobby Kontovan, sir."

"An' you're a commie!?"

"Oh, no sir—I'm a Catholic."

"Bull! Where are you from? Who sent you!?"

"From Topeka, sir. And we sorta sent ourselves, I guess."

LeMay stopped, his jaw twitching. The voice he heard was nervous, halting—just like a kid in trouble. It was slowly starting to sink in on him. Damnation! These weren't commies. These really seemed to be three ding-danged kids. Flying an airplane! From Topeka! American kids. *Boy Scout* kids! The very ones he'd been on the radio with all this time. He'd figured almost from the start that they were a young crew, idealistic maybe—a little renegade—but *this!?* What the hell!? "You really are a kid, aren't you? An American kid?"

"Yes, sir, sir," answered Bobby with a smart salute. "Gen-u-ine American through and through. Scout's honor, sir."

"And you flew this thing? To Cuba!?"

"Well, no sir, not exactly." Then he added hopefully, "But I flew it for a little while over the Gulf, and I helped start the engines and navigate. Plus I shot down that F-100, sir."

"That *what!?*"

"That F-100, sir. You shouldn'ta sent it after us. We were just trying to do the right thing, sir."

"The right thing? THE RIGHT THING!? What in blazes do you mean?"

"To stop the stand-down, sir," came a new voice.

LeMay spun around to his left. "And who the hell are you?"

"Colonel Riley, sir. The pilot."

"The pilot!? A colonel? I've had just about enough of this! Who made you a blasted colonel?"

"He did, sir," Tommy answered quietly, pointing to the Vice President. "He did it over the radio. It was a pretty quick ceremony."

Johnson looked down, sputtering, "Wall, I . . . you know, I just—"

"Can it! Everybody just shut up!" LeMay's head was about to explode. He wanted to shoot somebody bad. He glared at Johnson, then the airplane, then the APs, then the little freckle-faced midget colonel pilot. He looked back at the hulking plane and shoved his way through the circle of APs. He walked to the front gear and stared in amazement at tufts of wheat and twisted strands of what appeared to be some thick wiring streaming back from the strut. One huge tire was flat and lacerated, skewed crazily on its wheel. A piece of angle iron had penetrated the fuselage like a sword. "What the hell is all this!?" he roared.

"Um, VASI lights, sir. I think," mumbled Tommy, his head lowered. "Two rows of red, most likely."

LeMay opened his mouth to bellow when an airman rushed up, saluting, with a hastily scribbled note of further developments from radio reports. LeMay snatched them and read furiously. Crap! He chewed his cigar, scanned the report, then stared back at the short pilot and cooed menacingly, "Any other surprises for me, Riley? Would you like to introduce any more of your crew?" Then he shouted, sputtering, "Any more colonels in there!?"

"Oh, yes sir. This here is Mike. He's not a colonel yet, but he did the fine bombing work you saw awhile back."

"Fine bombing work!" LeMay screamed. "For what? What'd you bomb us for anyway? *And who taught you to fly an airplane!?*"

Tommy looked down at his tennies and mumbled, "We sort of taught ourselves, sir. I mean, it's not too hard if you follow the manual. But it's a real pig below 280 knots." He looked up at the general, squinting his eyes in the sunlight. "Next time I'll use partial flaps."

"Next time!? There won't be a next time! You're going to jail, young man. For a long, long time. Or maybe a firing squad! Whaddya think of them apples?"

Bobby didn't think much of them apples at all. "But sir," he interrupted gingerly, "I'm tellin' you, the Russians are up to something sneaky. That's why we did it, this whole mission. We figured they're using the stand down to put up rings of SAMs around the missiles they already have in Cuba."

"You *figured* that, huh?" spat out LeMay.

"Yes, sir. They're not taking the other missiles out, or they'd gladly have recon photos taken of it. They're bringing SAMs *in.* They're lyin'! And now we've got proof, I think. Won't know for sure till we develop the film, but this stand-down is just plumb-ass wrong and you know it."

LeMay paused, thinking, then drilled his eyes into Bobby. "Do you know your little stunt has been seen by just about everybody on this planet with a TV? And it's got half the damned Air Force flying off to their Fail-Safe points? As we speak?"

"Well . . . we hadn't planned on the Fail-Safe part exactly, but maybe that's a good thing, sir. See? Those Russians are pulling a fast one on us—they may be laughing at this silly ceremony, but they won't be laughing at a couple hundred B-52s coming at 'em."

"Yeah," added Mike. "How come you didn't figure this out yourself? Bobby figured it out in about five minutes." Mike held up a metal canister about the size of a coffee can. "You might want to go have this developed." He smirked and rolled his eyes. "No reconnaissance flights indeed. Wonder why? *Duh.*"

LeMay stared, his eyes blazing. Michael's gunpowdered face lowered at the challenge, and he shifted warily from foot to foot. Furiously, LeMay snatched the canister and looked at it. "This better be good, young man! This better be very good." Two airmen stepped forward at LeMay's barked command, saluting nervously. "Rush this to the Recon Lab. You've got five minutes! MOVE IT!"

The airmen whirled around and streaked off in a truck, siren blaring. Everyone watched it grow small in the distance, then squeal around a corner and disappear. There was a heavy silence. All the APs were still aiming their guns at the center of the circle. Criminy! thought LeMay. What exactly was going on here? World War Three, that's what—if he didn't do something, and fast!

He looked at the boys, gathering his thoughts, trying to get it all straight in his head. He then put his hands behind his back, and took a deep breath. Crap! "Well, gentlemen," he started gravely. "It seems that here's what we have so far: one stolen B-47 with major damage, from the looks of it. An overflight of Cuba, for God's sake! One extremely important ceremony ruined for all the whole wide world to see. Khrushchev is bonkers. Castro is apoplectic! I got VIPs in ambulances. I got VIPs cryin'. I got VIPs flat on their backs and blubbering like idiots! A bunch of expensive ejection seats full of god-knows-what scattered all over the ramp. Plus an entire hangar blown down back at Forbes, not to mention one government issue truck and its occupant wrapped up in a ball."

LeMay continued the tally, "Reports from every hick town from here to Florida are talking about major damage. Cows. Chickens. Barns. Glass. Plus a couple hundred rounds of 20 millimeter expended, and I don't even want to *think* about a million damned dollar F-100 scattered across tarnation, even if it was a commie

flying it! And now I've got three blasted KIDS telling me we don't
know what the hell we're doing diplomatically, so now we've got
half the U.S. Air Force charged up and on their way to Russia to
force the Soviet's hand. *Do I have it all?"* he barked. "Don't be
afraid to speak up, now—even though it could be your last words."
He rolled back on his heels and stared hard at the boys. "Anything
to add? Any bright ideas what to tell the president?" He cocked
his head toward Tommy and seethed. "Anyone?"

"Sir, um, can we just tell the president that we're sorry and we
promise not to do it again?" asked Tommy.

"Dammit!" roared LeMay. "I've still got half a mind to have
you boys shot!"

Bobby was especially depressed by that idea. He'd already
dodged some flak today, and he hadn't much liked it. Why, he had
a lot of living to do still—or so he hoped. "Say," he suggested
thoughtfully, "instead of having us shot, why don't you give us a
medal instead? Just wait'll you see the pictures!"

"What!?" LeMay snapped in disbelief.

"I saw it on 'No Time For Sergeants.' What a great movie! At
the end, they had to choose between shooting 'em and giving 'em
a medal, and they gave 'em medals and it all worked out just fine."

Michael nodded vigorously, "Yeah, a medal or a merit badge
or somethin'!"

Bobby's mind went into overdrive as he imagined girls swoon-
ing at the sight of him. An ace! With a medal! Yeah! He eyed the
fuming general and started rubbing the dried blood on his cowlick. "Lookit this! I could sure use a Purple Heart here. And so
could Michael there—looks wounded in action to me!"

"Shut up!" LeMay bellowed, chewing on his cigar. He ground
his jaw, trying to think. Everyone got rigidly silent, but Red Shirt
was still looking up at him with a silly-ass, pleading grin—still
trying to sell him on this ridiculous medal idea. More position
reports were coming in to him and the Vice President as the world
prepared for war. Russia was scrambling. Our forces were holding
at Defcon 3, missiles cocked. Great Britain was firing up their

fleet, and the Iron Curtain countries were going to full alert. France was having a late supper and couldn't be reached. Italy had surrendered.

A blue truck screeched up to the circle, and a man with a smock and white gloves ran over to LeMay. Johnson rushed to join them as the technician unrolled a strip of film, holding it up to the sky. The three men stood looking at it, silent. LeMay's jaw twitched. Johnson's eyes grew wide as he spun around toward the boys. "I say we shoot 'em!" he bawled. "Raght after I kill 'em!"

The boys' smiles disappeared.

"I hope you have a damn good excuse for this," LeMay told them savagely. "I don't think the president has much use for photos of Ford pick-ups driving into ditches and a bunch of bug-eyed cows!"

"*What!?*" The boys went white, and Michael had to hold onto Tommy's shoulder not to fall down. "Wait," yelled Michael. "I . . . I've got another one! That was a test cartridge! Let me back in—it's still there, I think. I stuffed it under a power pack. Please!" He rushed forward to the general, hands out, pleading.

A dozen weapons followed his movement. Christ, thought LeMay. What a day! He squinted at the towering hulk of the B-47 looming above them. Hard to believe something so big, so fast, something that had caused so much *shit,* could now be just sitting there, quiet. Like a huge, big, stupid, faithful idiot dog that had just chewed up a slipper and was waiting to be scolded.

"Go get it," LeMay growled, watching Michael's small form scurry back up into the belly of the jet. His gaze shifted off to the chaos on the other side of the ramp. Toy ambulances and tiny figures were running around amid the ruins of the bleachers and banners. TV vans were trying to get close to the bomber, blocked off at 200 yards by a blue line of armed APs. And the Vice President. Look at him. He had no idea what was going on here—or how to capitalize on it. That turkey just wanted somebody shot, and anyone would do at this point. God help us all if he ever became president, thought LeMay.

Michael plopped back out, rushed over, and handed the technician another canister. Then he rejoined his friends, still looking like he might faint.

"Try it again," barked the general. The technician spun around to the truck and sped off. LeMay then looked over at the three boys. Danged if they weren't standing at attention! And danged if they hadn't actually flown this huge thing to Cuba, blowing this bogus ceremony to smithereens! And double-god-danged if they weren't probably right. About the Russians and the Cubans and the missiles and all of it! I'll bet that film shows it, he thought. And now SAC is up there. Things were coming to a head, big-time! Time to earn your general pay LeMay, somebody better do something, fast—and that somebody is you! Time to get this show on the road!

"Sergeant!" ordered the general, snapping into action. "Take these boys to security, pronto! Lock 'em up tight and hold them till I come back."

"But," Johnson protested, "I thought we could shoot—"

"Enough!" LeMay interrupted. "These boys are right. I figured the Russians were up to something. You figured the Russians were up to something. Half the *world* figured the Russians were up to something. And these boys . . ." he spread his arms in a sweeping gesture, "just weren't going to listen to our high-faluting crapola anymore. They're the only ones around here without their heads in the sand." He addressed the crew. "Gentlemen, you've really pulled off a doozy here, I've got to tell ya'." The boys' chests swelled up with pride. "But you're going to jail now with the nice sergeant, till the President and I figure out what to do with you. Stealing a bomber, for Christ sakes! If I were you, I'd start praying."

Three little chests unswelled and the boys stared glumly at the concrete. LeMay nodded to Cold Eyes. "Put 'em in the slammer, sergeant. But first, get me to a radio. I've got a call to make."

In the Oval Office, the President listened tensely as LeMay's voice crackled through the speakers on his desk. Kennedy had

watched the whole unbelievable thing on TV along with everybody else, and had liked it, actually. Especially when the camera
showed the Vice President down on his hands and knees, sobbing.

"So General, this is big," radioed the high-ranking Catholic.
"What do you suggest we, ah, do?"

"Sir, my flyboys have piss in their vinegar now!" answered LeMay
confidently. "Lemme tellya!"

"Piss?"

"Yes, sir. Piss. Pee. You know . . . It's a saying, a manner of
speech, sir."

"In vinegar?"

"That is correct, sir. Vinegar."

"Hmmm. Interesting."

"Indeed, sir. But we're getting off subject. I'm looking at some
v-e-r-y interesting shots of Havana harbor right now. These boats
are crowded with SAMs, we've got 'em with their pants down!
Like it or not, what that plane did can't be un-did. SAC is up there
now, bub—we're at Fail-Safe. Better make the best of it. I say we
call 'em on it."

Kennedy sighed deeply. Bobby was in a snit, wanting him to
hurry up. He could sense him pacing outside in the hall. And an
hour ago those glad-handling ya-hoo students at that damn photo-
op. From where? *Arkansas?* Especially that pudgy one—almost
pulling his arm out of its socket—mixed in with all the other stuff
going on, it was just a lot on his plate right now. Commies cocked
and armed from the Ukraine to Cuba. Damn kids charging through
the South Lawn like cattle, trying to peek in. Advisers hovering
outside the door, and LeMay on the horn, ready to bust a nut.

He casually slipped a finger under the actress's shoulder strap,
rubbing her milky skin. Talk about caught with your pants down,
he thought with a sigh. Oh, well—he was President. El Presidente.
Screw 'em. Nobody jacks with Jack, at least not in the Oval. Still,
what the hell was he going to do with her? He couldn't help
himself, but knew that taking liberties like this was just crazy.
If only . . .

"Ooh, Mister President, sir. Your little Redstone rocket is—"

"Please, ah . . . stop now," he stammered. She pouted up at him. "That's a good girl."

He leaned over to the microphone, hitting the transmit button. "Okay, Curtis, hold tight," he answered. "Those photos are all we need. Time for hardball." He then reached across the desk, to the famous Red Phone, and sent the ultimatum. Through his interpreter, he stated: "Here's the, ah, deal. Missiles out of Cuba. NOW. And yes, we'll do the, ah, Turkey part, just to make it even. But don't try to pull any more of that, ah, Berlin silliness to change the subject. No more messing around. End of discussion. Yes or no."

With an armada of bombers circling menacingly around his grey, unkempt country, full of peasants walking sadly behind creaking wagons half-full of inferior potatoes, and with photos of the SAMs in Cuba and his sneaky plan symbolically blown to smithereens for all the world to see back at Offutt, Khrushchev knew he had no choice. He grunted a reply to his interpreter, who then muttered back to Washington: "O.K. We giveski."

The room was painted in that horrid military celery-green from the ceiling down to about waist level. From there down the walls were a more attractive battleship grey, including the floor. The chairs were grey metal, with a matching desk. No windows. Four rows of harsh fluorescent lights were mounted on the ceiling. A bright red light above the door cast a rosy glow on the AP's helmet and matched a red fire extinguisher on one wall. Cold Eyes sat balancing on the back legs of his chair, slowly tapping his billy club in the palm of his hand. He sneered at the three nervous boys lined up across from him in front of two APs, standing at attention. He zeroed in on the youngest one, with the burnt head and tattered shirt. Easy meat, he thought. The little puke. "You thirsty there, boy?"

"Yessir," mumbled Mike.

"Tough bananas, tough guy." He grinned, lifted the styrofoam cup to his lips and took a noisy slurp. "Now that's what I calls *goooood* coffee. Yessir re-bob. Good to the foist drop."

"You're still a moron," muttered Bobby.

"Shut up, ya little monkey." Cold Eyes pushed his chair off the wall with a bang. "I coulda had you's boys shot right here."

"Over my dead body!" snarled Bobby. He stopped and thought a second. "I mean, could not."

"Could too!"

"Could not!"

Cold Eyes jumped from his chair, his coffee cup spilling and skidding toward the center of the room. "Could damn too!" he yelled. He threw the billy club to the floor, and it clattered and spun a wooden dance in the tense silence as he snatched his .45 from his holster. He held it expertly with two hands and drew a careful bead on Red Shirt. "I could say you was tryin' to escape," he snorted. "Try me. Just make one teensy move, smart guy!"

Michael stepped forward. "You'd have to shoot me too, bozo," he said bravely. The pistol whipped toward him, and the hammer cocked back with a frightening click.

"Me too," said Tommy. He also stepped forward, daring the AP. "You'd have to do a lot of shootin' real quick and I don't think you've got the guts. You're just a big, fat bully!"

Cold Eyes swung his pistol from boy to boy to boy, sneering. "Well, well. Bully is it? I'll shows ya' bully! Talks about a target-rich environment! Only problem is, who gets it foist?"

In the tense silence that followed, one of the rear guards slowly drew his weapon, and carefully aimed it at the sergeant. "You can't shoot 'em, sarge."

"What!" sputtered Cold Eyes. He looked up nervously but still kept his gun moving slowly from target to target.

"The general said hold 'em—not shoot 'em. Please put your gun down."

"Dammit, airman! Whose side is you on?"

There was a dangerous silence as the third AP also drew his weapon, joining his partner. Guns swung one way, then another, everybody taking turns being in someone else's sights. Mutually assured destruction was a wacky concept, but it seemed to be working pretty well. They all stood there—silent, measuring, moving carefully and delicately. Almost-but-not-quite blowing each others' brains out.

The stand-off ended as distant footsteps grew rapidly: click, click, click, click, CLICK and the door slammed open. "Dammit!" roared LeMay, his eyes blazing. "What's going on in here? And why weren't guards posted outside like I ordered? Put those guns down!"

Cold Eyes turned toward the general and saluted so fast his pistol made an indent on his forehead. Everyone winced as he dropped his .45 and stumbled back, his helmet clanging against the fire extinguisher. "We uh, I sort of made the detoimination of guarding them from in here, sir," he squeaked as he slid slowly down the wall to the floor. His eyes were wide with surprise, but not really focused on anything in particular.

LeMay spat out, "And you made that *detoimination,* airman? All by yourself?

"Yethir. They ain't gone nowhere, thir," he dribbled. "An' ith thergeant, thir." He bent over and his cheek smashed flat against the floor, his tongue partway out. A little puddle of drool began to form on the concrete.

"The hell it's sergeant! It's airman, now!" LeMay glared down on the dazed figure. "And it's gonna be brownie scout if you don't get your ass out there in the hall and guard this door! No one knocks himself out on my watch!" He gestured angrily at the other two APs. "Get this slimeball outta here. Post yourselves outside this door, and throw some water on this turkey. Move it!"

"Yessir!" they chorused in unison, and scrambled to tug Cold Eyes away by his arms. His body bent compliantly around the doorframe, and the tips of his shoes made two thin, black tracks across the floor and out into the hall.

After the door slammed shut, the boys watched LeMay breathlessly. Mike was trembling, and almost preferred the gun battle they didn't quite have to what probably lay ahead. The general looked up at the ceiling, then down to the floor, shaking his head. The boys knew this signal only too well from their dads—they were going to Get It, plain and simple. LeMay clasped his hands behind his back, paced to the far wall, and turned smartly, looking directly at them. He forced a frown. Lord, but they were at attention again! He wished he had a whole squadron of men like this.

"Well, gentlemen," LeMay started carefully, savoring their discomfort. "Despite the Vice President's recommendations, the President agrees that we probably can't shoot you, at least not today, what with all these cameras around. Might look bad. Messy. .45s make such big holes, you know." He noticed the young bombardier's lips were quivering, and his eyes were watering. Good. "However, we could shoot you tomorrow or the next day, I suppose." Sniffles and nervous throat-clearings sounded faintly in the room.

Casually, the general reached over to touch the concrete wall, then again looked down at the floor, frowning. He shook his head. "Except for the dang ricochets in a room like this. Might get a good guy. Maybe we'd have to do it outside."

"B-but that's where the cameras are!" stuttered Michael, wide-eyed. " Y-you don't want to do that, remember? Maybe you could just ground us or something?"

"Hmm. Grounding. I suppose we could arrange something like that." LeMay stared at Michael, then the pilot, then Red Shirt, taking his time. "Ever hear of Leavenworth? I could ground you boys for, oh, about fifteen to twenty years in there. How'd you like that?"

Tommy did some quick calculating. Twelve plus twenty. Yikes! "I don't think we'd like that at all, sir. We'd sort of miss high school and college and everything. Heck, we'd be old." Not to mention poor Michelle, he thought. Doomed to being an old maid—knitting, gazing at the calendar, year after year, waiting faithfully for her tattooed man to get out of the clink. Of course he might get a chance with her at those conjugal thingies he'd heard about at recess—*hmmm.*

LeMay took the cigar from his mouth. "Yep, pretty old, son. Twenty years. And that's after the courts and hearings and the lawyers and all of that. Could go twenty two, twenty three, tops." He looked up, squinting at the lights. "But frankly, there's so much paperwork with federal sentences, I just don't know if I want to mess with it. Shooting is just so much quicker." He paused, noticing a few teary eyes. This was kind of fun! He sighed: "But this shooting thing just doesn't seem to be working out, either," he added, stroking the hard wall. "It just isn't. I don't think I could even *fit* a firing squad in here. What to do, what to do?" he murmured, sounding exasperated. "What to do?"

"We could mow your lawn for free," suggested Tommy. "Forever! And edge it, too."

"And sweep," added Michael.

"Oh, no," replied LeMay. "No, I have non-coms for that." He raised his eyes up to the ceiling again and sucked in a deep breath. After a moment, he exhaled slowly, shaking his head with final weariness. He had milked the Parental Pause for all he could, he thought, looking at the three nervous figures. Time for the coup de grace. "Soooo, if we can't send you to Leavenworth, and we can't shoot you, maybe we'll just have to give you that medal after all."

The three boys jerked their heads up, eyes almost popping out of their heads. What!?

LeMay looked down, inspecting his cigar seriously, then glanced at the boys with what could almost pass for a smile. "I liked that movie, too," he said. "Plus we have some really nice photos of Havana harbor, thanks to you. Really nice." He clamped the cigar back into his mouth. "Ever been to our nation's capital? There's someone there who'd like to meet you."

CHAPTER 15.

WE WERE HEROES ONCE, AND YOUNG

The air was stunningly clear in front of the White House. Flags snapped importantly in the fresh breeze, and the smell of summer and freedom was in the air. Tommy, Bobby and Michael sat surrounded by bishops and potentates, and there were rows of pinstripers and tuxedoed diplomats from all over the free world sitting at attention. The crowd below settled at the sight of movement on the podium. Robert Frost was introduced, and began the ceremonies with a classic poem. His knowing, scratchy voice sent "High Flight" by John Gillespie Magee soaring out through the warm air and into the hearts and minds of the hushed listeners, some holding back tears, some not.

> *"Oh, I have slipped the surly bonds of earth*
> *And danced the skies on laughter-silvered wings;*
> *Sunward I've climbed . . . "*

You could have heard a pin drop at the finish as he turned to find his seat, his helpers guiding the frail giant easily back to his place. The President rose to applaud and the crowd went wild. Soon after, the tumultuous clapping was directed toward Col. Riley and his crew as the President re-created their incredible mission.

Tommy gazed out at the cheering tens of thousands with their balloons and banners, all screaming in adulation. A guy could get used to this, he thought. The crowd surged, and breathed, and roared like a living thing! The President continued addressing the throng through a forest of microphones, occasionally glancing back at Tommy with a look of gratitude. Boy, was he embarrassed! He could barely hear the speech over the roar of the crowd, and wasn't really listening, but reliving the tense moments of air combat, the perfect (though slightly bumpy) landing, the proud airplane responding to him like an extension of himself, her spirit strong. Even with a blown engine and four holes in her sleek gut.

Tommy looked to his left. Good ol' Mike. His eyebrows and everything were starting to grow back. He sat ramrod straight, and a tear—another one!—crawled down his brave young cheek as the President singled him out for a few well-deserved words. Mike looked terrific in his Scout uniform. He was going to go places, that was for sure. Tommy hoped that they would stay in touch.

A nudge in his ribs brought his attention 'round to Bobby. He had spied a pretty girl in the adoring crowd and pointed her out—she was a looker, all right. Then Bobby made the finger going in and out of the circle sign. *That guy!* thought Tommy. Here they were, being praised by the biggest cheeses on the planet, and Bobby's got one thing on his mind. *"You wish,"* Tommy hissed.

All the families were there, of course. Tommy saw his dad in his dress whites, no less. Sheesh! He had never seen him wear those before, not even when Joey Bishop played that night at the Officer's Club. This occasion would be "points" in his dad's "career," he reckoned. He was pretty sure of that new bike now. A Huffy he bet, with the dual headlights. His mom was over there—next to Jackie—in her favorite dress, the blue one. His brothers and sisters all had on their best church clothes. He spotted Sister Redempta among a row of proud penguins and straightened up a little. Then he spied Michelle in the crowd, she was sure noticing him now . . . a little too much maybe. She made a kissy face, which both his sisters intercepted and spun around to help relay to him.

Tommy gave them The Look, and they whipped back around, giggling. He thought Michelle looked . . . old? Nope, not old, exactly. She was only twelve, for gosh sakes. Available? Maybe that was it, just too darned *available* all of a sudden. What was it with this gol-durned boy-girl thing anyhow? He hoped it would all start clearing up when he got to be a teenager.

At the end of the President's speech the Vice President got up to talk, but just then the fly-by began and drowned him out. Johnson started spinning around, looking up to the sky, yelling something. Thousands of grateful citizens rose to their feet and began cheering. They were all so proud, and many had teary eyes as they followed the path of the magnificent planes. Hundreds of them, jets and prop-jobs, from horizon to horizon, the oldest and the newest in perfect formation. High in the sky, out in front, in the position of honor—Tommy saw the lead plane. *His* plane. With a rebuilt #6 and four shiny new patches in her gleaming under-side. He just knew he'd be in one of those planes, someday. If he could only get an A on that darned math final next week.

As the Air Force Band struck up a rousing "Off We Go, Into The Wild Blue Yonder," the entire crowd stood as one, hands over their hearts, eyes skyward. The bright, spring heavens above were a dazzling blue. The clouds were like cotton balls, high in the sky.

"Breakfast! Time to get up!"

Tommy slowly opened his eyes and saw the formation of planes circling above him. He stretched and yawned, kicked off the covers, and rubbed his face. It was gonna be a busy day! He dressed, charged upstairs, and joined another noisy routine breakfast session.

"So," snickered Diane, "whadjya' dream about . . . Michelle?"

Tommy gave her The Look, and his two sisters giggled at each other and made kissy noises. He *had* been dreaming *something*, but it was all a little hazy now. There were the normal squeals and slurps and fights, and Tommy and his mom had a tie game going—one to one—as he blasted out the front door.

Ka*BAM!* The storm door slammed shut and Tommy Riley streaked off the small porch, cleared the hedge in an easy jump, then started picking his way through the muddy spots in the front yard. He heard a bomber starting up, way off in the distance, booming and whistling its shrill whine. He glanced up the street toward the bus stop, and saw three little birds in tight formation zip and wheel up the street, then angle off to the south. Tommy had almost made it to the curb, when out of the clear, blue sky, a voice sang out—in a beautiful church-choir soprano: "Don't slam that *dooooorrr!* How many times do I have to *tellll youuu!*" Cripes! Caught again, thought the young slammer. Two to one. Still, it was gonna be a great day, he could just feel it!

THE END

ABOUT THE AUTHOR

Tom Hanley is an artist, writer, surfer, pilot, and a regular guy. He lives in Hawaii with his wife and daughter. As a Boy Scout, Tom attained the rank of Tenderfoot. (He almost made Scout, Second Class, but had a little trouble with his knots.) He's a Leo—but not one of those, you know, loud and pushy ones.

Printed in the United States
1457100002B/106